BLUE SKY

ALANA ALBERTSON

EVERAFTER

Blue Sky
Copyright © 2018 by Alana Albertson
Cover design by Aria Tan of Resplendent Media
Cover Photography: Wander Aguiar
Cover Model: Jase Dean

Bolero Books, LLC
11956 Bernardo Plaza Dr. #510
San Diego, CA 92128
www.bolerobooks.com

To my parents—Joseph Chulick Jr. and Diana Viramontes Chulick

For once you have tasted flight you will walk the earth with your eyes turned skywards, for there you have been and there you will long to return.

LEONARDO DA VINCI

FOREWORD

This book has been a labor of love for me. As a biracial Mexican-American woman, I was hoping to shine a spotlight on the economic hardships in border towns. I hope you fall in love with Paloma and Beck the same way I did.

Love,

Alana Viramontes Chulick Albertson

BLUE SKY

THERE'S A BRIGHT LINING TO EVERY DARK CLOUD.

For ten weeks every year, the Blue Angels descend from the heavens and land in heEl Centro, California. The residents treat the pilots like gods. The city council members host black tie galas, little old ladies bring them homemade pies, and groupies wait by their rooms to satisfy their desires. Everyone worships them— everyone, that is, except for me. I hate the way they waltz into my poor town and romance all the residents only to vanish into the sky.

But even I can't afford to say no when I'm offered the chance to be the nanny for sexy, cocky pilot Beckett "Grind" Daly's baby girl, Sky. The job is my only hope to feed my family and maybe one day leave this town.

No matter how close I grow to Beckett, no matter how much I hunger for his embrace, I'll never let down my guard for this Devil in a Blue Angel's disguise.

CHAPTER ONE

TOMATILLOS

I stood in my mama's kitchen, peeling back the husks of the ripe tomatillos my neighbor had gifted to me. Even though I lived only miles away from the Mexican border, fresh produce was expensive, and purchasing my beloved tart, green fruit was definitely a luxury I couldn't afford.

Not when there was a constant, gnawing ache in my belly. Not when my little sister Ana María cried every morning because she wanted more food, but I had none to give her. Not when my other sister, Mónica, would often eat her only meal of the day at school because she had free lunch. Not when I had to feed a family of four on fifty dollars a week.

If only I had a job.

But my employment status wasn't from the lack of effort. No, not at all. I had literally applied to every job in the border town of El Centro, California, which had just recently been anointed "the worst place to live in America" by some huge national website. With the highest unemployment rate in the country at twenty-

1

seven and a half percent, my prospects were bleak. I lay awake most nights, terror gripping my body, shivering despite the sweltering desert heat, trapped in the hell that was my life, dreaming of an escape route.

In reality, I doubted that I would ever be able to leave my hometown. Instead, I would probably end up being buried here, but these days, even *that* wasn't a certainty. El Centro's cemetery recently went into foreclosure.

I clutched the tomatillos in my hands, rinsed them under the cool water, cut out their stems, and tossed them in a pan to roast. This spicy sauce would coat the chicken enchiladas I had just made from scratch. Along with a pot of cumin-spiced pinto beans and a batch of *arroz rojo*, we would be blessed with a rare, hearty dinner. Over the years, I had learned how to make delicious meals out of scraps. These enchiladas, along with oatmeal for breakfast and tortillas for lunch, would have to last my family for a week.

Ana María walked into the kitchen and clutched on my apron. "Where's Mama?"

At six years old, Ana María was a precocious little girl with amber-colored eyes and long brown hair that I made sure to braid every day, since Mama was usually too hungover to move, and that was if she even came home from her one of her frequent benders. Ana María was too young to learn the truth about our lives, though I knew I wouldn't be able to protect her forever.

"Baby, she's out working." And that was true, in a way. But Mama didn't have a real job, either. Her version of "working" was flirting with men at the local bars and offering them favors for a bit of cash.

"I am not a prostitute," Mama would swear up and down. "I just love men."

I didn't even try to argue with her any more. The fact that Mama had three children with three different dads, none of whom she married, let her decisions speak for herself. Not that there was anything wrong with a woman enjoying a healthy sex life. But she lavished attention on these countless men while she neglected her children, which was deplorable.

At least I didn't know who my father was, so I could sometimes close my eyes and pretend that he was a good man. Maybe he didn't even know that I had existed, and that if he found out that he had a daughter, he would rush to me and take me away from my mom.

If only Mama would tell me his name, I would be able to figure it out.

But my fantasy dad was the only good man in my life. Mónica's father was a deadbeat and a womanizer who cheated on Mama all the time before she kicked his sorry ass out. And Ana María's father was a hot-tempered alcoholic who would beat Mama until she could cry no more. The only other man around was my uncle, who also waged a losing battle with the bottle.

But growing up around these jerks, none of whom stuck around, told me all I needed to know about men.

Men were trouble. Untrustworthy. Only after one thing. At twenty years old, I was proud to say that I had never been distracted by a man, even though my soft curves and plump lips often made me a target for their leers. Sure, I had messed around with boys in high school, and had even lost my virginity to a good friend of mine who had wanted to date me, but I told him that I was not looking for a relationship. I vowed that I would never let any man get in the way of my dreams of leaving this town, and this life, behind.

But Mama had never known another way of living. She was only eighteen when she had become pregnant with me. Did Mama once have dreams of her own? Mama used to tell me, *"El sueño es alimento de los pobres."*

Dreams are the food of the poor.

Mama's future had blown away with the dust in this desert town. But my dreams were still real. Sometimes I closed my eyes and practiced creative visualization, something I had read about in a book. I pictured myself running a successful restaurant, living in a cute apartment, even owning a car. But no matter how hard I tried, I couldn't fathom a scenario where I would get an opportunity to change my life.

I just need a break.

I sat Ana María down in front of a coloring book and turned my attention back to the salsa. I sliced half a white onion while blinking back the tears that were not only from vapors but also from my despair, then pulled myself together and crushed two garlic cloves, chopped fifteen sprigs of cilantro, and halved and de-stemmed a serrano pepper.

My tomatillos were now ready, and when I removed them from the oven, their smoky scent filled up the tiny kitchen. I chopped the tomatillos and grabbed the *molcajete* to grind the salsa when my other sister, Mónica, burst into the room.

"Paloma, Paloma!" Mónica shrieked.

"What?" At fourteen, Mónica was definitely the rebel of the family, and already boy crazy. I worried that Mónica would end up just like our mother. To make certain that she didn't, I'd forced her to go on birth control this year. If only I could take custody of my sisters and get out of this town.

"Omg! Look at this!" She thrust a copy of the *Imperial Press* in my face.

"Ay, Mónica." I did not have time to read some gut-wrenching story in the newspaper. Just last week one of my high school classmates had been murdered in her apartment, which was only one street over from ours. The cops suspected drug traffickers, but it didn't matter. Another reminder that the only way out of this town was in a body bag.

"It's your dream job!"

Dream job? My dream was any job—I'd clean toilets, I'd mop floors, no job was below me. But with no car and nothing but a high school education, my prospects were bleak. And we needed the money now even more desperately than ever. The little help my mom received from the government went to food, and the rest was often squandered by her on alcohol. I choked back a sob. I didn't know how much longer we could all survive like this.

I grabbed the paper cautiously, refusing to get my hopes up again.

Looking for a full time live in nanny for my infant daughter. I'll be stationed in El Centro for ten weeks. Must be CPR certified. No drugs and no drama. Pay is $1000 a week. Will be taking applications in person January 4th at 4 p.m. at the Navy Lodge, El Centro, room 101.

I dropped the *temolote* I had been using to grind the salsa from my right hand. Did that say one *thousand* dollars a week for ten weeks?

Ten thousand dollars?

That money could be life-changing for my sisters and me. I could move the girls to San Diego and leave my mother and her destructive ways behind. I could rent a small apartment and send them to school out there, even get a job at a local restaurant to support them.

I stared at the old clock that was hanging on our cracked wall. It was quarter past two. The Navy Lodge was a few miles away, so I would have to leave enough time to walk. *Ay, Dios mío*, what would I wear?

I turned to Mónica and grabbed her shoulders. *"¡Ayudeme!* I need you to watch Ana María and pick me out an outfit. Something simple and classy. Nothing tight. I'm going to finish these enchiladas and bring them to the interview. Do *not* tell Mama where I went if she decides to come home."

Mónica's face dropped as she gazed longingly at the enchiladas. "Our enchiladas? What will we eat?"

"Beans and rice and tortillas. Military men like to eat. These enchiladas could be our ticket."

"Sí, entiendo. You got this. You're great with kids. If he hires you, I'll help out completely back here, no attitude, I swear."

My hand shook. How would this even work if I got this job? Who would take care of my sisters? My mom wasn't reliable. My only option was my uncle. He was a goddamn mess but at least he would be there—he never left his couch.

I stared at Mónica. She was completely capable of watching Ana María for ten weeks. If I was offered this job, we could make it work.

Mónica tilted her head. "I wonder if he's an Angel? I bet he's smoking hot."

A Blue Angel pilot . . . he had to be if he was offering one thousand dollars a week. No enlisted man in the support team of the Angels would pay that much money. An infant? Where was her mother?

For ten weeks every year, the Blue Angels descended from the heavens and landed in El Centro. The Angels were notorious as much for their sky stunts as they were for their land antics. They would hit the bars here, romancing the young local Mexican girls who dreamed of a life as a naval aviator's wife. It was like the *sucia* version of *An Officer and a Gentleman,* minus the happy ending; no Blue Angel had ever married a local girl.

But I didn't want to fall in love. I didn't believe in love. I had never experienced anything even close to love. I wanted a job. I needed a job. A job that could put food on the table, give me enough money to flee this town, and save my sisters from this fate.

My hand shook as I picked back up my *temolote* and finished grinding the ingredients. I dipped my finger into the *molcajete* and sampled my *salsa verde*. The delectable green sauce was perfectly spicy, yet tangy. I spread the mixture over the chicken enchiladas, crafted with homemade tortillas and lots of love, just like my late abuela had taught me. All of the lovers that Mama brought home couldn't get enough of my cooking. Abuelita would always say, *"Un hombre se conquista por el estómago."* The way to a man's heart was through his stomach. Maybe that was why Mama could never keep a man—she couldn't cook at all.

There would be hundreds of women, and possibly even men, applying for this job. I was amazing with kids and had pretty much raised my sisters myself. Even so, I needed an edge. When they were in town, these Angels would haunt the local restaurants, devouring the native cuisine. *Carne asada burritos, carnitas adobadas, chile verde, tacos el carbon*—those rich white boys couldn't get enough of our food. Maybe my cooking could truly be my ticket to a new life.

I grabbed a copy of my résumé from the bookshelf and placed it in my purse. Mónica walked back into the kitchen, holding Mama's best dress, a navy blue sheath with white trim. It was usually reserved for church, which was why it was in good shape. Mama hated to attend for fear she would be judged. A fear in this small town with her shameless behavior that was definitely warranted.

I slipped it over my head and looked at myself in the bathroom mirror; the reflection of a tired, slim, desperate girl staring right back at me. Well, at least the dress fit perfectly, not too tight or too baggy.

Mónica grabbed a little bag under the sink. "Let me do your makeup."

I shook my head. "No, this is a job interview, not a date."

"Right. And you need to look your best. Give me five minutes."

I gave up and let her have her way with me. I needed this job so badly it hurt. As Mónica started applying foundation, I exhaled and did something I hadn't done in years.

I prayed.

Once a devout Catholic, I had stopped going to church when my abuela died after being hit by a drunk driver. My abuela hadn't even been that old at only fifty-five. Without her guidance, we Pérez girls had fallen apart. Mama only cared about herself, and now it was up to me to be the adult in the household.

After a few more agonizing minutes of Mónica dabbing, blotting, and painting my skin, she finally released me.

"Look at yourself! You're beautiful. I would definitely hire you to watch my baby."

I looked in the mirror again, and this time I saw how green my eyes looked enhanced by the purple shadow and how my curled eyelashes made me appear awake even when I was getting by on only hours of sleep.

But more importantly, I saw an expression I hadn't seen in the mirror since I'd given up my college scholarship because I was afraid of how my sisters would survive without me.

I saw hope.

CHAPTER TWO

ENCHILADAS VERDES

I t wasn't supposed to be like this.

My beautiful wife, Catherine, should be sitting here with me now, playing with our little girl, deeply entrenched in the joys of motherhood.

We had been so excited to spend these ten weeks in El Centro with our daughter, Sky. Ten weeks that we would've been able to spend together without me having to fly to other cities for airshows. Catherine and I couldn't wait to return to this tragic town that despite having so little resources had welcomed us with open arms. We wanted to spend our three months here truly bonding as a new family. I couldn't wait to come home every night to my wife. I had dreamed of bonding with our daughter before I had to leave her again every week to entertain the public by doing aerial tricks.

Now, spending time with my little girl was the only dream I had left.

I pulled back the curtains in my room at the Navy Lodge and

jerked my head back when I saw that the line was wrapped around the entire hotel. There were men, women, even teenagers outside, all desperate for a chance to make a living in this border town.

I should forget this stupid idea.

Sure, I could've hired a nanny to travel with me from one of those fancy agencies. And I had definitely considered it. The ones I had interviewed had impressive résumés, but they had lacked heart. None of them seemed to truly need or even want to watch my baby.

I also could've left Sky back at home with her grandparents who had pretty much taken care of her alone last year while I flew around the country four days a week. But I had made a promise to my dying wife. A promise that I wouldn't leave Sky somewhere else to be raised when I was stationed somewhere for a few months. A promise that I would give someone the opportunity of a lifetime.

An even more importantly, I didn't want to be away from Sky any longer than I had to.

It had been my wife's idea to place an ad in El Centro's newspaper. We had lived here together last year, and Sky was born in this town. Catherine had loved the warmth of the people here, their hard work ethic, their perseverance in the face of adversity. When she'd had only moments to live, she'd made me promise that I would find a nanny out here when I returned. And dammit, I was a man of my word. Especially to her.

But how was I going to choose?

Sky cooed in the corner, happy in her swing. She was a happy, chubby baby, and thankfully a good sleeper, though recently she had been restless at night because she was teething. Since moving back here a week ago, the officers' wives had taken shifts helping to care for her when I was at work. I was grateful for their support, but it did nothing to soothe the ache in my heart from losing the love of my life. But as much as I was certain that I would never love again, I missed being around women. Their scent, their touch, their taste. My friends' wives offered to set me up with their friends, but I had no interest in dating. And the idea of having a one-night stand held no appeal to me. I needed to set a good example for my little girl and hooking up with random women I had no intention of getting serious with was not a step in the right direction.

Even so, I felt guilt that she didn't have a mommy. A woman in her life that would love her the way Catherine did. Her grandparents and I adored her, but we were no substitute for a mother's love.

I picked Sky up, planted a kiss on her forehead and took her into the other room where I rocked her to sleep and then placed her in her crib. Once she was out, I quietly exited the room.

As an officer, I was used to taking control, and had already planned a strategy for today. I was going to ask everyone the same question. *What are you going to do with the money?* And I knew exactly what I was looking for in that answer. I wanted someone who was selfless, wanted to help others, and had a clear plan of exactly what they would do with the money. I wanted to change someone's life. And I wanted someone who clearly loved children and didn't just see this as a job.

My buddy, Sawyer, opened the door to my room. "Ready?"

"Yup. Let them in."

Sawyer had offered to be crowd control. He was also an Angel, but—

unlike me—Sawyer was a womanizer. He had a girl in every city. Not that I could blame him—Blue Angels really were the rock stars of the air. But that kind of life had never appealed to me. Catherine had been my high school sweetheart. We had dated long-distance when I attended the U.S. Naval Academy in Annapolis, and after I graduated, we were married in the chapel. She had been a great wife. She had been faithful to me during my many deployments to the Middle East, had never once complained as I chased my dreams, supported me fully even when we spent years apart. All of our future plans had been cruelly ripped from us during what was supposed to be the happiest time of our life. All I had left of Catherine was our baby. And I would do everything in my power to give her the life Catherine wanted for her.

The first batch of people shuffled through the room one at a time, repeating their similar tragic life stories. Out of work for years, the money would go to feed their children, get out of debt, pay for medical bills. But with none of them did I truly think that this opportunity would change their lives. It seemed instead like a Band-Aid. And once the money ran out, they would be stuck in the same place they were before they had this job. I thanked every one of them and told them I would contact them tomorrow if they were chosen. Even my numb heart ached at the despair in these confessions. Maybe I had been wrong. Maybe I wouldn't be able to choose. Maybe I wouldn't find what I was looking for.

I closed my eyes and prayed to the heavens. "Please, Catherine. Help me out here. Give me a sign. Something."

After about an hour more of interviews, I had begun to lose hope. Then a girl with an incredible body entered the room. Her jet-black hair framed her angelic face, and her pale green eyes gazed at me over the casserole dish she was holding. I forced myself not to undress her with my eyes, but I couldn't help but notice how incredibly beautiful she was. She handed me a résumé and then cautiously peeled back the tin foil, and the scent of roasted tomatillos, corn tortillas, and cheese filled the air.

My eyes widened when I saw the enchiladas verdes. My favorite. Catherine and I had spent last winter trying every Mexican restaurant in El Centro on a quest for the best enchiladas. Was this my sign?

"Hello, sir. My name is Paloma Pérez. I would be honored to apply for the nanny position. I'm a hard worker, and I love babies. I raised my sisters pretty much myself. I was also valedictorian of my high school class and I am CPR certified. And I cook, too. I'd be happy to cook for you every day. Would you like to try these enchiladas? I made them from scratch—even the tortillas and the sauce. It's made with fresh, roasted tomatillos."

My stomach rumbled, and my mouth watered in anticipation of this home cooked meal. I had been existing on fast food, ramen, and pizza since my wife had passed, but I needed to get my act in gear for the upcoming season. I had to be one hundred percent focused on flying, or my fellow pilots could be killed. Even worse, I could crash into a crowd of innocent spectators. After Catherine had died, the Navy had offered to give my slot to another pilot, but I had quickly shot down that idea. No way. I had worked toward this dream my entire life. Catherine would be livid if I stopped living my life to mourn her. I had to push forward, no matter how much it hurt. For Catherine. For Sky.

"I'd love to. Thank you, Paloma. I'm Beckett Daly. Nice to meet you."

Paloma's face brightened into a smile and she looked around the room's kitchenette. "Can I get you a plate? A drink? I would've brought something. I'm so sorry."

"Hey, don't apologize. I'll get the plates." I stood up and grabbed two plates from the cupboard, utensils, and a wide spatula. I fought the urge to pop open a beer in front of her and instead reached for two glasses which I filled with water. After I served the food, I sat down at the table and invited Paloma to sit next to me.

I dug my fork into the enchiladas, and the second the bite hit my mouth, my taste buds were in heaven. The enchiladas were not too mild, not too hot. Just perfectly spiced, tart and fresh. Before I could come up for air, I took another bite, and then another. I devoured one of the enchiladas on my plate and became completely lost in this amazing dish. For the first time since my wife died, I felt satisfied. Catherine would've loved them.

But she couldn't. She was dead. And here I was gorging myself on this applicant's food, enjoying this delectable dish, feeling happy.

Hell, I felt guilty eating enchiladas without Catherine.

I pushed back my plate.

"These are delicious."

"Thank you, Mr. Daly."

"I go by Beck. Where did you learn to cook?"

"My grandmother taught me. I love to cook. I can make anything you like to eat. All the Mexican specialties, of course—flautas, burritos, tacos. But I can learn anything else you like. Hamburgers, spaghetti, meatloaf. You name it, I'll make it."

Her desperation hung thick in the air, and I wasn't ignorant to the fact that there were still at least a hundred other people in line. I had to give everyone a chance, but I was entranced by the girl sitting in front of me. And I'd be lying if I didn't admit that I was insanely attracted to her, despite myself.

"So, tell me, Paloma, how would you spend your day with my daughter, Sky? She's nine months old."

She grinned. "Oh. I love that age. We would have so much fun. I don't believe in any screen time and I don't watch television. We would sing songs, play games, take walks around the base, go to the park. I would read to her every day and go to the library. I'd be available for any playdates with any other babies on base. And I have this Mommy and Me yoga video I used to do with my sister. Ana María loved it."

I winced. Catherine had bought a bunch of Mommy and Me yoga DVDs. She had dreamed of doing them with Sky. It had completely slipped my mind until Paloma mentioned it.

Yoga. Another sign.

But I wasn't convinced yet.

"What would you do with the money you would earn as my daughter's nanny?"

She gulped and took a deep breath. "I'll be honest with you, sir. My mom is a mess. She had me young, she drinks, and runs around with men. I take care of my two sisters, and we often don't have enough food to eat. They are good girls, but I worry about their future. I want them to go to college. There aren't any jobs around here in El Centro. I have a high school degree, but I turned down my college scholarship because I just couldn't abandon my sisters here with my mom."

Her voice cracked, and I was worried that she would cry. Paloma had just said that her family was hungry, yet she had given me food.

She spoke rapidly as if she had interpreted my silence as a reason to up the ante. "I would take the money and move to San Diego. Leave this town forever. It would be enough to get a tiny studio apartment. We are used to being crammed into one room. I would get a job and attend college part-time. It would be a struggle, but we would make it work." She paused and bit her lip. "Please give me a chance, sir. I won't disappoint you. This opportunity would change my life."

Bam. And there it was. The sign I had been waiting for hit me over the head like the sound of thunder crashing on my plane. I had struggled with my faith daily since my wife had died, and Paloma's presence forced me to remind myself that even though I was in deep pain, I was blessed. I had a great career, a beautiful daughter, had been married to a wonderful, loving wife, and had food to eat. Had Catherine sent our baby girl and me this message?

"I hope this isn't inappropriate, but do you have a boyfriend? I'm not interested in having any drama."

"No, sir. I don't have a boyfriend, or any desire to have one. I don't date at all. My only focus is on taking care of my sisters and getting a job."

I paused. Her sisters. If her mom was so irresponsible, who would watch them if she took this job?

"This is a live-in nanny position. You would have to spend the night. Who would watch your sisters?"

"Oh, you don't have to worry about my sisters. They would stay

18

with my uncle. I've spoken to my sister, Mónica, who is fourteen, and she has agreed to step up and help with our youngest sister, Ana María, who is six, if I am blessed enough to get this job."

She bit her lip when she mentioned her uncle and I wondered if she was lying about him being able to take care of them. She had also mentioned she had turned down a college scholarship to take care of her sisters. Couldn't her uncle have watched them then? Maybe he was willing to take care of them for ten weeks, but not forever.

My heart constricted in my chest. I had gotten her hopes up. I couldn't let her down now. But I had to let her know what she was in for by working for me. And I had to see if she would be good with Sky.

"You would have to be up at night to take care of Sky. I would love to get up with her, but I have to have a good night's sleep, or I can't fly. Your room would be on the opposite side of the home. Would you be okay with that?"

She nodded her head vigorously and then lifted her eyes which met mine. As they locked in intensity, I felt, even if only for a moment, like we shared a deep connection. "Yes, sir, that would be wonderful. You won't hear a peep out of me. And I will do my best to keep her quiet."

"When I come home from work, I would like some time alone with my daughter. You will be free to go home for a few hours and see your sisters, which could work out because it would be after school. I keep to myself most days, and to be honest with you, I'm not a pleasure to be around. My wife passed away nine months ago."

A lump grew in my throat, and I stopped talking. Nine months. Had it been almost a year? Why did every second without

Catherine seem like an eternity? If living without her for nine months had been so painful, how could I bear to spend the rest of my life without her?

I wasn't ready to express my grief to this girl. "I don't mean to be rude, but I have no interest in being your friend. Our relationship will be strictly business."

"Yes, sir. I understand completely. I won't bother you at all. If I'm given this job, I will just be so grateful for the opportunity."

Sawyer opened the door. "Beck, the line is getting anxious."

"Give me a minute." I turned back to Paloma. "Would you like to meet my daughter?"

"I'd love to."

I opened the door to the bedroom where, despite the noise, little Sky was still sleeping contently. I carefully watched Paloma. Her face lit up when she saw Sky. I didn't sense anything fake about Paloma's smile.

"She's so precious." Paloma whispered, and she knelt down by the crib.

I stood back for a moment to watch Paloma. She kept her gaze on my daughter and didn't even seem to notice that I was still in the room.

And I had no more doubts. Deep in my soul I knew that Paloma was the woman who was meant to be my nanny.

I motioned her to leave the room and grabbed my phone to text Sawyer.

Send them home.

"Paloma, thanks for meeting with me. I'd like to offer you the position contingent on checking your references."

Paloma stood in front of me, her chin quivering as tears welled in her eyes. "You mean it, sir? Of all these applicants, you chose me? I've never had any luck in my life."

"Yes. I choose you. And it isn't about luck. We are both in the position to help each other. I will still call your references, and I will run a background check, but if everything checks out, you will start in two days. Will everything check out? No convictions? Nothing I should know about? Tell me now so you don't waste my time."

"No, sir, none. I have lived my life honorably and honestly. I have never done any drugs, never been drunk. I'm determined to make something of myself. I can't thank you enough for giving me this opportunity."

"No. Thank you. I have your number, and I'll call you tomorrow afternoon. Thank you for the enchiladas. They were delicious."

Before I could stop her, Paloma flung her arms around my neck. My breath hitched; I hadn't been this close to a woman since my wife died, and I didn't have any desire to cross this line with my nanny. Even so, heat rose in my body and I imagined slamming her against the wall and fucking her. Instead, I hugged her back, enjoying the warmth of her tight little body before she pulled back fast.

She averted her eyes and her cheeks blushed. "I'm so sorry, sir. I know that was inappropriate, but I'm just so happy. It won't happen again. This is the best day of my life. Thank you. I won't disappoint you."

My mouth became moist and I fought the urge to kiss her. Then I read myself the riot act.

Don't fuck the nanny.

I had to break the awkward silence. "Wait. Take the rest of the enchiladas. They were delicious."

"Thank you, sir."

And with that, the beautiful Paloma Pérez walked out of my hotel room, leaving me with my lone enchilada. Tonight, I had my first home-cooked meal in years, since Catherine never really cooked. I cracked open a Corona, cut a lime wedge, and pushed it inside the bottle. One sip and my nerves relaxed. Another bite of the gooey enchiladas and warmth filled my soul.

I knew Catherine was looking down on me.

CHAPTER THREE

BURNT TOAST

I raced home as fast as I could while being careful not to drop the remaining enchiladas. Every thought in my head filled me with confusion.

Me? Did he really say that he planned to hire me?

He couldn't possibly be serious. There were hundreds of people outside his room. Why would he choose me? Was it really as simple as me bringing him the enchiladas?

His baby Sky was adorable. She looked just like her daddy, but had blonde hair. Was her mom blonde? How had she died?

And I hated to admit it, but Mónica had been right about him— he was hot. Gorgeous, even. Ugh, I should not be thinking about my future boss like that. His dark hair, his piercing blue eyes, and the sexy scruff hiding his chiseled face. And that was just his face. His body was ripped. I had tried not to stare at his tattooed bicep. When I hugged him, I couldn't help but melt into his rock-hard chest. But even if I wasn't his nanny, he was way out of my league. I pictured his wife to have been some tall gorgeous, classy blonde, with bouncy golden curls and killer legs. In other words, nothing like me.

That must've been why he chose me—I must be her complete opposite. I was sure he wasn't remotely attracted to me. Which was a good thing since he would be my boss.

All that mattered was that I had a job!

I burst back through my door, and the scent of burnt toast immediately overtook my nostrils.

Great, Mama was home.

I didn't want to tell her about the job. Not yet. Not until I knew for certain that I had it. If I told her now, she would try to sabotage it, because she needed me to take care of the girls. And even though she didn't watch them, she didn't want us to move. She needed the girls so she could continue to get money from the government. Mama's greatest fear was that I would get a job, get custody of the girls, and leave her. Then she would have no money, no place to live, and no one to make her food. It would serve her right.

"¿Dónde estabas?" she barked at me, the thick stench of cheap liquor still on her breath.

"None of your business. Where were you? You didn't even come home last night."

Her eyes fell on the enchiladas. "Why are you bringing *my* food to another house when we are starving? And why are you wearing my nice dress? Were you with a man?"

I forced myself not to explode at her. "No, Mama. I'm not like you."

Her hand lifted, and before I could duck, her hardened palm

24

slapped against my cheek. "Don't talk like that to me, Paloma. I am your mother. I would never talk to my Mama the way you speak to me."

I pressed my hand against my cheek to ease the sting. "Yeah, well I wouldn't either. Abuela was a good mother. You are cruel and selfish. I wish you had died instead of her!"

The second those words left my mouth, I regretted them. Not because I hadn't meant them, because I had. But I shouldn't have stooped to my Mama's level. After twenty years of emotional abuse and neglect, I was a wreck. I needed to get away from living with her before I lost my mind.

But first, I needed to use her abuse as a way to get what I wanted.

"I don't feel safe here anymore. I'm going to take the girls tonight to stay for a few weeks at Tío José's. If you argue with me, then I'll press charges because you just hit me. Your choice."

My mama looked away from me. "You can go. I don't want you here anyway."

Good. Step one went off without a hitch, unless you counted me getting slapped. Now I just needed her to sign over custody. I placed the enchiladas down and went to get the girls from our room.

Mónica greeted me at the door.

"Did you get it?"

I placed a finger over her mouth and closed the door.

Once safely inside, I whispered, "I think so! He said he would like to offer me the job and would call me!"

"Oh my God! Lo! You did it! When do you start? Do you really think he's going to hire you?"

I nodded. Even Ana María started jumping up and down, though I wondered if she understood what we were talking about, and how this job would change our lives.

I glanced around our small room. We all slept together on a queen mattress without a frame. But we had dressed it up with homemade pillows, and I had made sure to secure a Princess Elena blanket over the border so Ana María would have something special. But even her pretty blanket couldn't brighten up this dump. With linoleum floors, cracked walls, and one bathroom for the four of us, I would be embarrassed if Beckett ever saw where we lived. But I was grateful to have a roof over our heads.

I wondered what Beckett's home was like. I had been on the base once with my uncle, who had been a maintenance man there before he had been fired. I remembered thinking that the officers' homes seemed so grand. I bet the kitchen had new appliances. I couldn't wait to cook in it, and to take Sky to the base park. Was this really happening to me? Why was I afraid that tomorrow he would call and let me know he had found someone else?

But even if he kept his word and gave me this job, getting through the next ten weeks would be brutal. Especially for my sisters. My uncle would definitely agree to watch them, but he was an alcoholic. And Beck had said that I'd be off work every day in the afternoon, so I was hoping I'd be able to pick the girls up from school and be with them until they went to sleep. And honestly, what other choice did I have? They couldn't stay with my mother because she often didn't come home. It was only for ten weeks. They would be fine for ten weeks. That had to be.

Mónica grasped my hands. "So, then what? After the ten weeks, we can move to San Diego? How are you going to get Mama to sign over custody?"

My heart dropped. I prayed this wouldn't blow up in my face. My Mama could screw this entire thing up. If she found out about the job, she would embarrass me and show up at Beck's house. And Beck definitely wouldn't want my mother around his daughter. But I had to put on a brave face for Mónica. "Whoa. *No cantes victoria todavía.* Let's not get ahead of ourselves. I haven't even started the job. He could call tomorrow and say he changed his mind."

Her face dropped. In a way, she needed this more than I did. I had already lived two years of my adult life like this. Mónica wouldn't tolerate it. The second she turned eighteen she would flee this town, any way she could, whether it was on the back of a motorcycle or hitching to San Diego. My sister was not the type of girl to stay here and tough it out.

I placed my hand on her shoulder. "Let's go eat. I brought back the rest of the enchiladas. And remember, don't tell Mama. I will deal with her when I start the job."

I opened the door, expecting to find Mama scarfing down the food, but instead, she had vanished again. Fine by me. I was pretty sure she didn't like my sass, but her moods no longer concerned me.

I plated the enchiladas for Ana María and Mónica, and we sat down around the kitchen table.

I hadn't said grace since my abuela died, but tonight I wanted to. To honor her. To honor the gift of this job. To honor the food on our table.

"Bless us, O Lord, and these your gifts, which we are about to receive from your bounty. Through Christ our Lord. Amen."

Mónica gave me a quizzical look but didn't question me. "Amen."

"Amen." Sweet Ana María looked so adorable clasping her hands. A chill passed through me. What if something happened to the girls while I was at work? Would they be okay?

They had to be okay. Had to be. This had to work. But I couldn't stop thinking of all the ways this could go tragically wrong.

Mónica scooped a big bite of the enchiladas. "These are so good. Definitely why he hired you. And, of course, because you look sexy in that dress."

I shook my head, completely in denial of what I had felt during the interview. He was so ridiculously hot, looked like he walked off a movie set. But his tone with me was serious and his eyes looked sad. But at least a couple of times during the interview, I could swear he was attracted to me. The way his eyes lingered on my body when I first walked in, how hard he embraced me back when we hugged. But that was probably wishful thinking. "No, it was nothing like that. He did ask me if I had a boyfriend but made it clear to me that he didn't even want to be my friend. I mean, his wife died last year. It's all so sad. He seems like a really good man."

A good man. Those words hung heavy on my lips. What was a good man? Did I even know? Had I even met one? My uncle was a hard worker, had provided for his family, and had been faithful to my aunt, but he fell apart when he has lost his job. Became a nasty drunk and my aunt left him. Now, he was even more of a mess. And in his drunken stupors, he was violent. He had once choked my aunt.

"Was he hot?"

I exhaled. I didn't want to tell Mónica how sexy Beckett was, how once during the interview I became entranced with his eyes. But I had no one else to confide in but her. "Yes, Mónica, he was. So gorgeous. He was over six feet tall with the most incredible body, and had the most beautiful sky-blue eyes. But I could tell he had a bad boy streak in him. I mean, his arm had a bunch of tattoos. And he smelled so good."

Mónica squealed like the schoolgirl that she was. "Damn, girl. Forget working for him. *Marry* him. Does he have a brother?"

I eyed her. In my dreams. Though I had vowed not to even consider dating seriously until I had a college degree, could support myself and my sisters, and was stable, a man like Beck seemed completely unattainable.

"Ay, Mónica, you're crazy. I'm not going to marry him. He's my boss. He wouldn't hit on me anyway. I highly doubt I'm his type. His daughter has white-blonde hair. I'm sure his wife was some gorgeous rich, educated classy woman. And she just died a year ago."

But at some point, he would move on, right? I couldn't imagine a man as sexy as him being single forever. "Even when he's finally ready to date again, I highly doubt that he would be interested in some poor chica from El Centro. And by that time, we will be in San Diego starting our new lives. He's a Blue Angel. He can get any woman he wants. The prettiest girls in the world."

Ana María finally seemed to comprehend our conversation. "You are the prettiest girl, Lo."

I leaned over and kissed her forehead. She was so sweet. She deserved a great childhood. A princess room instead of a cheap blanket. I bet Sky had the best nursery. Probably with one of those plush cribs from Pottery Barn and designer baby dresses. I tried not to be jealous, but sometimes I couldn't help it. Why did some people have so much when I had so little?

Mónica pinched me. "All I'm saying is that it *could* happen. Just like *The Sound of Music*. We could be like the Von Trapp family."

I laughed. "Yeah, but I can't carry a tune. You are silly. Get your head out of the clouds. Best case scenario, I truly get this job, and we take the money and start over in San Diego. We can have a good life and make something of ourselves. But I promise you— I'm not going to fall in love with my super-hot boss. I want him to respect me, not see me as some girl who would use sex to get money. It would be gross, because he's paying me. I want to teach you girls your own self-worth. That you have something to offer the world besides your body."

And I meant every word I said. Maybe one day, after we had moved to San Diego, I would meet a nice man who would treat me right and accept my sisters as part of his family. But until then, I would happily remain single.

We spent the next hour actually enjoying ourselves. Laughing, fantasizing about our new lives in San Diego. Mónica dreamed of working in a clothing store to get discounts and spending her weekends hanging out at the beach. And Ana María wanted to take dance lessons and learn how to ride a bike. Those little things in life that most people took for granted would be huge for us.

I cleared the table and Mónica started doing the dishes. Then, my phone beeped.

Mónica and I shared a glance, and we ran over to it. She grabbed my phone first, but I stole it out of her hands.

My heart skipped when I read the text from a phone number with an 850 area code.

Paloma, this is Beckett. I enjoyed meeting you tonight and loved the delicious enchiladas you cooked. I already checked your references. Your teacher couldn't say enough good things about you. Sky is a bit restless, and I have to report to base early tomorrow for a meeting with the Captain. Is there any way you could start tonight?

CHAPTER FOUR

COLD PIZZA

I looked out the window for Paloma. I had texted her an hour ago, and she still hadn't arrived. To be fair, I had asked her to come over at the last minute. But she had been so eager for this job, her tardiness shocked me. I had already notified the security guard at the gate to allow her on base. What was the holdup?

My fingers shook, and I knocked back another shot of whiskey. I hated to admit I was nervous. I had not spent any time alone with another woman since Catherine died. Yes, Paloma was my employee but having her in our home felt illicit. This home had been my little slice of paradise in the desert, my home with Catherine. Her presence still lingered in the air, and I wanted to keep her to myself just a little while longer. Every day without her felt a little more final.

Sky had finally fallen asleep, but I knew she would be up in a few hours. I could always get her back to sleep, but I really needed a good night's rest. I started flying again tomorrow.

I grabbed the final slice of pizza from the box on the counter. It was cold, but it didn't matter. Though it was filling, it didn't satisfy me. I was craving more of the enchiladas Paloma had made earlier.

I glanced down at my phone and saw a message.

Paloma: I'm here. I didn't want to knock or ring the doorbell.

What the hell? I hadn't heard a car drive up.

I peeked past the curtain, and Paloma eagerly waved back at me.

I opened the door.

"Sorry it took so long for me to get here. I had to drop my sisters off at my uncle's place and then walk back here."

Walk?

Dammit, I hadn't even realized she didn't have a car. I looked down at her worn tennis shoes. Man, was I so entitled that it had never crossed my mind that this poor girl had probably walked four miles today to come to this interview, go home, and come back? "No worries. I'm sorry. I should've offered to pick you up. You shouldn't be walking alone at night. I assumed you had a car."

She shook her head. "No, I don't. It's okay, though. I like walking. But I do have my driver's license in case you need me to take Sky to appointments. I took driver's education in high school. Got an A."

The excellent driver without a vehicle. And my rich ass owned four. Granted, one was Catherine's, but I also had a truck, a sports car, and an SUV.

Paloma's hair shone in the moonlight, and I couldn't help but notice again how beautiful she was. Her lips were naturally pouty, and her breasts were full. I fought off my desire. Maybe I should've hired an old grandma type to watch Sky.

"Come in."

"Thank you, sir." She walked through the doorway, clutching a small duffel bag, and fidgeted. Her nice dress from earlier was gone, and now she was wearing a grey T-shirt and black pants, which hung low on her hips. Based on the high school graduation date on her résumé, Paloma had to be around twenty. My mind flashed back to what my life had been like eight years ago when I had been her age. I studied hard during the week at Annapolis and partied harder on the weekends. My parents had given me a car for my high school graduation and always sent me spending money in addition to my salary from the Navy. I never had to work for food. I guess I never considered how good I had it.

"Paloma, my men call me sir. As I said in the interview, you can call me Beck. *Mi casa es su casa.* That's about the only Spanish I know—I took Latin in high school and Arabic in college. You are my employee, but I want you to be comfortable here. After all, you are watching the most important person in my life."

"Yes, sir, I mean, Beck. Sorry, that will take a while to get used to."

I smirked. Did she see me as some old guy? "I'm not that much older than you. I'm twenty-eight. How old are you? Twenty-one?"

"Twenty. I'll be twenty-one in October. It's just . . . you're my boss. You already said that you had no interest in being my friend, which I totally understand, so 'sir' keeps it professional for me."

Man, I must've come off like an asshole. Professional was one thing, but I didn't need to act like a dick. I'd been so wrapped up in my grief that I hadn't interacted with another woman alone outside of work. This was supremely awkward. "I did say that. I meant that you are my daughter's nanny and our relationship should be about her. We won't be socializing together alone as adults. But, of course, I want you to be comfortable, and if you need anything, like a ride, don't hesitate to ask. I'm here for you. Let me show you to your room.

She nodded and quietly followed me to the guest bedroom. Catherine had decorated it last year. It was simple and feminine. Just a bed, a desk, and a dresser.

But one look at Paloma's beaming face and I realized that my version of simple was her version of luxurious. "This is so beautiful! I've never had a real bed."

This girl was blowing my mind. "Glad you like it."

"I love it." She dropped her duffel bag and sat on the edge of the bed. I noticed her eyes were tearing up. I had been burying my own emotions for so long, I blinked hard to prevent myself from tearing up also.

Man, this was intense. And it was only the first night.

I had an overwhelming desire to help her. To change this girl's life. After ten weeks of working for me, she would have enough money to move away, attend college, and support herself. If she was as hard of a worker as she claimed, I bet she would be successful. This job could be life-changing for her. And it would all be because of Catherine's wishes. Catherine's legacy.

Sky let out a soft cry. Perfect timing, because I wanted to show

Paloma everything before I went to sleep. She followed me to Sky's room, and I scooped my angel up.

Sky greeted me with a coo and a stretch, and my heart melted. At nine months old, she was so innocent and sweet. But I was racked with guilt thinking about how I could never give her the life she deserved. A life with a mother who loved her.

"She's so precious! Can I hold her?"

"Of course." I handed Paloma my daughter. Paloma's face lit up, and Sky smiled. A sharp pang hit my chest. It killed me to see another woman hold my daughter. My last memory of Catherine was her holding Sky one final time. One final kiss before she was taken away from me.

I looked away. "Her changing table is fully stocked. She has a bottle ready in the fridge. I have a bottle warmer. Have you ever used one?"

Paloma shook her head no. "I just usually submerged the bottle in warm water."

"It's easy. Let me show you."

I led her to the kitchen and taught her how to use it. She learned quickly and fed Sky while I watched.

After Sky finished her bottle, I gave her a kiss. It was time to go to bed.

"It's late. I'm going to crash. I have to be at work at six. Make yourself at home."

"I will. Don't worry about Sky. She will be great. I'm excited to get to know her. I love babies."

I turned to walk to my bedroom but stopped when I felt her hand on my arm. Her touch sent a jolt to my cock.

"I just really want to say thank you. You have already done more for me than anyone in my life."

I swallowed and my voice cracked. "Don't thank me, Paloma. Thank my wife, Catherine. This was her idea."

CHAPTER FIVE

HUEVOS RANCHEROS

Beck went to his bedroom and I couldn't help but stare at him as he walked away.

From his sky-blue eyes to that rock-hard body of his that couldn't be hidden under his black T-shirt and grey sweat pants, Beck was complete perfection. And he was all man. Sure, I had had crushes on high school boys, but nothing had come of them besides sloppy kisses and late night unsatisfying liaisons in the back seats of their jalopies. I imagined making love to Beck would be different. He was older, he was masculine. He was in control.

And he was also kind and thoughtful. He had credited his decision to give someone in this town a life changing job to his wife. He could deflect all he wanted. I knew he was a good man.

I would make sure that Beck didn't regret hiring me for one second. This place would be spotless, there would be three home-cooked meals a day, and his baby would be spoiled. After ten weeks, he wouldn't know how to live without me. Too bad I'd be living my life in San Diego.

My nerves rattled. First night alone in this home with Beck and Sky. And I couldn't quit worrying about my sisters. Ana María cried when I left her at my uncle's place. I hoped they'd be okay there. I just prayed he wouldn't get drunk and go on one of his rampages.

But what could I do? I felt so helpless. I had to make this job work, so I could give them a better life.

I cradled this beautiful baby girl in my arms.

"Sky, you are such a happy baby. Yes, you are! Look at those toes!"

She had these fat little cheeks and the brightest smile. She was so lucky to have such a loving daddy who adored her. The pang in my heart hurt even more, not knowing if my own father even knew I existed. I wasn't sure how, but one day I would learn his identity.

Sky yawned so I went to her room, changed her, gave her a kiss goodnight, and placed her into her crib. I was delighted when she barely fussed and drifted to sleep.

I couldn't believe I was getting paid for this. I'd do it for free!

I left the room and considered turning in, but I wasn't ready to crash yet. I walked around the kitchen and noticed that the floors were a bit dirty, so I grabbed a mop, poured some liquid soap into the bucket under the sink and scrubbed the floors.

I had always enjoyed cleaning. Since I'd never owned anything nice, I liked to keep the few things I had in great shape. I couldn't understand why so many people spent money on a gorgeous home yet kept it dirty.

After I finished with the floors, curiosity got the best of me; I had to see a picture of his wife.

I grabbed a towel to dust and stopped the second I saw a picture of his wife, Catherine. He had said her name tonight, and the tone in his voice had crushed me.

She had white blonde hair, like her daughter, and big brown eyes. Her skin was flawless, and her smile was warm. So gorgeous and super happy. At least it looked like she'd always lived a dream life.

When did she die? How did she die? Was it from a disease like cancer or from complications during Sky's birth? Whatever the cause, it was completely tragic.

I continued my fight against the dust bunnies and ended up at their wedding picture, which was in a frame on the mantle. Wow, it looked like a fairy tale. All the groomsmen were dressed in their white uniforms, holding swords above Beck and Catherine, who were kissing under the arch. Catherine's gown was long and flowing, and Beck was clean shaven and handsome in his uniform. They looked like the perfect couple. Truly in love.

He must've been my age in that picture.

I couldn't imagine being in love, let alone marrying, so young. But we clearly came from very different backgrounds and led completely different lives.

With my mind pondering their life, I went back to my own room.

My own room!

I couldn't believe it. I had always slept with my sisters. I didn't even know what privacy was.

I changed into my pajamas and placed the baby monitor next to my bed. I set my alarm for four-thirty a.m. and drifted to sleep.

When the alarm went off, I woke, complete refreshed but panicked. Had I not heard Sky? I hope she hadn't woken in the middle of the night and I hadn't heard her. What if Beck had to get up with her? He would fire me for sure.

I quickly changed and rushed into her room. She was still miraculously asleep. I went back to my bedroom and brushed my teeth. And though I normally kept my hair up in a tight ponytail, I brushed it out, the waves cascading against my chest. Mónica had packed a cosmetic bag for me. And for the second time in recent memory, I decided to put on some makeup. I washed my face, dabbed on some tinted moisturizer, curled my eyelashes, rolled the mascara wand on them, and put on a light lip gloss.

Now, it was time to cook breakfast.

I took the monitor to the kitchen to prepare breakfast. After a quick survey of the refrigerator, I realized I didn't have too many options. Clearly a bachelor, or in this case, a widower, lived here. We definitely needed to go grocery shopping later today.

But I would make do with what I had.

I started brewing a pot of coffee, and then gathered the ingredients. I had eggs, store-bought salsa, tortillas, oil, avocado, and pre-shredded cheddar cheese. I opened the jar of salsa and poured some into a cast iron skillet. Once the salsa was bubbly, I cracked four eggs into the pan, covered them with the lid, and set the stove to simmer. I warmed some oil in another pan and fried the tortillas. Finally, when everything was cooked, I plated the tortillas, scooped an egg and some salsa onto each, sprinkled them with cheese, and placed a sliced avocado on top. The lack of cilantro and queso fresco was unfortunate, not to mention the store-bought salsa and refrigerated tortillas, but I hoped the meal would taste great anyway.

As I was pouring the coffee into mugs, I heard footsteps in the hallway. For some reason, my hand was shaking.

Once he came into view, I did my best not to drop the coffee pot. Holy hell, he was fine. He was wearing a sexy smirk and a tight blue flight suit with a zipper down the middle. My first thought was how much I wanted to see what was under his flight suit. I tried not to stare, but I couldn't help myself.

"Morning. How did you sleep? Is Sky up?"

"No, she's still asleep. I slept great, thank you. She didn't wake once."

"Great." His eyes narrowed at the plate of food and then his gaze turned to the shiny, spotless kitchen floor. "Look, Paloma, you don't have to cook and clean for me. I hired you to watch Sky. That's it. You aren't my maid or my cook."

"Oh, I know. I love to cook. And I love a clean house, especially one as beautiful as this. If I'm going to live here for ten weeks, I want to keep it clean. I hope you don't mind."

He shrugged. "No, I definitely don't mind. I appreciate it. Thank you. We used to have a maid come once a week. I can still hire one, so you can focus on Sky."

Control your face, Paloma. He lives a completely different life than you.

"Oh, no. I'll be fine. It's just the three of us. I'm happy to clean when Sky naps." I couldn't fathom why he would want to waste money on a maid. It couldn't be that hard to keep this plate clean.

"Okay. Thank you."

I took his plate of food and placed it on the kitchen table with his coffee. "Do you like cream and sugar in your coffee? I did the best I could with what you had—you didn't have any cilantro and I had to use salsa from the jar. I can go shopping later today."

"I like my coffee black. I'm sure the food is great." He dug his fork into the eggs, and then he shoved them into his mouth. For a moment, I was jealous of the eggs.

I studied his face as he ate his food. His eyes brightened, and a smile formed.

"These are amazing. I usually have a bowl of cereal. My wife never liked to cook, and I'm never home. But I can grill a mean steak."

A wave a satisfaction overtook me, but I felt guilty for being secretly happy that his wife never cooked. Was I a horrible person? I couldn't fathom having a hot, sexy husband like Beckett and not wanting to take care of him. But we were clearly from different cultures. It sounded like they had a strong marriage. Maybe she worked also.

"I saw a picture of your wife. She was very beautiful." I stopped there. I wanted to ask how she died, when she died, how she lived, how they fell in love, everything, but I had no right to ask these questions.

His tone lowered. "Yes, she was."

He finished his food in silence. But at least he ate every bite.

He handed me a slip of paper. "Here's all my contact information. You clearly have my phone number, but when I'm flying I won't be able to answer it. If there is any emergency at all, please contact my command. Today will be an easy day, getting back into the swing of things. When I get off, I'll come back here and then you are free to leave to go see your sisters. I can give you a ride wherever you need to go."

"Oh, that won't be necessary. It's not too far and I like to walk," I lied. It was two miles down the road. I would've most definitely accepted a ride, but I didn't want Beck to see where my uncle lived. Or worse yet, have Beck meet my Uncle who could quite possibly be in a drunken stupor. So, I would walk, knowing that my traveling time would even further shorten the time I would be able to spend with my sisters.

"Okay. Do you have any questions?"

I hesitated but then I spoke. "Just one. Do you want me to speak to her in Spanish?"

He pursed his beautiful lips for a moment. Ugh, why had I said that? Maybe he didn't want his daughter to speak Spanish, and now he was probably worried he would offend me.

"If not, no worries. I can speak English."

"No, Spanish is great. Her mother wanted her to be bilingual." He downed the rest of his coffee. "But then you are going to have to teach me, so I know what she is saying."

I laughed. I'd love to teach him Spanish. First word that came to my mind was *cómeme*, eat me. My mind was way too dirty.

I pushed that thought out of my head. "*Bien*. I'll sing songs to her, and read her books. If her next nanny also speaks Spanish, she will be fluent." I paused and gazed into his eyes. "As for you, I'm happy to teach you."

Sky cried and we both jumped up.

He reached his hand out to stop me. "Wait, let me get her. I want to see her before I leave."

45

I nodded, and he left the table. He came back a few minutes later, holding her. Seeing this handsome man wearing a flight suit while holding his daughter was almost too much to bear.

He handed Sky to me and for a moment, our bodies met. A shiver went through me. He was so sexy, I couldn't stand it. I fantasized about him throwing me up against the wall and fucking me until I couldn't see straight.

God, Mónica had been right. I was totally already dreaming about him. What the hell was wrong with me? Here I had the opportunity of a lifetime to leave my town and start a life, and I was already distracted. This kind man had offered me a job, a home, and I was repaying his generosity by lusting after him.

I was no better than my mother.

"Bye, Paloma. I'll see you later."

"Bye! Have a great day! Don't worry about us."

I couldn't help myself from watching him walk away. Once I shut the door, I warmed Sky's bottle. Excitement filled my soul.

After changing and feeding Sky, we had read books, played peek-a-boo, and cuddled on the sofa. I enjoyed every second of being around this sweet baby girl. I inhaled her scent, kissed her toes, and finally put her in her swing.

In ten weeks, I would have a new life. I would be free from this town. And I owed it all to the little girl in my arms.

CHAPTER SIX

SOGGY CEREAL

I reluctantly entered my car. This would be the first time I would be leaving Sky alone with a stranger. I had used another babysitter in the past in Pensacola, but she was the daughter of a fellow Naval Officer. I pushed down the nausea in my stomach. It was only for a few hours. I had checked all of Paloma's references. Double-checked. Hell, I'd run a background report on her. Clean as my jet. Sky would be fine. But I couldn't help feeling nervous leaving my baby with someone I didn't know. I'd made the stupid mistake of Googling "nanny horror stories." I'd read one about this bitch who had offed the kids in her care. If someone hurt Sky, I'd kill them with my bare hands.

But clearly, I was paranoid. Paloma seemed great. Amazing, even. And man, could she cook. The eggs she'd made this morning blew me away. Better than most of the bougie brunch places that Catherine used to drag me to. I could definitely get used to Paloma's cooking. Beat the chow hall, hands down.

And she was ridiculously sexy. I wondered what she slept in last night. I imagined her wearing nothing but a tight tank top and sheer panties. But I had to get my lust for her under control. I would not cross that line with her, no matter how much I wanted to fuck her.

I wasn't ready to date anyone seriously, but I didn't know how much longer I could go without having sex. Being so close to Paloma, inhaling her scent, staring at her incredible ass, was almost too much temptation for me. I never thought I'd be with another woman besides my wife. She was it for me. But for the first time since she died, I craved another woman. But that woman couldn't be Paloma.

I drove to my command and checked in. Time to fly.

Charlie, the lead pilot, debriefed me. Charlie and his wife has welcomed Catherine and me to the squad when I had been a newbie. Though he was an excellent pilot, for some reason I didn't fully trust him, which was a huge problem when flying. I didn't know why, but there was something off about him. Like he was just faking his good guy persona.

Sawyer greeted me at the door. "Hey man, how's the hot nanny? Did you fuck her yet?"

I shook my head. Sawyer would never know the true meaning of love. At least I knew what it felt like to completely love a woman, even if it had ended in excruciating sadness. But the guy had had a rough upbringing—no role models like I had had in the relationship department.

"Nope. Not going happen. She works for me." I looked down at his soggy cereal. "She did make me an amazing breakfast. *Huevos rancheros.* From scratch."

Sawyer shook his head. "Man, she cooks too? Damn, I wish I had a baby, so I could hire her. I'd be doing her over the kitchen counter while she wore nothing but an apron."

Our other friend, Declan, walked over to Sawyer. "You are such a misogynist. You would fuck your own nanny? That's called sexual harassment. Stop being such a pig."

Sawyer laughed. "Whatever. Both of you have zero game. I'm going to give Beck here a pass since his wife died last year, but you won't shut the fuck up about your high school sweetheart, Declan. Both of you need to move on. I get it—you loved them. But they are no longer in the picture. Are you guys going to be celibate for the rest of your lives? We are motherfucking Blue Angels! There are only six of us in the entire world. We are more elite than the Navy SEALs. Stop letting them get all the pussy. It's our time to shine. The other three guys on our squad are married. You are my wingmen. And that's legit, not even a catchphrase."

I grabbed my helmet. "I'm here to fly, not to fuck. And you won't be an Angel forever. In a year, we'll all be attached to deployable units. You're a Marine, Sawyer. You'll probably be dropping bombs over North Korea. Don't you want someone to miss you while you are gone?"

His jaw clenched. "Someone to cheat on me while I'm gone? No thanks."

"Not all women cheat. One day you will get it. You will look at a woman and the entire world will melt away and it will only be you and her. You won't think of anyone else. A super model could beg you to fuck her and you wouldn't even consider it. You will love her more than flying. Until then, you're welcome to hook up with all the groupies. Gentlemen, I'm ready to fly."

Declan grabbed his helmet, too. "Let's go."

I greeted the other three pilots, and we walked to the runaway. Next week we would start practicing our formations and our aerial maneuvers, but today we were just supposed to reacquaint ourselves with our F/A 18 Hornets after the winter holiday.

One look at my plane and chills filled my body. I stroked the nose of my other baby. This hunk of steel was my home and it was the most beautiful plane I'd ever seen. My hand ran over the yellow paint that displayed my name for the entire world to see. Lt. Beckett Daly. Catherine and I had taken a bunch of pictures standing in front of it the day I saw my own plane for the first time. She'd been heavily pregnant but had looked so beautiful and proud. For years when I had deployed, I had been worried about being shot down by the enemy and leaving her a widow. I had never once considered that she would be the one leaving me.

Once I climbed inside the cockpit, the rest of my troubles faded. The only thing that mattered when I was flying my plane was making sure I landed on the ground safely, especially as an Angel performing for crowds of thousands. The risk of death was real in the diamond formation, where we flew as close as eighteen inches to each other.

I loved it. I couldn't imagine doing any other job.

I secured my harness and my lap belt and began to taxi on the runway. I made a call to the tower and once I was cleared for take-off, I accelerated and headed towards the heavens.

Time to pay a visit to my wife.

CHAPTER SEVEN

TORTAS

I dressed Sky in a cute onesie with yellow ducks on it and placed a headband bow on her head. She was so adorable. I made the band from some fabric I had bought from home. When I had searched through the accessories in her room, I had found no embellishments, which made me sad. Had her mom not had time to purchase them? Maybe she was sick while she was pregnant. Or maybe she and Beck didn't know until Sky was born if the baby would be a boy or a girl. Sky was a gender-neutral name. And many of her clothes were unisex. I realized I knew nothing about this sweet baby in my arms. I wanted to respect her mother's intentions on how to raise her, but since I knew nothing about Catherine, for now, I would keep this feminine bow in her daughter's hair.

I heard the car pull up and my heart raced. Beck was home. It was one o' clock and if I left within the next ten minutes, I'd be able to make it to my sisters' school by the time they were dismissed.

The door opened, and Beck's blue eyes widened when he saw Sky.

He scooped her out of my arms and kissed her forehead. "Nice bow. I don't remember seeing it before."

"That's because it hadn't existed. I just made it myself. I brought over ribbons and threads. I hope you don't mind."

He turned to me and smiled. "It's cute. Thank you. How was the first day?"

"Great. She's an angel. You lucked out. How was work?"

"Incredible. There is never a bad day flying. I've been an Angel for a year, but every time I get in that plane, I can't believe how lucky I am."

A burning sensation filled my stomach. How cool was it that this man had this prestigious job? Clearly he was whip-smart and a hard worker, but I was so envious of his accomplishments. Being around him was a blessing. He inspired me to let nothing stand in the way of my goals. I wouldn't be a nanny forever. I would graduate from college and start my own restaurant. My dreams were finally in reach.

"Oh, that's awesome. Glad you had a good day. Are you hungry? I made lunch. Just tortas—we really need to go shopping."

He looked at the plate of grilled ham and cheese sandwiches, which technically weren't tortas because I didn't have the right bread but at least I had made a spicy aioli from scratch. I wondered how spicy Beck liked his food—normally I would pickle jalapeños, but I would slowly test his tolerance for heat.

"I can eat. You are off now if you want to leave."

I needed to leave. But I wanted to stay spend as much time with

Beck as possible. "Yup. I'll leave in a few minutes." I handed him his sandwich, some chips, and tall glass of water. There were beer bottles in the fridge, but I hoped that Beck didn't drink during the day like my uncle did.

He gave Sky back to me, sat down at the table, and took a bite of his sandwich. After a moment, he gave me a thumbs-up. "This is a great sandwich. Seriously. I would pay ten dollars for this. You are a really talented cook."

I beamed with pride. "Thanks." Many people had complimented my cooking, but for some reason, Beck's approval made me giddy.

"So Paloma, tell me what it's like living in El Centro. It's so hot now, I can't imagine it in the summer."

I closed my eyes and remembered the sweltering nights, sweating in my apartment with no air conditioning. I didn't want to complain but I wanted to be honest with him. "It's brutal. Every day is over one hundred and seven degrees, so we don't go outside much. That's how I learned how to cook. I would stay inside most days. It's really rough for the younger kids because they can't go outside, and our place is so small there isn't much room to play. That's one of the reasons I can't wait to move to San Diego." San Diego. A place I had never even visited. I was so sheltered.

He winced. I didn't know if he was pitying me, but I felt self-conscious just the same. "You should. There is a chance I'll be stationed there next year."

Oh my God, really? That would be amazing! We could fall in love and both move there, and I could have a hot fighter pilot boyfriend. God, I was so pathetic—he wasn't even remotely interested in me. He had just asked me to leave his home and I was sitting here ruining his lunch by hanging around. I had to play it cool. "Oh really?"

"Yup. I love San Diego. Perfect weather. Amazing beaches. I was going to try to get stationed there next, but Catherine wanted to go home to Virginia. Her folks live there. And that might be wise because when I deploy again, I will need a guardian for Sky."

I nodded my head like I thought that was an excellent idea, which I supposed it was. There went my fantasy of having a future with Beck. "How long do you deploy for?"

"Depends. Nine months, maybe up to a year. Whatever the Navy needs. And I have no control over where I get stationed. I can request a certain place but there is no guarantee. So who knows? I could still end up in San Diego."

Oh. There was still a glimmer of hope. How amazing would that be if we met in El Centro and ended up both living in San Diego?

But no matter what, the deployment would suck for Sky. She would be without both of her parents. No day-to-day consistency in her life. "The deployment sounds tough. What about your parents? Can they watch her?"

"They live outside of San Francisco. They are great, but don't really want to raise a baby. They travel a lot, go to the opera, attend many social events. That's not really an option."

That didn't surprise me at all. I could tell that Beck was very wealthy by the cars he had parked out front and the amount of money he was paying me for my job. I definitely wanted to be comfortable in life, but I had no desire to be that rich. "Well I don't know much about Virginia, but I bet it's really nice. I've never been to San Francisco either"—I paused, not wanting to open up to him too much. But then I just blurted out—"or San Diego for that matter." Ugh. I sounded so pathetic.

Beck's jaw dropped. "Are you serious? You live two hours by car from San Diego. I can fly there in forty-five minutes. You never even went there on a field trip?"

I wanted to laugh but didn't want to be rude. "Field trip? No. Our school played a football game in La Jolla once, but my mom wouldn't sign the permission slip. Ana María was a baby, so I had to stay home and take care of her. But I'll be able to go after this job ends. I can't wait to see the ocean. And for that matter, I've never been on a plane. What is it like?"

Beck's eyes bulged. I wanted to know what he was thinking. Probably how pathetic I was. "It's exhilarating. You are on top of the world. I love everything about it. The adrenaline rush, the excitement, the thrill. Tell you what, I'll take you for a spin . . . in my plane."

Oh my god. Was he flirting with me? "What? Are you serious? Is that even allowed?"

His mouth closed and widened into a grin. "Of course, it's allowed. We have a passenger seat for a reason. The whole point of the Blue Angels is to do PR and recruitment for the Navy and the Marines. We take up news reporters, family members, friends . . . beautiful women."

Whoa. Did he think I was beautiful? My heart beat rapidly in my chest. My eyes met his. I wanted him to know how much I craved him, even though I would never ever make the first move. "I'd love that."

His knees touched mine under the table. "Then it's a date. I have to head to San Diego for flyover change of command ceremony anyway next month. My friend's wife can watch Sky. I'll show you around the city. You will love it."

Ay, Dios mío! I was so excited! I wanted to jump up and down and kiss him. But I still told myself he was probably just being nice. It would be like a pity flight. Even so, I wanted to believe he had ulterior motives. "I can't wait." I glanced down at my watch and noticed the time. Dammit. I had to leave now to get to my sisters. "Oh. I have to go. I'll be back later."

"I can take you. I don't mind."

"No, thank you. I'll walk." A ride would be so much easier. But no. I couldn't risk him seeing my uncle's place. He might think that giving me this job was a bad idea because they had to stay there. And he'd be right. It was a bad idea. But I needed this job as a way out.

"Okay. I'll see you later. Thanks again for the sandwich, Loma."

Loma? Was that his nickname for me? "You're welcome."

He took the last bite of his sandwich, finished his glass of water, and then stood up. He walked toward his room, and a few minutes later, I heard the water start. A chill ran over my body. Beck was naked in the same house as me. I couldn't stop imagining what Beck looked like with water streaming down his chest. I wanted to jump into that shower with him. I wanted him to make me come so hard that I could forget the hell that was my life.

But my attraction to him wasn't just physical. Ever since I'd first met him, his presence has awoken a hunger inside me that I didn't know existed. I wanted to know everything about him. He was so worldly and cultured.

I wondered what it would be like to be loved by a man like him.

CHAPTER EIGHT

TORTILLA SOUP

After the first few weeks of flying, I was exhausted. I had adapted back to my routine effortlessly. It helped that I didn't have to worry about Sky when I was working. Paloma had been such a blessing. I couldn't have asked for a better nanny. Not to mention a cook. She had made me three meals a day, despite my protests. She never complained once and was always on time. And Sky seemed as happy as a lark.

I wanted to do something nice for Paloma. Maybe take her shopping. Spoil her.

Hell, I wanted to fuck her.

But that was totally out of the question. I wasn't going to reward her kindness by hitting on her. And I didn't want her to think she had to hook up with me because I was her boss. So, I would put myself in check and just appreciate how lucky I was to have found her.

I pulled up to my home and was greeted by Paloma who was holding my little girl.

"Hi sweetheart. I missed you," I said to Sky, but I meant it to Paloma as well.

"Here's your daddy." Paloma finally handed her to me, but Sky let out a cry.

Ah fuck. I tried again to grab her, but she clung to Paloma like a magnet, snuggled against her breasts. Not that I could blame Sky —I wanted to stick my face in Paloma's breasts also.

"It's okay, sweetie," she said as she hugged Sky. "I'll just hold her until you are done with your lunch. I made you tortilla soup."

Sounded good to me.

"You sure? You are off if you need to leave."

"I'm in no rush. I'll stay a bit longer."

Sky's last babysitter couldn't wait to leave every day and Sky never seemed to care that she was gone. Now Sky was already becoming attached to Paloma. Was I going to take another care-taker away from my daughter? And what would happen next year when I was stationed at my next base? At some point I would have to deploy again. My own parents would never watch her and though Catherine's parents offered, they were so cold that they would probably ignore her. They had even mentioned that they would maybe even put her in full time day-care. I didn't have a problem with day- care but I didn't see why they couldn't watch her since they were retired.

Who would sing songs to her at night? Who would love her when I wasn't around?

I studied Sky interacting with Paloma. Sky smiled and clapped and pulled Paloma's hair. Suddenly, I wanted to be the one pulling Paloma's hair while she screamed my name.

Ah fuck. It had been so long since I'd had sex. But I couldn't think of the nanny like that, even if she was wearing an apron wrapped tightly over her clothes. The tie in the back accentuated her amazing ass. I pictured her wearing nothing but that apron as I took her from behind.

Fuck, Sawyer was right. I really did need to get laid.

At least I was about to eat another great meal. The kitchen smelled like lime and spices and I couldn't wait to taste the soup. Hell, I couldn't wait to taste Paloma. Well if my cock wasn't going to be satisfied, at least my stomach would be.

Still holding Sky, she placed the bowl of soup in front of me. "How was your day?"

"Great. How was yours?"

"Perfect! Sky and I had so much fun today. I took her to story time at the base library and then we danced."

I took a big scoop of my tortilla soup and the warmth immediately soothed my stomach. I had never had a version like this with a clear broth base instead of a tomato one. It was filled with big chunks of avocado, wedges of lime, and shreds of chicken. A dollop of sour cream accentuated the flavors and freshly toasted tortilla strips gave it an extra crunch. I loved it. I wished I could eat like this every day.

Maybe I could.

"This soup is excellent. Thanks."

"You're welcome." She bounced Sky on her lap, but I noticed that she checked her phone. Was she looking at the time? Was she late going somewhere?

Every day since she had started, I came home after work and

Paloma had made me a feast. After she handed me Sky, she would leave.

And she never told me where she was going. She said it was to see her sisters but how did I know that was true? Maybe she had a man.

Not that it had been any of my business. I had made it very clear from day one that I didn't want to be her friend. That I didn't want to hang out with her or even be in the house with her unless I was asleep or at work. I didn't want to get to know her.

But the curiosity was killing me. Who did she see every day for hours? Was it a boyfriend? If it was, I'd be pissed. Not because I wanted her, but because that would mean that she had lied to me. I couldn't stand liars. And I didn't want some jealous boyfriend getting mad that she slept in my home, that she cooked for me, cleaned my place and took care of me even though I did my best to keep my distance.

Which was becoming increasingly hard because she smelled so incredible.

Fuck it.

"So, what are your plans today?"

My question caught her off guard and her eyes widened. "Oh, just going to see my sisters."

"Do you want me to give you a ride?"

Her cheeks flushed. I had definitely not meant that type of ride. Though I'd be game to give her the ride of her life.

"No. I'll walk. It's a beautiful day."

It was not a beautiful day. Though it was January and seventy-one degrees, there were high winds that would kick up the dust in her face. It was so gusty that we might not even fly tomorrow. The chill was setting in and by the time she returned tonight, it would be in the forties.

"It's going to be cold tonight. I don't mind picking you up when you are done. Just text me."

"I'm good, but that's really kind to offer."

Why was she being so evasive and secretive? Was she embarrassed by where she lived? I wasn't going to judge her by her home. She was so fucking hot, I bet she had a man.

I must've been horny as fuck because I sat there staring at her while I finished my soup. I imagined her naked, riding some douche, as she screamed *Ay, Papi,* while she came. Then he probably flipped her over and plowed her as he spanked her incredible ass.

Dammit, I had been watching way too much porn. And last night I had even searched for hot Latinas on Pornhub. Maybe Sawyer was right. It had been a year. I was still a man. I loved my wife; I always would. But I really, really needed to get laid.

But definitely not by my nanny.

I finished my soup, and she handed Sky back to me after giving her a kiss on her head.

"Bye. I'll see you later tonight."

"Bye."

I watched her walk out of the door, and then paced for a moment. Something was off with her. I knew she was keeping a secret from me, and I was determined to find out what it was.

CHAPTER NINE

BURRITOS

I hurried down the road once I walked off base. The arches in my feet ached, but my heart was full. Was I imagining that Beck was falling for me? Over the past few days, he had been talking to me more after work and always engaged with me when I returned at night.

The way he looked at me made me weak and I was pretty positive he wanted me. I knew how a man looked at a woman that he desired. With hunger in his eyes.

But even if he was attracted to me, that didn't mean he was going to cross the line and hit on me. Beck was a man of morals and principles. I didn't think he would risk ruining our working relationship.

Unless.

Unless he wanted something serious with me.

And there was no sign that he felt anything more for me than just lust. Oh well, I could dream.

The minutes stretched into an hour, and the fierce wind hit my face. I should've accepted Beck's offer to give me a ride, but I didn't want to do anything to ruin my job.

A low rider car drove by and some men whistled at me. "Cuánto cuesta?"

How much? What, did I look like a prostitute? Maybe they thought I was my mom. I put my head down and increased my pace, hoping they would just drive by and leave me alone. Luckily, they did.

This whole situation sucked. I hated being away from my sisters. Mónica had told me that Ana María had been crying herself to sleep and who knows what kind of trouble Mónica was getting herself into. At least, I hadn't heard from my mom.

I raced down the street and finally reached their school. Ana María was sitting outside in front of a tree.

"Hi sweetie. Did you have a good day at school?"

"No."

"Why not?"

"There's the daddy daughter dance next month. And Rosa said because I don't have a daddy, I can't go!"

Fuck. My throat tightened. I remembered exactly how it felt to get those fliers. Stupid school. Why did they have those events when it just made some people feel left out? Every year when I found out about that damn dance, I wanted to hide at home and not ever go to school again. Mónica would be missing it also since they went to the same school which was a TK-8th grade. I wanted to weep for Ana María. I wanted to weep for Mónica. I wanted to weep for myself.

"Baby, I'll take you."

She shook her head. "You are my sister, not my daddy. That will make it even worse. Everyone will laugh at me."

"Tell you what. I'll make it up to you. Once we get to San Diego, I'm going to have enough money for you to take dance classes. And then you can go to so many dances."

"Really? That would be the best. I love you." She wrapped her arms around my neck.

"I love you, too." I adored her. I didn't resent at all that I had to take care of my sisters. I wanted to give them everything.

But I couldn't give them a male role model. A father. Someone who would love and protect them the way Beck loved Sky.

I had to focus on what I could give them. A roof over their heads, food in their bellies, and clothes on their bodies. I still had hope that I could do right by them.

My moment of hope was quickly dashed when I spied Mónica walking out of school, holding hands with a boy.

Oh hell no.

"Mónica! Let's go."

"Can I hang out for a bit?" She pressed against his boy's chest and he touched her bottom.

My own body tensed up. "No. We have to leave now."

The boy wrapped his arms around my sister and kissed her. God, she was only in eighth grade. I was doomed. I didn't know how I would get through the teen years with her alone.

But then again, I had been messing around with boys when I was her age also. But I had been determined to make a better life for myself. I didn't know if Mónica would emerge from high school unscathed.

She slowly walked toward me.

"Who was that?"

"Oh, just Jaime. He's just a friend."

I rolled my eyes.

"Do you normally kiss your friends?"

"Just the cute ones."

Ay, Mónica. I swear. But I didn't want to lash out at her today. No doubt all the girls in her class were talking about the father-daughter dance today. Maybe some of them even had dresses. I remembered when I was in eighth grade it was my final chance to go to the dance. I had prayed that Ana María's dad would take me. I had left the flyer on the kitchen table for weeks. Finally, I had worked up the nerve to ask him.

And I'll never forget what he said.

"I'm not your father."

That night, I had run away from home for the first time. Drowned my sorrows in the kisses of a high school boy. Lost my virginity in the back seat of his father's car. Trying to numb away the pain.

I wiped away a tear.

I stopped at the grocery store to pick up some food for dinner for the girls. Beck had already paid me for my first three weeks. But I was careful to save the funds for everything but food. I needed every penny I earned for once I arrived in San Diego.

We walked over to my uncle's apartment. Unfortunately, he was at home, sitting there like a sloth, holding a bottle of tequila like it was glued to his palm. Ever since he had been fired from his job and his wife had left him, he had given up hope. Not that I blamed him. It was hard enough to get a job in this town, and once you lost your chance, it rarely came back around.

"Hola. Did you bring any food?"

"Yup. I'll start cooking now."

I quickly headed to the kitchen and sautéed and seasoned the meat. As I was wrapping the mixture into the tortillas, I saw that my uncle was going through my purse.

Oh hell no. "Tío. What are you doing? That's my money."

"I'm watching your little brats. You should pay me."

No. I couldn't pay him. That would defeat the whole point of taking this job. "No. I need to save it. Please give it back."

He grabbed a bunch of twenties and I wanted to cry. I ran over to him.

"Give me my money back or I'll call the cops."

He laughed. "If you call the cops, I'll tell them that you dumped your sisters here. And they will take them away."

Fuck. That could definitely happen. But I needed this money. "Please. Once I get more I'll send you some. I promise. I need this money to move."

He didn't flinch and put the money in his pocket.

Rage took hold of me and I lunged toward him, but he grabbed his tequila bottle and hit me across the face with it, sending shards of glass everywhere. A sharp pain radiated above my eye, and when I reached up to my head, I could see blood on my hands.

Mónica screamed. "What the hell, Tío José?"

He grumbled something and went to his room.

"You okay, Lo?"

Blood dripped down from my brow and on to my shirt. I sat in the middle of the living room, crying.

Mónica got a towel and hydrogen peroxide and dabbed my face. It stung.

This wasn't working. I had to get my sisters out of here.

"Come on, We are leaving."

"Lo, we have nowhere to go. We can't go to mama's. If she isn't there and the cops come by, they will take us in foster care. Just finish your job. We need you to."

I shook my head. "No, I can't leave you here with him. He's a drunk. A thief. An abuser. This was a stupid idea."

"He never touches us. It's only for three months. This is our only way out. I keep Ana María away from him. We will be fine. I don't have any money for him to take, and I clean the house. We stay quiet."

I was impressed how mature she was being, watching my sister. I wish she could just be a kid, even thought I had never been one. But she was right. I had no choice. Otherwise the girls could end up in foster care, and I would never get them back. I had to make this work somehow. This was my only way out.

I hugged Mónica and Ana María. "I love you girls so much. We will get through this. Please be strong for me."

And I prayed again. For another miracle. If I could only get through this job, I just knew we would be okay.

CHAPTER TEN

HAMBURGERS

The hot water beaded down my chest as I scrubbed my body. An image overpowered my mind of Paloma in the shower with me.

I tried to push the fantasy of her naked body out of my head, but it wouldn't budge. I imagined water cascading between her full breasts and down her curves. Turning her around and taking her from behind, grabbing her round ass as I fucked her tight pussy.

Dammit. I was her goddamned boss. I was no better than Sawyer. I couldn't think of my nanny like that. What the fuck was wrong with me?

It had to be that I was just missing my wife. And that I was horny as fuck. Catherine had had a difficult pregnancy—she was bedridden for most of it, so we had been unable to make love. But that hadn't bothered me in the least. All I wanted was a healthy baby. I had prayed so much that Sky would be okay, never thinking that in a cruel twist of fate that I would lose my wife instead.

But God had other plans in store.

Something about Paloma intrigued me. I didn't pity her; it was nothing like that. I admired her. She was so strong. Many people would've given up with the lot she had been dealt. Drowned their sorrows in liquor, drugs, or sex. But Paloma seemed so positive and upbeat. I couldn't believe she had never left this town.

I can show her the world.

My wife had been dead for nine months, and I had finally accepted the fact that she was never coming back. For the last nine months, I had never thought seriously about another woman. But now, everything seemed different. Was I falling for Paloma?

I mean, it had been Catherine's idea for me to hire a local nanny when I returned. And she had told me in her final words that she loved me and wanted me to be happy.

Even so, I felt guilt. I turned my rage toward myself and took a calming breath.

I toweled off and got dressed. These thoughts were normal. I had no reason to be ashamed. I couldn't help my desires, but I was in control of my actions. And I was an honorable naval officer. I would not hit on my daughter's nanny. I wasn't that guy.

I walked down the hallway, and realized that Paloma was already home. She must've come in while I was in the shower. I wished she had joined me. Dammit, there I went again.

Her hair was wavy and wild, and I couldn't help but think that her hair would look like that after sex. Maybe she had just had sex with her hidden boyfriend.

Stop, dude. You have no right to know about her personal life.

She was sitting on the sofa, and Sky was playing in her Pack n' Play. Instead of greeting me like Paloma normally did, she remained quiet. As I approached her I noticed that she was looking down at the floor.

Maybe she could sense that I wanted her. I had to stop flirting with her.

"Hey. How are your sisters?"

"Good."

She still didn't look up at me. Something was wrong.

"You okay?"

"Yup, just tired. There are leftovers in the fridge if you are hungry."

Yeah, something was definitely wrong. I didn't mind at all if she didn't want to cook for me. I could take care of myself, and her for that matter. But her voice was low, and she had still not looked up at me.

I sat down next to her and a lump grew in my throat when I saw a big, open gash above her forehead.

What the fuck?

My vision clouded. "Paloma, what happened to your face?"

She covered her face more. "Nothing. It was stupid. I tripped walking and fell. There was some glass in the street. I'm fine."

She was lying to me. But I wasn't angry. I could tell from her slumped posture and the despondent look on her face that she was embarrassed.

I took her hand and she started crying. Before I could stop myself, I pulled her into my arms.

"Hey, listen. You can tell me anything. I'm not going to be mad, I just want to take care of you. What happened? Did some guy hit you?"

"It was my uncle. He went through my purse and stole my money. When I confronted him, he smashed his tequila bottle over my head."

Ah fuck. I clenched my fist. I wanted to kill that mother fucker for touching Paloma.

But then a chill came over me. Paloma at least was safe in my house now. Her sisters were with this jerk now.

"Are your sisters still with him now?"

She nodded. "Yes. But don't worry about them. They will be fine. He's good to them."

My chest constricted. Here I thought I was giving this woman the opportunity of the lifetime—and I was—but I didn't realize that by doing so, I was also putting her and her family in danger. She was the sole caretaker of her sisters, and now her sisters were living with an abuser to care for my daughter.

"He just assaulted you, Paloma."

"He won't hurt them. He's fine except when he drinks."

"How often does he drink?"

Her voice dropped. "Every night."

Yup. Nightmare. What had I gotten myself into? I could fire her, so she could go take care of her sister, but she was so great with Sky. And it wasn't fair to fire her when she had put her sisters in danger to take this job. She needed this job, this opportunity. And I was starting to have feelings for Paloma. She was incredible. And I wasn't the only one who thought so. Her references had been stellar. Everyone praised how hard working, smart, kind, and determined she was. Her teacher had even told me that she had begged Paloma to accept her college scholarship, but Paloma wouldn't consider leaving her sisters behind. I respected the hell out of her decision. And I wasn't sure that I would've put off my dreams of being a pilot for my own family.

Her refusal to chase her dreams to take care of her sisters doomed her to stay in this barren town.

And now, to take this job, I had forced her to leave them in a dire situation.

This was a new year. My old life died with my wife. Catherine hadn't wanted me to wallow in my grief, but to instead help others less fortunate. It didn't seem right to have Paloma's sisters suffer so she could work for me. Especially since I was living in a four-bedroom, two-bath home paid for by the government.

I couldn't believe what I was about to say.

"I'm not sure this is going to work out. I don't want your sisters to have to stay in an unsafe situation."

Her bottom lip quivered. "Oh, please, Beck. They will be fine. Please don't fire me. I really need this job. This is the best thing that has ever happened to me. They are my problem, not yours. They won't interfere with my work or my care for your daughter."

Dammit. I had definitely not said that right.

"I'm not firing you. But I have a big place here, and I'll be working most of the day. Your sisters are welcome to stay here."

Her eyes bulged. For a second, I thought she would immediately accept my offer, but she shook her head. "No. That won't be necessary. They are fine at my uncle's. I'm sorry I bothered you with my problems. I should get Sky ready for bed."

Had anyone ever done anything nice for this girl? "Sky is fine right now. Look, I insist. You can't focus on my baby if you are worried about your sisters."

She met my eyes and didn't look away. "Nope. It's out of the question. I don't need your help."

I was enjoying her little defiant streak. I loved that she wanted to earn everything herself. But I had received favors in my life that had helped me achieve my goals. And I was going to give her one.

"Then, I rescind my job offer. If your sisters don't stay here, you can't work here. You will be too distracted to concentrate. That's my offer. Take it or leave it." *There, that ought to do it.*

Her mouth slackened. "Wait, what? Are you sure? You really want them to stay here? Are you kidding me?"

"Yes, I'm serious. It's only for seven more weeks until I go back to Pensacola. It will be nice to have some laughter around here."

Tears welled in Paloma's eyes. "*¡Ay, Dios mió!* I can't believe this. This is the best day ever. I promise they will behave. And they love babies. We will keep this house clean, and we will be quiet. You won't even know we are here."

"I'm going to call Declan to come over and watch Sky and we can go get your sisters.

"Beck, you truly are an angel. I can't thank you enough."

She wrapped her arms around my neck and kissed my cheek. I fought the urge to kiss her back.

Ten minutes later Declan showed up. I quickly debriefed him about Sky, who was still asleep.

"We will be back in an hour. Call if you need anything."

The second we left base, I was struck at once by the poverty around me. I had noticed it last year, but it had seemed less heartbreaking. But now, with Paloma by my side, the barren landscape was painfully in focus. There were so many empty businesses with boarded up windows and chained off buildings littered with graffiti. An elderly man pushed a cart of food down the road and a young woman clutching a baby begged on a corner. It was around seven at night and the wind had kicked up the despair with the dust.

"Turn here. It's that one there."

I turned to an apartment building which looked more like a prison than a home. Was this where her uncle lived? Where her sisters were staying? And she walked here every night? Hell, I didn't even want to park my SUV out here. I'd even considered packing my gun.

She opened the door. "I'll go and grab them."

"I'm going with you."

She shook her head. "No, that's fine. I won't be long."

"Paloma, he hit you over the head with a liquor bottle. I'm going in."

We walked up the stairs and Paloma pushed the door open.

Her sisters were cuddled up on the lumpy sofa, but her uncle wasn't in the room.

"Beck, meet my sisters, Mónica is the older one and Ana María is the younger one. Girls, this is Beck. Gather your things. You are going to stay with us."

Ana María's eyes opened wide and Mónica's mouth gaped open.

"En serio?"

"Yes, I'm serious. Come on, let's go."

I heard a door open and some middle-aged man walked over to me, his face red and his eyes blood shot. "Who are you and what are you doing in my house?"

I didn't want to fight with him, though he deserved to be punched in the face. But I didn't want the girls to see any more violence or this loser to press assault charges on me. I just wanted to get out of this house as soon as possible. "I'm Paloma's boss.

Her sisters stared at me. Ana María's hair was braided, and she had big brown eyes and a sad smile. Mónica was wearing a tight shirt and shorts.

I knelt down to Ana María. "Do you girls want to go to McDonalds?"

"Yes!" Ana María jumped up and down.

Her uncle walked up to me and the stench of the liquor on his breath made me recoil. "The girls are my family. They stay here."

"Yeah, well I'm going to take them with me. Looks like you got your hands full here. Is that weed I smell?"

"Yeah. What's it to you? It's California. It's legal."

"I'm aware. But you shouldn't be smoking around young kids. Come on girls, let's go."

Paloma gathered the girls' clothes. I grabbed their bags and we went to my SUV. Her shoulders slumped, and she looked almost embarrassed.

Mónica stood next to me. "I can't believe you are going to let us stay with you. Is it true there is a pool on base?"

A pained expression crossed Paloma's face. She turned to me. "I'm sorry. They are just excited. They don't know how to swim."

Ah, fuck. I had no idea how much the little things I took for granted would mean the world to these girls.

Once we got into the SUV, I turned to them. "Yup, there sure is. And there are even swim lessons. Would you girls like to learn?"

Ana María's eyes became wide. "Are you serious? Did you hear that Mónica? We can take swim lessons!"

A wave of satisfaction took over me. "Yes. I can sign you girls up. After we eat, we can go to Target and buy swimsuits."

Paloma placed her hand on my arm. "Stop. That's not necessary. We don't want to owe you anything."

"You don't owe me a thing. Let's go shopping. Seriously, it's on me. No strings attached."

"I can't accept any gifts."

Man, she was tough. "You represent me on base. I don't have anything for the girls' room. Please, it would make me happy."

She shrugged. "I guess."

I felt bad that I was making her uncomfortable.

Mónica squealed. "Lo, can I get bikini?"

"No, you can not. You are only fourteen. You can pick out something modest." She placed her hand on my knee and a jolt went to my cock. "You really don't have to do all of this. I can never repay you. Actually, you can take it out of my salary."

I loved how humble she was and that she didn't want anything for free. "It's really my pleasure. I know I told you in the interview I didn't want to hang out with you, but honestly I've been so depressed since my wife died. It will be good to have you all around and keep me distracted."

She squeezed my leg. "If you need to talk, I'm a good listener."

Maybe I did need to talk. I had refused to talk to a grief counselor, and I never really opened up to my buddies.

We hit the drive-thru and the girls had Happy Meals, I ordered a Quarter Pounder with Cheese, and Paloma had a Filet-O-Fish. We stuffed our faces and then I turned into the shopping mall and parked in front of Target. When we exited from the SUV, Mónica whispered something into Paloma's ear which caused Paloma to blush.

I grabbed a red shopping cart, and they followed me into the store.

"Okay, ladies. So, seriously, let's get whatever you need. Clothes, some stuff for your bedroom, toys, school supplies. Don't be shy, it's on me."

Paloma whispered in my ear. "Seriously, I don't feel comfortable with this. Maybe just a few things."

I grabbed her hand, caressing her soft skin. "I want to. Please don't mention it again. And grab another cart."

"Okay, I'll make it up to you."

I wanted to ask how, but I shut my mouth. I wasn't offering to buy her stuff, expecting any sexual favors. Quite the opposite. No matter how hot I thought she was, I refused to get involved with her. It wasn't ethical, and I was a man of morals.

We zoomed around the store and the girls picked out clothes, swimsuits, bedspreads, and some toys. I picked up some supplies for Sky. Then I looked into the cart and noticed that Paloma hadn't picked anything for herself.

"Hey. I'm serious. Buy some new clothes. Whatever you need. Do you have a swimsuit? Maybe you can take Sky to the pool. I think there is a baby class." Hell, I knew there was a Mommy and Me class. Catherine and I had looked into it.

"Okay." She walked over to the rack and picked out a black bikini. Heat flooded my cock as I imagined her body covered in that thin fabric barely covering her huge tits, her wide hips, her tiny waist, and that incredible ass. I'd definitely have to go to the pool with her, to make sure some dickhead like Sawyer didn't hit on her.

I wanted to get home to Sky. We made a final pass to the grocery section and Paloma paused over the spices, but then walked away.

"Get whatever you need. If anything, you are saving me money by cooking."

"I was just looking at the saffron. I've always wanted some, but it's super expensive. I don't need it."

"If you make me paella, you can buy it. I had some in Spain and it was incredible." In Spain. On my honeymoon.

"It's twenty-two dollars. A waste of money."

I grabbed the little bottle. "Not if you make me paella. Okay, let's go."

I paid, and we walked out of the store. Pride filled my chest when I looked at their happy faces. The girls giggled in the back seat when talked about how much they couldn't wait to see their room. After suffering through all my grief, giving someone else joy made my heart leap.

Paloma made another quick stop at a grocery store, and then we went back to base.

As I pulled up to my house, I couldn't help but notice how at ease I felt around Paloma and her sisters. They were under the assumption that I was helping them out, but in reality, they were saving me.

CHAPTER ELEVEN

PAELLA

The next night, the house was buzzing with excitement from the girls. Ana María loved her princess bedspread, and Mónica was experimenting with her new makeup. Both of them had been perfect angels so far. I was proud of them. Beck was watching television while holding Sky.

And I was stressing out in the kitchen.

I had never made paella.

And this was Beck's favorite dish. I most certainly did not want to screw it up. I had started on the chicken broth, refusing to buy it from a can. This had to be the best paella Beck had ever had. I didn't care that he'd had it in Spain—mine was made with love.

I began to strain the chicken when my phone rang.

Ugh, my mother.

I had to get it.

I stepped outside, making sure to speak in Spanish so Beck couldn't understand me.

"*Hola?*"

"*Hola?* Where are you? Where are the girls? My brother said you took them away with some man."

Great. Good news travels fast. "None of your concern. When was the last time you were home? They are safe. That's all you need to know."

"Don't you speak to me like that. You must respect me. I am your mother."

I exhaled. I had to do this. I had to do this now. It was a long time coming, and I didn't have a moment to waste. Once she knew about my job, she would do anything to sabotage it. "Yeah, well about that. I want you to give me legal custody of the girls. We can do this the easy way or the hard way. The easy way is you sign over your rights. The hard way is that I take you to court for abandonment."

Her voice became quiet. "You would do that to your own mother? How dare you. I won't give up my babies. You have no right."

"No, you have no right. I swear, Mama, don't try me. I have records of everything. No court will let you keep custody. Don't make me fight you. Think of it as a relief. You don't have to worry about us anymore."

And then I heard a soft sob. "Paloma, you must know. I love you. I love the girls. I tried, *mija*, I did. It was just so hard."

"I know it's hard. But where there is a will there's a way." I lowered my voice. I needed to give her an easy out. "Mama, look. Just sign over your rights and once you get your act together, you can see the girls again. I'll be leaving El Centro in a few months. I have a job. But I'll come back and visit. And if you stop drinking, I'll let you see them."

"Job? What job?"

I was surprised my uncle hadn't mentioned that Beck said he was my boss. "Doesn't matter. I have to go. The girls are fine. I'll call you in a week. Bye."

And I hung up the phone. I wasn't heartless, but I was done with her excuses. I had to focus on the girls and our future.

But even so, my heart broke for her. There was something in her voice that made me feel compassion for her despite my hatred for her. She said she had tried? Had she? I didn't remember her making an effort. Maybe things were different when I was a baby. If she would only open up to me about my father, then maybe I could possibly understand where she was coming from.

I walked back through the door and found Beck standing in the kitchen. I couldn't help but stare at his biceps busting out of his white T-shirt.

"Are you okay?"

I wiped my hands on my apron. "Yup. Great."

He pressed his lips. "Who were you arguing with?"

I refused to lie to him. "My mother, but don't worry. She doesn't know where we are. She won't bother us."

He placed his hand under my chin. "You are amazing, do you know that?"

I choked back tears. I wasn't used to compliments. "No, but it's nice to hear. You're pretty great yourself. You are so generous."

His body brushed against mine. I held my breath, wondering what it would be like for him to kiss me.

I turned away from him. "I need to get back to the paella, or we won't eat tonight."

"Right, I just wanted to make sure you were okay."

"I am. Thanks."

I started scrubbing the mussels while I cooked the *sofrito* by sautéing onions, garlic, and parsley. The smell from the fragrant saffron and broth mixture filled the kitchen. I was in heaven. Spanish chorizo, shrimp, mussels, chicken—this dish had it all. I was ready to feast.

Mónica set the table, and when the dish was finally done, I served everyone. I poured Beck a glass of red wine and watched his beautiful mouth as he took his first bite.

He reached across the table and grabbed my hand. "Paloma, this is the best paella I've ever had."

CHAPTER TWELVE

FRENCH TOAST

Saturday morning I woke with a hard-on and a mission.

To see Paloma in her bikini.

Ever since she had bought that damn thing, I couldn't stop fantasizing about seeing her in it. And today was the day.

I took a quick shower and threw on my board shorts and a T-shirt. I never even woke during the night anymore to take care of Sky. I would've been happy to on my nights off, but Paloma would always grab her before I woke. And I was so well rested, my flying drills had been as tight as ever. I couldn't thank Paloma enough.

How would I live without her?

Her sisters had kept to themselves and had been quiet since they moved in a few days ago. But that bothered me. They were almost too good. As if they didn't consider this to be their home. Today I wanted to see their personalities. I wanted them to feel comfortable around me.

I opened the door, and the smell of cinnamon and vanilla over-took me.

Sure enough, Paloma was in the kitchen, and Mónica was playing with Sky on the living room floor.

My coffee was already waiting for me. "Morning. I made French Toast. It will be ready in a minute."

"Morning." I resisted the urge to kiss her on her cheek. It would've seemed so natural, so innocent.

Paloma was always cheerful, but I knew that she hid pain behind her bright eyes. I wanted her to cry in front of me, be vulnerable, trust me. I would have to earn her trust.

I scooped up Sky and kissed her. Her goofy smile brightened my world.

"Girls, do you want to go to the pool today?"

Mónica's eyes widened. "Yes. We would love to! Paloma, can we go to the pool?"

Paloma shot me a pointed glare. "After you do your chores. Breakfast is ready."

I strapped Sky into a baby bouncer and sat at the table.

Paloma handed me a plate of thick French toast. But it wasn't any old French toast. I took one bite and my taste buds danced. The whipped cream was infused with cinnamon and the minute my fork sliced into the bread, thick chocolate oozed out. I couldn't believe I was eating like this every day. Man, I hope Sawyer never comes over here. Even the womanizing confirmed bachelor would take one look at her and one bite of this food and would sweep her off her feet.

But I wanted to keep her to myself.

"This is delicious. If you keep cooking like this, I won't fit into my flight suit."

Paloma smiled. "Please, you are in perfect shape. You need fuel for your body and your plane." She paused. "Look, we all can't swim. I'm happy to take Sky to the pool, but I'm worried about the girls. Is there a lifeguard on duty?"

She was so adorable and non-presumptuous. "Yup, but you won't need a lifeguard. I was on the swim team at Annapolis. I'll teach you."

Her cheeks blushed. "Okay. Thank you."

At least I had made progress with her. She had stopped questioning me when I offered to do something with her and the girls.

After breakfast, the girls did their chores—vacuuming and cleaning bathrooms for Mónica and dusting and putting away toys for Ana María. I bathed Sky and dressed her in a cute ruffled swimsuit with a matching bonnet. Then, I slathered her in sunscreen until her skin was opaque with lotion.

My breath hitched when Paloma walked out from her bedroom. She was wearing a tank top and shorts, but I could see the bikini underneath. I couldn't wait to get to the pool and see even more of her incredible body.

"Let's go."

We walked over to the pool. I could feel all the eyes on us as I signed us in.

We placed our belongings under a cabana when Brittney, Charlie's wife, waved over to me.

Dammit. I didn't want to talk to her. I just wanted to watch Paloma take her clothes off.

But I couldn't ignore Brittney.

I whispered to Paloma. "I'll be right back. That's my buddy's wife."

I walked over and hugged her. She wore a black one-piece bathing suit and a big brimmed straw hat, and her face was painted with makeup. I would never understand why women wore makeup to the pool. Catherine always had, even though I had told her that I preferred her without anything on her beautiful face. I loved how Paloma never seemed to wear anything but lip gloss on her full lips.

"Oh, Beckett. How are you? How is little Sky? I just can't get over that poor angel living without her mother."

"We're hanging in there. Sky is great. She has a great nanny."

Brittney's eyes focused on Paloma who was holding Sky. "Oh, that's lovely. I'm glad you found some help. Who are the girls with her?"

Man, she was nosy. "Her sisters. They don't know how to swim. I'm going to teach them today."

She lightly punched my arm. "Wow. Well aren't you generous. I'm happy to watch Sky if you need me too. Actually, my sister Laurel will be coming out for a visit next week. Maybe we could all get together. Go out to dinner."

I swallowed the lump in my throat. I had met Laurel on several different occasions when Catherine was still alive. Laurel was pretty, sweet, and kind, but I was not interested in going on a double date. And even worse, I couldn't stop thinking about my nanny.

I was a wreck. I should've hired a nice grandma to watch Sky so I wouldn't be drowning in temptation.

"Thanks, Brit. I'll let you know if you need help with Sky. I'm not ready to go out anywhere though. But maybe I'll see you around base."

"Okay. Have a good time at the pool."

I turned around and saw that Mónica was now holding Sky. Paloma was still dressed and as if she was waiting for me to watch her, she caught my gaze and slowly lifted her shirt over her head, as her hair cascaded around her breasts. Then before I could blink, she shimmied her shorts over his hips. My heart pounded in my chest. She was more beautiful than I had imagined. I wanted to rip her bikini bottoms off with my teeth and feast in between her luscious thighs.

I needed to get a grip.

Seeing her in her bikini should've satisfied me, but it didn't.

Now, I wanted to see her naked.

CHAPTER THIRTEEN

ICE CREAM

Beck stared at me and I was certain he was checking me out. And for once, I was proud to show off my body. After years of being modest, I liked having him as my audience.

His eyes locked with mine as he ripped off his shirt. Hot damn, this man was fine. His chest was defined but not massive and he had tattoos on his arm. I noticed an angel and wondered if he had gotten that for his wife. He also had a rosary, and I wondered if he was Catholic. I was living with this man and I didn't know enough about him.

Mónica handed him Sky. I walked in front of him and took my steps into the shallow area of the pool.

Beck had bought some arm floats for Ana María who looked adorable in her Elena of Avalor swimsuit. I looked around the pool and noticed that a few people were staring at us. Did they wonder why we were here? I shuddered, and it wasn't from the cool water. I was probably paranoid but the sharp feeling that I was completely out of place overtook me.

Beckett placed Sky in a baby floatie and I pushed her through the water. "I'm going to help Ana María for a bit. I'll be right back."

Mónica sat next to me and we played with Sky. "Lo, he totally wants you."

I splashed her. "Stop, he's just being nice."

"Whatever. Men aren't nice unless they want something. Trust me."

I laughed. "Trust you? What do you know about 'men'? You are fourteen."

"I know a lot. I watched Mama, no matter how you tried to shield me."

Great. I needed Mónica to witness a respectful relationship between a man and a woman. She was too young to remember Papa and Abuela's relationship since he died when Mónica was Ana María's age.

Sky was loving the water and seemed to be a natural like her daddy. And Ana María was having the time of her life splashing around in the pool.

Beck then took Mónica for a spin around the pool. He held her body straight as she kicked on the paddle board. I was so impressed by his patience. Mónica kicked her hardest. I glanced up at the sun and couldn't remember the last time I had been so happy. My belly was as full as my heart.

When Mónica returned, Sky started to get antsy. I took her out of her floaties and took a step out of the pool when Beck grabbed my arm.

"Wait. Your turn."

What? I shook my head. "No. Sorry. I'm too old to learn. Let me get her out of the sun."

He turned to Mónica. "Would you take Sky and Ana María out of the pool? I'm going to work with Paloma for a bit. Then we will get ice cream."

"Sure, take your time."

Mónica grabbed Sky from my arms and Ana María followed them out of the pool.

I stood in the shallow end staring at Beck, hoping he couldn't read my mind.

He placed his arms around me and led me a bit deeper into the pool. I could swear all eyes were on Beck and me. I noticed the lady he talked to seemed focused on us, even though she was wearing sunglasses.

"Beck, come on. I'm embarrassed."

"You want to move to San Diego, right? You need to learn how to swim."

I was happy just feeling his arm wrapped around me. "Everyone is watching us."

He pushed back my hair. "They are all just looking at how beautiful you are."

Did he say I was beautiful? This was a dream.

He handed me the kickboard and lifted my waist up, so I was straight like an ironing board. "Kick, Loma. I got you. Just kick."

Loma. He had started calling me Loma. It felt illicit, intimate.

I wanted him to be proud of me. So, I kicked as hard as I could as the water splashed on my face. And then miraculously I started moving around the pool. Granted, Beck was guiding me. But even so I felt strong, invincible even.

He finally released me, and I gave him an involuntary hug. Our wet bodies pressed against each other with only the thin fabric separating us. I wanted to stay in this moment and lose myself in Beck's embrace.

But I quickly realized all eyes were on us at the pool. God, what did these people think? This widower hugging the nanny. How inappropriate.

I raced out of the pool and Mónica handed me a towel.

"Don't!" I scolded when she opened her mouth.

"What, I wasn't going to say nothing. Just that you are a good swimmer."

Her tone was teasing. What kind of example was I setting for them? I wanted to rush back to our place and lock myself in the room, alone with my embarrassment.

But Beck placed his hand on my back and smiled.

"Let's get ice cream."

"Yes!" Ana María said, a little too loudly.

We went to the concessions cart and we each ordered a cone of swirl soft serve.

Ana María looked up at Beck, with ice cream dripping down her face. "Beck?"

"Yup, sweetie."

96

"Thank you. This is the best day ever."

CHAPTER FOURTEEN

PASOLE

P aloma's sisters had settled into my home quite nicely. I drove them to school on my way to the base and went with Paloma to pick them up when I got off work.

But the normalcy was getting to me and the guilt of Catherine's death was eating me up inside. My life was moving on without her. It wasn't right.

After everyone had gone to bed, I crept out into the living room, craving my solitude. I turned on a war flick and opened a bottle of whiskey.

The whiskey soothed my soul, each sip numbing my pain, swallowing my indecision. Would I be betraying Catherine if I pursued Paloma? Would hitting on Paloma be considered sexual harassment? I didn't just want to fuck her; I wanted to kiss her, make her happy, take care of her the way she took care of me and Sky. I needed to make sure my feelings for her were more than just loneliness and lust.

After an hour, I heard Sky cry. Fuck. I didn't want Paloma to see me like this. I stood up to head back to my room, but before I could walk, Paloma walked into in the living room, holding Sky.

"Oh! I'm so sorry, I had no idea you were up. I'll take Sky to her room and leave you alone."

I studied her tight little body under her night slip. I could see the outline of her nipples and her panty line. I was aware that I was buzzed and wanted to vanish as quickly as possible before I embarrassed myself, or even worse, hit on her.

"No, you stay here. I'm going to bed."

She placed her hand on my chest. "No, wait. Don't go. Are you okay?"

"Yup." She could surely smell the liquor on my breath. I didn't want her to think I was a drunk like her uncle. "Just tired. I'm going to crash."

Her eyes dropped to my waist and she moistened her lips. I realized I had no shirt on, having removed it earlier because it was hot as fuck here, even in January. Fuck, this was my house, but I felt like a jerk just the same. It was totally inappropriate for me to be half-naked around her.

"Are you hungry? I'm starved. Let me cook you something."

Well, damn, if she insisted. "Fine." I sat back down on the sofa.

"I'm just going to feed Sky really quick and put her back down."

She turned and walked away, and I didn't even stop myself from staring at her tight little ass.

I read myself the riot act. I would in no way shape or form hit on her since I had been drinking. I was not that man.

I zoned in on the TV. Paloma appeared twenty minutes later and headed straight to the kitchen.

The scent of *chiles* and garlic filled the kitchen. I had no idea what she was making, but I couldn't wait to taste another one of her delicacies.

Hell, I couldn't wait to taste her.

Another twenty minutes passed, and she brought me a bowl of some red soup with chicken and a slice of lime.

"It's *posole*. Good after a few drinks. Normally, I would make *menudo*, but it takes three hours."

Damn, she saw right through me. "Thanks." I took one bite and the spicy broth soothed my stomach. "Babe, you're an incredible cook."

Fuck, had I said babe?

She placed her hand on my thigh. "Glad you like it."

I wanted to throw her over the sofa and fuck her. Instead, I calmed my cock down and finished the soup, savoring every bite. What would it be like to live with this woman? I knew I was paying her, but she seemed to genuinely like taking care of me which felt so strange to me. Catherine loved me for sure, but she never doted on me. Never. We had a very equal relationship. We shared all the chores since we both worked, and neither of us ever cooked anything outside of grilled cheese and spaghetti. Even my own mom was never the nurturing type. I never thought I wanted a woman who was very traditional, but I couldn't help but love every minute that Paloma was pampering me.

But it wasn't just one-sided. I fought an overwhelming desire to pamper her too. Rub her feet, give her a massage, make her come.

Fuck. Stop.

I finished the soup and she finished hers.

I grabbed her hand. "Let's go outside."

Her face contorted. "What if Sky wakes?"

"I'll grab the monitor. Come on."

She covered herself with her hands. "Let me change."

I didn't want her to change. I wanted to look at her incredible body in the moonlight. "We're just going to sit in my truck. It's hot out."

"Okay."

I grabbed a blanket and the monitor, and we snuck out of the front door like two teenagers absconding into the night. It felt so illicit.

I threw down the blanket and we sat in the truck. I resisted the urge to wrap my arms around her, kiss her, tell her how much I needed her. But it wasn't the right time. Not now.

I took her hand and traced the constellation with her. "Look up, Loma. Look at the stars. Do you see Orion?"

She nodded and then sucked in a breath. "Wow, it's beautiful. Are you into astronomy?"

"Yeah, I wanted to be an astronaut. Still might go for it after I get out. My degree is in aeronautical engineering."

"Oh, so you're a genius." She gave me a playful pinch and then leaned into my arms. Her skin was so soft, and she smelled like honey and bananas. I wondered if she tasted like them, too.

"No, I just liked to study." But I didn't want to talk about myself.

I wanted to know everything about this strong, beautiful woman in my arms. "What about you? What do you like to do besides cook?"

"I don't really know. I mean I liked to read in school, especially about other countries. But I haven't really been exposed to much. I just want to travel, enjoy life."

Despite the physical chemistry, we were such a match in other ways. I knew I made her feel safe and protected, and she made me feel loved. She wanted to travel, and I would be stationed around the world.

I could make her happy.

She placed her head on my chest. "Can I ask you something?"

"Anything."

"What happened to your wife?"

Anything but that. My heart sank. I didn't want to think about my dead wife when I was looking up at the stars with Paloma.

But she was taking care of my daughter. And me. She had a right to know. Especially since I was dying to kiss her.

I took a deep breath. "Catherine was my high school sweetheart, but her parents moved to Virginia our senior year, so we dated long distance. I was accepted into Annapolis, and she went to Washington and Lee, near her folks, so we were still long distance in college. We got married when I graduated, and my first station was in Nevada. She got a job doing social work, which she loved."

"Social work? She must've been a great person."

"She was. She really cared about people. But I deployed so much, we barely saw each other. When I was selected as an Angel, we decided to try for a baby, because even though I'd be off flying for the year, at least I would be stateside. She got pregnant immediately."

I looked up to the heavens. It was time to lay my heart on the line.

"But she had a brutal pregnancy. Nothing went right. She was sick, and we were worried about Sky's development. I was flying all over the country, so I couldn't be with Catherine." I hadn't even been there with her the last year of her life. I'd been too focused on being a great Angel.

A dullness ached in my chest. "She was overdue, so the doctor decided to induce her. But she wasn't progressing fast, so she had to have a C-section. Sky was born healthy, and it was the best day of my life."

And it had been. I was a dad. I was so proud of my beautiful wife. We had savored that day in the hospital. I couldn't wait to go home and pamper my wife while she recovered.

I gritted my teeth. What happened next, I would never for the rest of my life come to terms with. Had it been my fault? Maybe if I had noticed the signs sooner, maybe she would still be here. "But then Catherine got sick. She had a strep infection from the surgery. The doctors tried to save her, but it was so aggressive. She died when Sky was two days old."

The guilt came in waves, eating me up. But no matter how much I loved her, I couldn't save her.

I had failed her.

And there was my truth. I had told Paloma, told someone. Everything. No secrets.

Her hand grabbed mine, and I didn't push it away. "I'm so sorry,

Beck. That is awful. But she would be proud of you. You are such a great man. And a great father. Meeting you was the best thing that has ever happened to me. I mean it."

And at that moment, I broke. I didn't realize how much I needed to hear that. As a man I wanted to be strong. But sometimes, even men need to cry.

Paloma wrapped her arms around my neck. And I hugged her back. I pressed her body so hard against mine. This was wrong. She was a girl who worked for me. A girl who I refused to destroy.

But after a few more moments of her in my arms, my resolve broke. I couldn't wait another moment to kiss her. My hand cupped her face and she leaned up toward me, her plump lips already parted. We both paused for a moment, as if to acknowledge the last seconds before this kiss would change our lives forever.

I brushed her hair back and my lips took hers, softly at first. The second she opened her mouth a bit more, my tongue probed her. She tasted like cinnamon and sweetness and I wanted to devour her. An electricity pulsed through my body.

"Paloma, you are so beautiful. I'm crazy about you."

Her beautiful mouth upturned into a smile and our kiss turned raw, hungry, unbridled. I needed her, I craved her connection. Her hands ran down my body, stroking my arms, and caressing my chest. Then she straddled me in the truck and my hands grasped her incredible ass, rubbing her onto my cock. Her hair glowed in the moonlight and I wanted to make love to her under the stars.

"I'm crazy about you, too. I can't believe this is happening right now."

Neither could I. Our chemistry was electric, and it woke a part of me that I had thought died with my wife.

I buried my head in her chest and kissed the tops of her breasts. She let out a little moan that caused a sharp pang in my cock. I wanted to be inside her, make love to her, tell her that I would take care of her, that I believed she had been made for me and Sky.

She slid next to me and her hand rubbed against my cock, exploring its length. My own hand pressed against her pants, and I was excited by her wetness.

"Beck, I . . . I we shouldn't be doing this."

Ah fuck. My hand pulled away and I looked at her in the eyes. "We can stop now. I don't want you to feel pressured into anything because you work for me. But I want you to know, this isn't a fling for me. I've never met anyone like you.

Her shoulders relaxed. "I've never met anyone like you either. You don't look down on me. You appreciate me for who I am. I don't feel judged. You are kind and generous and sweet. But . . ."

There was always a but. "But what, babe."

"But you are leaving in next month. And I'll be leaving also. I don't want to get my heart broken. I don't want to make things weird. So, unless we have a future together, I can't do this.

Ah fuck. I was sure we had a chance, but it was complicated. I didn't even know where I'd be stationed next year. And though I was crazy about this girl, I wasn't in love with her. Not yet. But I thought of her every moment of the day, even when I was flying. I dreamt of her at night. I craved her.

And honestly, this was the most passionate kiss I had ever shared.

But I couldn't give her my word. My forever. We were not there yet. So, I did the honorable thing. I always did the honorable thing.

"I can't promise you forever tonight, but we could make this work. Let's cool off and talk tomorrow."

"Sounds good."

I pulled her into my chest and she fit perfectly. And I knew the answer to all my earlier questions.

I was falling for my nanny.

CHAPTER FIFTEEN

GUACAMOLE

I woke extra early with a spring in my step but fear in my heart. Beck had kissed me! I had wanted him so to kiss me so badly but when it finally happened, I panicked.

This kiss was electric. The way it started sweet but turned hungry. The way his lips claimed mine. The way he caressed my body.

But minutes after our lips touched, doubt took over my mind. This could all go terribly wrong. He was my boss. He was about to spend the next nine months flying around the country performing at air shows. And then, who knew where he would be stationed. I didn't want this to be a fling, but I didn't see a path for making this work. So I backed off.

And now, I was wondering if I had ruined my chances forever.

I gasped when I saw Beck walk out of his room in his white dress uniform. Though I could barely control myself when I saw him in his tight blue flight suit every morning, his sexy white uniform was a million times hotter. He looked handsome, classy, and completely out of my league.

I wondered what it would be like if Beck was my husband, if Sky was our daughter, if this house and this life was mine.

But I was quick to realize not only was that not the situation, there was no possibility of that ever happening. Beck was an educated, wealthy Blue Angel pilot. Despite the kiss, we didn't have a future together. In other words, he was way, way, way out of my league.

I exhaled. *Say something, dammit.*

Mónica beat me to the punch. "Wow, Beck. You clean up good."

"Thanks."

Beck's blue eyes narrowed at mine. He was clean-shaven and smelled like chicory and amber.

I clutched Sky to my chest, as if she was a security blanket that would help hide my lust for her dad.

"You look handsome." Ay, I was so lame. Was that the best I could do at flirting? The poor, simple nanny hitting on the rich, cocky fighter-pilot hunk.

He licked his lips. "Glad you think so."

Mónica's eyes bulged. Before she could open her mouth, I kicked her and gave her a "don't you say a word" look.

Beck was clearly just trying to make this less awkward. He was a gentleman.

He grabbed some chips and plunged them into the guacamole. I had made snacks and put out drinks for his friends that were about to stop by and pick him up.

He touched my hand and heat jolted through my body. "Lo, I shouldn't be home too late. These work functions are such a drag. I'd rather be home with you and Sky. Charlie and his wife will be here soon."

Did he really mean that? He probably just meant be home with Sky and since I was her nanny, I was included in that sentence. He couldn't possibly mean what I thought he meant, what I wanted him to mean, what I dreamt he would mean.

That he wanted me.

"We'll be here. Have fun."

The doorbell rang. I left Beck with the chips and opened the door. A wave of nausea hit when the people standing in the doorway came into view.

Another man was dressed in his dress whites standing next to the woman we had seen at the pool. But they weren't alone.

Next to them, was a tall blonde woman with huge fake breasts pushing out of her tight red dress and stiletto heels strapped to her feet. A wave of noxious perfume hit my nostrils, but the scent wasn't the reason I wanted to vomit.

This woman was clearly Beck's date.

"Oh, hi! My name is Laurel. You must be Paula, the nanny. I've heard so much about you."

Funny, I've never heard anything about you. I wanted to scream, yell at Beck, run back into my bedroom like an insolent teenager. "It's Paloma, like Picasso."

"Well, isn't that a pretty name," she said with a thick southern twang. "What a beautiful baby. Cutie, just like her daddy." She pointed at Beck. "Can I hold her?"

"Sure." I handed Sky to Laurel, and the baby immediately started crying.

Laurel held Sky at an arm's length, as if she had never held a baby before.

I took a big step backward and shot a hurt look at Beck. His mouth gaped, and his brow was furrowed. Was he shocked also?

No. It wasn't that. He was probably ashamed of me. It was one thing to kiss me in his truck when the world couldn't see, it was another thing to tell his rich friends that he was slumming with the nanny.

My cheeks burned with shame and my body felt impossibly hot. I needed to get out of there before I embarrassed myself and Beck.

He and his friends would probably laugh tonight about the poor Mexican girl who fell in love with her boss. How delusional and pathetic I was to ever think I had a chance with this Blue Devil.

I looked back at Laurel, who was now holding Sky closer. As if on cue, Sky spit up all over her. Curdled milk and strained peas stained her dress.

That's my girl.

Round one.

Sky: 1 Laurel: 0

Mónica let out a laugh. I turned to her and gave her another dirty look.

"Oh my. She must be ill. Here, take her."

Laurel handed Sky back to me.

"Beck, may I use your bathroom to freshen up?"

"Sure, it's down the hall."

I grabbed Sky and took off as fast as I could to her room.

How had I been so wrong? I had been sure that Beck had been falling for me. After our kiss under the stars last night, I had felt something. A connection. A spark. I had been certain he had felt it too. His face lit up when he saw me, and he no longer asked me to leave every afternoon, so he could be alone with Sky. He had finally opened up to me about his marriage. I had never felt closer to anyone as I had to Beck last night.

But I was naïve. A man like Beck could never love a woman like me. I came from the wrong side the tracks. He belonged at a country club, and the only way I would gain entrance to one would be through the door marked "employees only."

When he was finally ready to move on from Catherine, he would marry someone like Laurel, not me.

I placed Sky carefully on the changing table. But before I could stop myself, I started crying. The sobs came, and I couldn't stop them. I changed her as quickly as possible and lifted her up, then sat in the rocking chair.

The door opened, and I was horrified to see Beck standing there, watching me.

"Lo, can we talk?"

I shook my head and kept it tilted downward. I didn't want to talk to him and I refused to let him see my tear-stained cheeks.

He came closer toward me. "Look, I had no idea Britney was bringing her sister. Laurel is just up here visiting. There is nothing going on between me and her. This is a work function, not a date."

Sure looks like a date to me.

I choked back my sobs and tried to calm my breathing. I didn't want his pity.

I forced myself to speak. "It's fine. Go, have fun. She's really pretty."

He was now standing above me and sat on the bench next to the rocking chair. He brushed back a lock of my hair. "She's not as pretty as you."

Wait, what? "Beck, that's not funny. Please stop flirting with me. I know you don't mean it. I'm sure you just got caught up in the moment last night. And it's okay. I can't help how I feel about you. I get it—you're some gorgeous rock star pilot, and I'm just the nanny. I'm sorry about my behavior. I won't let it interfere with my job. Please, just leave me alone."

But he didn't leave. His hand brushed against my cheek, cupping it.

"Lo, I'm crazy about you, too."

My heart fluttered, and I wanted to pinch myself. Was this really happening?

He leaned in closer to me and my heart leapt. Was he going to kiss me again? The first kiss could've just been written off as a moment of passion, but a second kiss couldn't be ignored.

I lowered Sky into the crib and leaned toward Beck. Our lips were as close as could be without touching. I looked up at him one more time. This couldn't be happening. I felt like in a second, his friends would open the door and laugh at me, like this was a cruel joke.

But no one opened the door.

This was so wrong. He was my boss. I was his nanny.

Then why did it feel so right.

I couldn't catch my breath. Nerves, excitement, dreams pent up in my body. His eyelids closed and our lips met in perfect, forbidden bliss. He pulled me closer to him, and the kiss turned from sweet to hungry.

¡Ay, Dios mío!

I kissed him back. He tasted like salt and lime and lust, and I wanted to drink him in like a margarita.

He finally pulled away and I opened my eyes. He had a devilish grin, and I didn't see a hint of regret in his eyes.

But had these kisses ruined this job which was the only good thing that had ever happened to me?

"We can't keep doing this," I said.

"Yes, we can. And I plan to do it again. I've got to go. But wait up for me. I'll get out of there as soon as I can. And Paloma, you are way more to me than just the nanny."

Then he kissed his daughter's head.

And with that, he walked out of the room, leaving me counting the minutes until he returned.

CHAPTER SIXTEEN

CANAPÉS

I licked my lips, savoring the taste of Paloma. She was even sweeter than I had imagined. Our kisses had been everything that I had fantasized they would be—innocent, warm, loving, yet passionate, and hopefully a hint of what was to come.

"Bye, girls."

Mónica shot me a dirty look, probably suspicious of Laurel, but Ana María ran over and gave me a hug. A lump grew in my throat. I was not only crazy about Paloma, but I adored her sisters. My new life as the lone male living with four women felt right. It had only been a few weeks since Paloma and her sisters moved in, but I already couldn't imagine living without them.

Laurel waited for me by the door. Her perfume overpowered me, and I couldn't help but think about how different she was from Paloma. My stomach tightened with guilt. I didn't want to go out tonight, especially with Laurel. But I didn't have a choice. As I had told Paloma, this was a work function, not a date.

Laurel touched my uniform. "Beck, that baby of yours is so cute. I'm so sorry she's feeling sick."

"She wasn't sick earlier. She had just tried peas for the first time."

"Oh. I don't know anything about babies. But I could learn."

I resisted the urge to roll my eyes and make a smartass remark. I didn't care if she knew anything about babies or not. I had no desire to date her.

I only wanted Paloma.

We all climbed into Charlie's SUV and to my dismay, Laurel sat in the middle seat right next to me.

Ah, hell. I didn't want to be rude to her, but the only woman on my mind was Paloma.

"So Beck. Your nanny seems nice. I think she has a crush on you," she teased.

I didn't appreciate her passive aggressive way of trying to find out what was going on with me and Paloma. I fought the urge to tell Laurel that the crush was mutual, that my lips were still burning from Paloma's heat, that I wanted to fuck the shit out of my nanny. But I didn't want to start any gossip.

"She's an amazing woman. I have never met anyone like her. She has such a positive attitude even though she's had a rough life."

Her face contorted, and I could see that my response didn't satisfy Laurel. "Well, she must be special. So, who's going to watch Sky when you go back to Pensacola?"

With any luck, Paloma will come with me.

Man, was I being interrogated? I was done with this conversation. "I'm just taking everything day by day." I turned my head and looked out of the window. Thankfully, Charlie arrived at the banquet hall. Good, time to get this event started so I could get back home to Paloma.

I exited the vehicle and didn't even bother opening Laurel's door. I wanted to make it clear now that this wasn't a date.

We entered the banquet hall which was decked out. There was a ridiculous ice sculpture in the center of the room, expensive linens and designer silverware on each table, and elaborate flower arrangements adorned every corner.

In the past, Catherine and I would appreciate the elaborate set up. But now, it seemed gaudy. All this wasted money, especially knowing that many of the residents of this town were hungry.

For some reason, I thought that I would be the one to show Paloma a whole new way of life. But she was the one who was opening my eyes up to the world.

I greeted our fellow pilots. Sawyer was flirting with tall redhead and Declan was nursing his drink while making small talk with the commander's wife. Yup, another fun night.

I walked over to a table of food and grabbed a plate. But nothing excited my taste buds. The spread consisted of smoked salmon on cucumber slices, shrimp on rice crackers, caviar on puff pastries, and sausage stuffed mushrooms.

I would rather be home feasting on one of Paloma's meals.

Hell, I'd rather be feasting on her.

I quickly said hi to the commander and engaged in thrilling small talk about the weather. Luckily, another pilot stole him away from me.

Laurel walked up to me. "Do you want to dance?"

I winced. I didn't want to turn her down, but I didn't want to lead her on either. "I'm really not in the mood, Laurel. It's nothing personal."

Her face tensed up and she bit her lower lip. She gave me an understanding nod and then walked away.

Great now I had hurt her feelings.

I needed some air. I stepped outside the building, hoping I would be alone, but within minutes I saw Charlie exit the building.

He walked over to me and put his hand on my back. "You okay, man?"

"Yup."

"No, seriously. I know you miss Catherine. Hell, we all do. She was a great woman. But she would want you to be happy. Laurel has always had a crush on you. I know she's coming on strong, but she's a great girl. I think she's just nervous."

Maybe I was wrong about Charlie. Unlike Sawyer and Declan, Charlie appeared to be stable. And he was right—Catherine would want me to be happy also. She had even told me that before she died.

"I appreciate that, but I'm just not ready yet," I lied. I was ready. I would never stop loving my wife. But my feelings for Paloma were strong. They were real.

Charlie looked me straight in the eye. "It's the nanny, right? You're fucking the nanny? Hell, I don't blame you. She's fine as fuck. I'd love to be *livin' la vida loca* with her. But it's a rebound dude. Don't fall in love with the help."

My chest constricted, and I had to force myself to unclench my fist. I wanted to deck the motherfucker, but I was in uniform outside an officer party for the Angels. I wouldn't risk my career over his stupidity.

"Don't ever talk about her like that again, got it? She's not some fetish. She's honestly the sweetest, kindest, most selfless woman I have ever met."

His eyes bulged. "Wow, you are already whipped. She must be incredible in the sack."

Fuck my career. I raised my fist and clocked him in the jaw. "I warned you, dude."

I gazed toward the banquet hall. The last thing I wanted to do was spend the night snacking on canapés while schmoozing with a bunch of pretentious assholes who didn't have a clue how good they had it. After only a few weeks living with Paloma, my entire world view had changed. Yes, my wife died, and I'd miss her until my last breath. But I had a great life. I was blessed. I had a beautiful daughter and my dream career. I was financially stable, had every opportunity for my future and had traveled the world. Paloma had never even seen the ocean.

"Give my regards to the CO, your wife, and her sister. I'm going home."

He rubbed his jaw. "Dude, I'm sorry. Just come in. I didn't know you were serious about her. It was a joke."

"It's fine, man. I just want to be alone."

"At least let me give you a ride. You didn't even bring your own car."

Give me a ride? I remembered the first night that I hired Paloma, how she had walked miles to get to her job. At night. Alone. An attractive woman. I was a fucking man. A goddamn United

States Blue Angel. My entitled ass drove a half a mile daily from my home on the base to the hangar. I had no idea what it was like to wear threadbare clothes and have worn shoes a size too small. And I never ever suffered from hunger. Hell, I wasted food before I met her.

"It's a beautiful night—I'm going to walk."

Walk straight home to Paloma. And kiss her until the dawn broke.

CHAPTER SEVENTEEN

FLAN

After I got the girls to sleep, I paced in the living room. God, what had just happened? Beck had kissed me again. Once could've been an accident but twice now meant that the first kiss hadn't just been in a fleeting moment.

But now, everything was so confusing. He was my boss. Not that he took advantage of me, hell no. I wanted that kiss probably more than he had. But even so, it was wrong. It was distracting. I had to stop this now. Before it got out of hand.

It was only nine o'clock and I didn't expect him home for a few hours. He was probably dancing the night away with beautiful Laurel. Maybe he was kissing her? He probably only kissed me because he was horny and thought I was easy. From all the men I had seen around my mother, I realized that men didn't have many standards. They were happy with any warm body. Or even a cold one for that matter.

To distract myself, I decided to make some flan. It was so easy to cook and the girls loved it. It was also soft enough that Sky could try it. I started adding sugar and a tablespoon of water to a pan and placing it on the stove until it reached the desired dark color. Once it had, I removed the pan from the heat and scooped the hardened sugar into a pie pan. Then, I mixed eggs, La Lechera Condensed Milk, Media Crema, a can of evaporated milk, and some vanilla. Once blended, I poured this mixture into the mold, filled a baking pan with water, and baked it at 350 degrees for an hour.

But Beck still wasn't home yet.

I was about to scour the kitchen counters as a way to deal with my anxiety. But the door opened, and Beck stood there with a sheepish grin.

I opened my mouth to tell him all the ways that these kisses were wrong. To tell him all the reasons why this could never work. All the reasons why no matter how much I wanted him, nothing would come from these kisses but heartbreak. Especially mine.

But no words came out of my mouth. Instead, my weak heart ran to him like a scene from a movie, and before I could come to my senses his lips covered mine.

But this time, we didn't stop at a kiss. A hunger that I didn't know existed in me exploded. Beck scooped me up in his arms and carried me to his bedroom, a room I had only briefly been in, as I had tried desperately to respect his privacy.

He gently laid me down in his big king size bed. I was drunk on his scent.

"Wait, Beck. Is the event over?"

"No," he said in between kisses. "I just couldn't wait to be with you any longer. I've wanted to kiss you for so long."

"Really?"

"Yes, really."

I wanted to get lost in the moment, lost in him, and turn off my brain.

But I had never been one to get lost in the moment. I prided myself on being the sensible one, the responsible one.

"But, we should stop. I'm your nanny."

He laughed. "No, you're Sky's nanny. You're my woman."

Ay! Could this man be any more perfect? His words filled me with delight. I kissed him back and allowed myself to be present. I savored the taste of his mouth, the scent of his cologne, the strength of his touch. My hand glided down his body and I rubbed over his length. It simultaneously excited me and petrified me. The last time I had seen a naked man was when one of my mother's johns walked out of our one bathroom in the middle of the night. He stood there buck naked and when his eyes met mine, I swore he was going to rape me.

But for once my mom had saved me. She had lured him back to her room. The one thing I'd say for her, is that she never allowed us to get abused.

My hand reached for the shiny gold buckle on his belt. As I tried to undo it, he stopped me.

"No, tonight is all about you. Let me worship you," he said as he continued to kiss me.

Worship me? I tensed up. The thought of having pleasurable sex was foreign to me. I'd had sex before, but honestly, I had never really enjoyed it. And I had never been in love with my partner.

He finally pulled away from my lips. "Are you okay? Look, if you want me to stop, say the word and I will never touch you again. But don't back out because you're scared. I give you my word that I won't hurt you."

I wanted to believe every word he said. But how could what he just said be true? Of course he would hurt me. He was leaving next month to go to Pensacola and fly around the country, and I would move to San Diego. His wife died just last year. Was I the first woman he had kissed since she passed? For some reason I thought I was. I was clearly a rebound. An amazing man like him would never get serious with the nanny. This was a fairy tale. And no matter how much I had prayed that they were when I was Ana María's age, I knew fairy tales weren't real.

But I didn't want my dream to die. I wanted to drown in his kisses, live in his world, and believe for once in my own happy ending.

"I've never been better. And no, I don't want you to stop. I want to kiss you forever."

Joy flooded my body. I wanted him, I needed him.

But any delusion I had that I was in control quickly vanished when he scooped me up and threw me down on the bed. He ripped of his shirt and I gasped—mesmerized by his body. His shoulders were broad and perfectly sculpted. The scruff on his beard prickled my skin as he savagely kissed me, pressing his incredible body into mine. I could feel his hard cock against my thighs. I was desperate to feel him inside of me.

"You are so beautiful, Lo," he said between kisses. His mouth made its way down to my neck and I arched my back. He pulled the strap of my slip down and blew kisses on chest. His tongue darted over my nipples and I moaned. I was already so turned on and we weren't even naked yet.

For a second, I thought he was going to take it slow, but my sweet, patient man had vanished. He was replaced by an animal. A man that I never even imagined in my deepest fantasies. His lips made a tight seal around my nipple and his tongue flicked it. I never knew I could feel so good, so loved, so hot, so sexy. I writhed under him, desperate for more of him, more of his mouth, more of his soul. My arms wrapped around his back, pulling him into me, begging for relief.

His mouth gave my other nipple attention as his hand reached down to my thigh. He hiked up my slip, exposing my panties, and then kissed down between my thighs. Suddenly, my body tensed up and nerves took over my mind. What if my mom was right and men just wanted one thing? What if he fucked me and then fired me tomorrow? I rationally knew that he was a great guy and not possible of such betrayal and dishonesty, but my fear consumed me.

He was so in tune with me that he stopped and kissed my lips again and looked me in the eyes. "Relax, baby. I'm crazy about you. You're beautiful. I'm not going anywhere."

Whoa. His words soothed my anxiety. I refused to question him. Not today. Not now.

He pulled my tank top and pants off and stopped to stare at my body. I had always been self-conscious of being leered at by men, but I loved the way Beck's eyes studied me.

"Perfect. Seriously, Loma, you are so sexy."

He made his way back down to my panties and blew over the

fabric before he pulled them down. His lips pressed against me and he licked down my center.

Ay! My hand grasped the top his head. His warm tongue felt delicious against my folds. I was so wet, and he ate me like I was his favorite dessert.

The pressure built between my legs as he licked my clit and I didn't know if I could hold on. This felt so much better than I could've ever imagined. My belly coiled and my breath hitched.

"Oh Beck!"

Before I could hold myself back, pleasure rippled through every inch of my body and I exploded into ecstasy. I felt like I was going to black out but instead I giggled uncontrollably.

Beck gave me a final lick and then looked up at me and grinned.

I sat up and reached for his pants again, wanting to return the favor, but he stopped me.

"Hey, not tonight babe. We have the rest of our lives to be together."

And with those words, a lump grew in my throat. This was truly happening. Beck had feelings for me. He saw a future.

Then why was I waiting for this to blow up in my face.

"Oh no! I forgot I had flan in the oven!"

I threw on my clothes and raced out of the bedroom, just in time to save my dessert. Beck joined me a few minutes later and we indulged in the creamy treat. And my life was as sweet as my flan.

CHAPTER EIGHTEEN

BACON AND EGGS

Paloma snuck out of my bedroom at dawn, wanting to ensure that her sisters didn't wake up and see her in my room. I had insisted that I would wake up with Sky, so Paloma could get a good night's sleep.

She would need it. I planned to wear her out tonight.

When she and the girls woke the next morning, I had a surprise for them.

First things first—I was going to cook breakfast. Definitely wouldn't be as delicious as Paloma's food, but it would be filling. Perfect for a road trip.

I threw the bacon into the pan and started the coffee pot. My heart brimmed with excitement. No more telling Paloma how I felt. Today, I was going to show her that I was serious about having a future with her.

I walked over to the kitchen table to clear it and noticed that there was one of Mónica's papers from school crumbled up. I opened it up and my heart wrenched.

A Father Daughter Dance.

Paloma had told me that none of the girls knew their fathers and that she didn't even have a clue who her dad was. I couldn't even imagine that. My father was the best man I knew. Without his guidance, I was sure I'd be a womanizer like Sawyer.

When I had been with Paloma last night, it had been only about her. I wanted to be with her, hold her kiss her, make love to her, make her feel good. But now I realized that being with Paloma met so much more.

It wasn't just about her. I needed to do right by her sisters.

The bacon sizzled in the pan and I flipped it over.

Paloma emerged from the room wearing a tank top with no bra and low-slung pajama bottoms—definitely less conservative that the fully dressed woman I was used to seeing in the mornings.

"Morning, sunshine."

I walked over to her and gave her a kiss. A confused look graced her face.

"Are you cooking? Do you know what you are doing?"

Smartass. "I can feed myself, Loma. I did eat before you came into my life." But honestly, the only thing I wanted to eat was her again. I wanted to devour her nightly. Last night, my balls were in a world of hurt. But I was a patient man and I wanted to wait until she felt more comfortable about dating me. To ensure her that I wasn't using her.

Her eyes glanced over at my packed suitcase. "Are you going somewhere?"

I removed the bacon from the pan and patted it dry with some paper towels. Then I cracked some eggs to fry in grease.

"*We* are going somewhere."

Her brow furrowed. "We? What are you talking about?"

"Babe, I'm taking you to San Diego. The girls too."

She bit her lower lip. "Today?"

"Yes today. Tomorrow I have to fly over Coronado for a Navy SEAL graduation. We can stay at my buddy Grant's place."

"How are we getting there? We can't all fit in your plane."

"Right. The narrator on the squad is going to fly my plane to San Diego. It's good practice for him. He will be taking over my slot next year. I'll drive."

Tears began to well in her eyes. "San Diego! Are you serious? Can we go to the beach?"

"Woman, we are staying on the beach. The base in the on beach."

"Oh my god!" She ran over to me and threw her hands around my neck and kissed my lips. I pulled her into me and kissed her back, savoring her taste as I pressed her against the sink.

"Well well well, guys. Good morning to you," Mónica said.

Paloma pushed me off of her, but I pulled her back into me.

"Morning, Mónica."

Paloma's cheeks reddened, and she whispered in my ear. "I didn't want her to know until we became serious."

"Well, know she knows and we are serious. We have nothing to hide."

Paloma exhaled and buried her head in my chest.

I turned to Mónica. "Mónica. Do you want to go to San Diego today?"

"You serious?"

"Yup. We are leaving in an hour."

Mónica ran over to me and hugged me. "I can't believe it. Lo, can we drive around and see where we are going to live?"

Paloma and I made eye contact and her face seemed to fall at the same time that my heart dropped.

San Diego.

Where they had planned to move after I left El Centro. It was only a month away, but it seemed like an eternity.

It was too soon to ask her to move with me to Florida, but I couldn't imagine my life without Paloma. Without her sisters. And it wasn't even about me and how I felt about her. What about Sky? Paloma spent more time with her than I did, though that wasn't by choice. We were deep into our training schedule now and I couldn't imagine having anyone else take care of Sky. I no longer worried about Sky when I was out flying. I completely focused on my men and my formations knowing that Sky was being loved and attended to. I would either have to hire another nanny back in Florida or ask my in laws to watch her. For the next nine months, I would be traveling every week around the country to different air shows. And then she needed someone to love her when I would deploy next year. Sky needed stability. And I needed someone to miss me while I was gone.

But I had a month. One month to ease into this conversation. One month to make decisions.

"I'm sure Beck will show us around. I'm going to wake up Sky." Paloma left the kitchen.

I turned my attention back to the eggs and plated the food. Ana María walked out in her favorite Dora the Explorer nightgown.

Mónica ran over to her. "Ana María! We're going to San Diego."

"Today?"

"Yes. Today!"

Ana María clasped her hands together and turned to me. "Can we see the baby tigers?"

The tigers. They had been all over the news. A baby tiger had been caught at the border and the Zoo Safari Park had rescued it.

"Sure. We will go to the Zoo Safari Park and the beach."

Mónica ran down the hallway almost plowing over Paloma and Sky.

"Mónica, Beck said we can go to the beach and the Wild Animal Park. Can you believe it?"

Paloma looked up at me and her confused expression from earlier turned into a hopeful smile. "Yes. I can."

And this time, Paloma kissed me. In front of Mónica. In front of Ana María. In front of Sky. I kissed her back.

We had nothing to hide.

CHAPTER NINETEEN

FISH TACOS

We packed our bags, loaded up Beck's car, and headed off for our trip to San Diego. Nerves and excitement mingled inside my belly. I couldn't believe this was actually happening. Beck and I had hooked up again and now I was on my way to see the ocean for the first time in my life.

He reached across and put his hand on my thigh and I melted. I loved being in the car with him. I felt so safe. Maybe it was because he was a pilot, but I loved the way he was completely in control. I couldn't wait to see him fly tomorrow.

After two hours on the road, we finally arrived in San Diego.

Our first stop was the Zoo Safari Park to see the tigers. It was inland, so I had still yet to see the ocean, but I was thrilled nonetheless. Beck bought us all tickets. He held my hand as we walked into the park. I had never seen anything like it this place.

First, we stepped into the butterfly garden. They flew by our heads as we marveled at their vibrant colors. Their jeweled colors mixed together like an abstract painting by nature.

"Paloma! Look!" Mónica yelled.

A gorgeous Monarch had landed on Ana María's nose.

Ana María giggled, and I had never seen her so happy, so full of joy. I held Sky and pointed out the different butterflies to her, naming the colors in Spanish. She clapped her little hands and Beck put his arm around me.

Mónica's face beamed. "This place is awesome." Even she was having fun.

We walked over to the Lorikeet Landing and bought some nectar.

A gorgeous bird with a lapis colored head and orange, yellow and green feathers landed on Mónica's hand and lapped up the nectar out of her little cup.

Joy filled my body and for once my outlook for the future was as bright as the San Diego sun. The girls and I had never ever been to a zoo. I had learned about animals from books, not from nature. We had so much to experience.

Our final stop at the Zoo Safari Park was to see the tigers. Two baby tigers frolicked together like kittens, fighting over a ball of yarn. I couldn't believe I was seeing these wild animals up close.

I pressed my hand to Beck's chest and we kissed under a bamboo canopy. "Thank you. You don't know what this means to me."

"You're welcome, babe. I just want to make you and the girls happy."

Swoon. I didn't want this day to end.

After we left the zoo, we stopped for dinner at this incredible taco place, *¡Salud!,* in Barrio Logan. I was impressed that Beck knew about this restaurant, with its authentic Mexican food, handmade tortillas, and churro ice cream. The Mexican murals on the wall made me feel like I was home.

I took a bite of the fish taco. It was beer battered on a warm tortilla and adorned with cabbage, *cotija* cheese, *pico de gallo*, and dressed with a creamy sauce. "This is so good! How did you find this place?"

He paused for a moment and took a sip of his blood orange beer. "My wife and I used to come here. She loved Mexican food."

I smiled, and it wasn't even forced. I loved that Beck could be open with me about Catherine, especially now that he and I were romantically involved. I didn't ever want him to feel that he couldn't talk about her, especially in front of Sky. If it worked out between us, the ghost of Catherine would always be present in our home. But I wasn't jealous of her. If it wasn't for her, I would've never met Beck. I hoped that she would want Beck to find happiness and for Sky to have a mother. And I prayed even harder that I would be the woman for that job.

After our amazing lunch Beck drove us across the Coronado Bridge. The view of the ocean was breathtaking. It was even bluer than I imagined, and the boats and naval carriers docked in it added to its beauty.

Beck parked near the ferry landing and my sisters and I ran to the shore and dipped our toes into the sand. I felt like such a dork but for a small-town sheltered girl like me, the warmth of the sand, the cool breeze blowing on my face, and the chill of the ocean meant the world to me. I wanted to live in this moment forever.

Beck strapped Sky on his chest and took my hand. "What do you think? Is it everything you thought it would be?"

"Yes, it is. And more. I can't believe I'm here, with my sisters, with you, with Sky." Tears welled in my eyes. "I'm just so happy."

He placed his arm on the back of my head and kissed me passionately. "I want to make you happy. Before I met you, the only reason I wanted to live was for Sky and for my job. I had become so angry, so bitter about losing Catherine. But seeing the world through your eyes, has completely changed me. I need you, Lo, and you need me too."

I didn't get a chance to respond before the girls joined us and we began to build sand castles. Ana María giggled and Mónica was checking out the boys on the beach.

Life couldn't get better than today.

CHAPTER TWENTY

ENERGY BAR

The next morning, I woke up early and headed to the Naval Air Station North Island to prepare for the flyover. It was an easy Delta formation—all six planes would fly in a tight triangle over the Change of Command ceremony for the Commander of the Naval Air Forces. It was good practice—our first air show was two months away.

I had only two months left with Paloma.

We spent last night at my buddy Grant's place. Grant was a Navy SEAL. I had deployed with his Team once and supported them in a combat mission. Though they were on the ground doing the dirty work, my life had also been at risk. Our planes could be shot down at any time. What if I died overseas on my next deployment and orphaned Sky?

I pushed that thought out of my head. I quickly snacked on an energy bar to give me the fuel I needed to fly.

Sawyer and Declan greeted me with fist pumps. Charlie, on the other hand, gave me a curt nod. We had not really talked since I'd punched him. Which was fine by me.

Sawyer addled up beside me. "What are you doing tonight? Do you want to hit the clubs downtown?"

I shook my head. "Going to dinner with Paloma. Don't you get tired of that scene? A different woman every night?"

Declan's eyes bulged. "Seriously? Are you guys together?"

I nodded. "Yup. It's new, but I'm crazy about her."

Declan placed his arm on my shoulder. "Congrats, man. She's beautiful. As long as you're happy."

I appreciated Declan's support. He was a great guy. I hoped he found someone to help him get over his ex.

Even Sawyer seemed happy for me. "Me too, Beck. She seems sweet."

"She is." Now that I had told three of my fellow pilots about Paloma I was tempted to tell the world. Shout it from the roof tops.

There was only one person I dreaded telling.

My mother.

We were not close by any stretch of the imagination. Even so, I always craved her approval. She had loved Catherine. And Paloma was so different from my wife. All my mom cared about was her image and status. She loved to boast to people that she had a Blue Angel as a son. And I highly doubted she would embrace the nanny with open arms.

But I wouldn't live my life to make my mom happy. I wanted to be happy. I wanted Sky to be happy. And that was all that mattered.

My fellow pilots and I proceeded to walk in unison to our planes. The crowds cheered but it was nothing like the roar of the normal air shows. I had asked Grant to take Paloma and the girls to the beach to watch me fly. Knowing that she would see me soar, filled me with pride.

Our planes took off and adrenaline consumed me. I focused on the paint on Sawyer's jet, making sure I was perfectly aligned and in formation. We soared in the air and took a right turn toward the Naval Base Coronado. A quick flyby over the ceremony and then we headed west toward the ocean before landing back at North Island. Piece of cake. All in another day's work.

When I disembarked from my plane, I marveled at how beautiful San Diego was. I had so much fun yesterday at the zoo. San Diego would be the perfect place to raise Sky and enjoy all the attractions here. We could take her to Balboa Park, Legoland, all the beaches, all the gardens, and the weather would always be perfect.

And Paloma would be here.

The more I thought about it the more I was certain I was going to put in my orders for San Diego.

And that way—I could stay with Paloma.

CHAPTER TWENTY-ONE

SPAGHETTI

O ur weekend in San Diego had been glorious. I was more determined than ever to move there.

But now, I was wondering how I would live without Beck and Sky.

I didn't even know what I wanted anymore. What if he asked me to move to Pensacola with him? It wasn't out of the realm of possibilities since he still needed a nanny. But even if he asked, I wasn't sure I'd say yes.

I was crazy about him. Did I love him? I thought I did but I wasn't sure yet. Even so, I didn't want to be a nanny forever.

Since we returned from San Diego, we had been busy with school and flying. And luckily I hadn't heard from my mother or my uncle.

I had just cooked a huge batch of spaghetti and meatballs, using fresh tomatoes for the sauce and both pork and beef for the meat mixture.

Beck couldn't stop raving about it and even had seconds.

But Mónica hadn't touched her food. She was pushing it around her plate with her fork.

I knew something was wrong.

I sat down next to her. "Are you okay?"

"Yup. Fine."

But she wasn't fine. I could tell.

By now, Beck was sitting down on the sofa, looking at his phone. I noticed that Mónica was staring at him and biting her lip. What was she up to?

After a few more minutes, she finally got up from the table and sat down next to Beck, a worried look on her face.

"Beck, can I ask you a question?"

Ay, Dios mío! No! Suddenly I knew exactly what she was going to do. Something I had done six years ago when I had been her age.

My heart hurt.

She was going to ask him to the daddy/daughter dance.

Don't do it!

"Sure. Anything."

Dammit. I couldn't watch. This was a fucking train wreck.

Beck was a great man, but he was under no obligation to take my sisters to the daddy/daughter dance. I didn't want him to feel pressured.

"Uh, well next week there is this dance, the father/daughter dance. I know you're not my father. But, I was wondering if you would take me and Ana María to it. If not, no worries. I understand."

My eyes watered up, and I craned my neck like one of the goddamn people who stops to watch an accident.

Please, Beck. Please say yes.

The room went silent. I tried to read Beck's face but I couldn't.

He took Mónica's hand. "I'd be honored."

Yes! I wanted to run over there and jump on him.

Mónica's face brightened. "Really? You wouldn't mind?"

"Not at all. There's one catch though."

Oh great. What? Was he flying that day? I knew he couldn't switch his schedule. I understood that but would the girls?

"Oh, what?"

He grabbed his keys. "We need to get you both dresses."

God, could I love this man anymore?

Mónica jumped up and squealed. She ran into the other room and grabbed Ana María.

I ran over to Beck, sat on his lap, and kissed him, for once not shy at all if my sisters saw us. "I can't believe you did that. You don't know what this means to me. What it means to them." I paused. I had been unable to know my feelings about him until now. But they were finally clear. "I love you."

Beck cupped my head in his hands and kissed me. *"Te amo."*

He loved me, too? In Spanish no less? I couldn't believe this was my life right now. I was in love with a totally hot, accomplished, educated, classy pilot who was a wonderful father and loved my sisters. And he had just said he loved me too. This was really happening for me.

Ana María ran out. "You;re going to take us shopping? Can I get a pink dress?"

"Yup, let's go."

I wanted the girls to bond to Beck without me hanging around. "I'll stay back here with Sky if you don't mind."

The second they left, I burst into tears. I was so happy for my sisters. I had remembered seeing those fliers in school, ripping them up, shame burning my cheeks. Sometimes the mean girls would taunt me. "Paloma isn't going to go to the dance because she doesn't even know who her father is." I would never engage with the girls but secretly I was devastated. Even worse, they were right.

I didn't even know my father's name.

Abuela had talked about him only once. She said that Mama had snuck out of the house repeatedly and then became pregnant. Mama had never uttered his name and my birth certificate said unknown where my father's name should've been. My only connection to him were my green eyes.

The not knowing his identity was the worst part. Maybe he wanted me. Maybe he had looked for me. Or maybe he didn't even know I existed. When I had been Ana María's age, I had dreamt that he would find me and whisk me away from my mother. But after the weeks turned into years, I had given up any hope of ever knowing the identity of my sperm donor.

A few hours later, the girls returned. Mónica had chosen a long purple dress and Ana María picked a sparkly pink princess dress and matching shoes.

I helped the girls get ready for bed and returned to find Beck sitting on the sofa. I felt breathless and my body throbbed for him.

I no longer wanted to wait. I wanted him to make love to me.

I wrapped my arms around him and we kissed passionately. Desire radiated between us.

And I didn't need to say another word. Beck threw me over his back and carried me to his bed.

CHAPTER TWENTY-TWO

CHERRIES AND PINEAPPLES

I carried her into the bedroom and threw her on the bed. Her face broke into a nervous laugh. We'd been messing around since I'd first kissed her in my truck, but I had been hesitant to fuck her until she knew that I loved her. That I didn't just want to fuck her. That I wanted to be with her. Right now. Forever.

And she had said she loved me too. Now, I had a new goal. I wanted no distractions from my mission, to make her come.

I attacked her greedy little mouth, and she passionately kissed me back. With fire in her eyes, she met me kiss for kiss. I had never in my life experienced this kind of electric, clothes ripping passion. My previous sex life had been warm and loving, not raw and unhibited.

Tonight, I was going to fuck Paloma.

She removed my shirt and her hands ripped on my belt buckle. I was still busy kissing her mouth, her neck, her chest. I unbuttoned her dress and unhooked her bra. Her tits were fucking gorgeous. Plump and oval shaped. I buried my head in between her chest before my mouth suckled on her nipples. They were like two perfect cherries, tart and sweet and red. I could stay here forever. I planned to.

Paloma had succeeded in removing my belt and my pants dropped to the floor. I stood beside the bed, not sure what Paloma was about to do but not wanting to pressure her into anything. She was young and though she had told me she wasn't a virgin, I wasn't sure how sexually experienced she was.

"Can I suck your cock?"

Whoa. Okay, that answered that question. Hearing her say cock rattled me. The excitement of Paloma's dirty mouth made my cock even harder than it already was, which I didn't even think was possible.

"Absolutely. And Paloma, you never have to ask that question. The answer will always be yes. Suck me, baby."

Her eyes lit up and she crawled over the bed spread until she was laying on her belly. Her hands reached around and grabbed my ass and then she wrapped her mouth around my cock.

I exhaled. Man, this was incredible. Catherine had never really enjoyed giving me head, and I hadn't wanted to push her. But Paloma seemed to enjoy it. I placed my hand on the back of her neck and guided her rhythm. She hummed and flicked her tongue around it, giving me the most intense pleasure. Then she placed her hand at the base of my cock and used her fist to rub up and down while she kept her mouth on the head. Jesus. I was about to come, but I didn't want to just yet. Not like this.

I wanted to taste her.

"Babe," I urged her off. "Lay down."

She bit her bottom lip. I climbed up on the bed spread and removed her panties. Her pussy was so fucking beautiful. Nicely trimmed in a triangle, dark and delicious. I kissed up on her thighs. I grasped her with both of my arms and placed my head in between her legs.

I gave one slow lick down her center and she gasped.

The sight of her spread in front of me, her hair cascading over her nipples was almost too much to bear.

I devoured her pussy and she tasted like the sweetest treat—like a sweet juicy pineapple. Two beautiful little lips. I licked her lips and rubbed my thumb over her clit. Her breath sputtered, and she began to moan. I increased my pace, loving every second of this. I could eat her forever, I was drunk on her scent. I could tell she was close, so close so I reached up my other hand and rubbed her nipple causing her body to thrash.

She finally came all over my face and I lapped up her nectar.

Now she was ready for me.

I reached over to grab a condom out my dresser and I slowly rolled it over my length. I pressed my body slowly over hers, gripped my cock in my hand, and slowly entered her.

She gasped as I pressed further. She was so fucking tight. I was dying to get inside her. She gripped my ass. "Fuck me, Beck."

Yes, ma'am.

I thrust deep and paused for a moment to stare into her eyes. I needed her to know that I loved her. That I never wanted to fuck another woman but her.

I grabbed her hips, shifted her forward, and cupped her breasts. Her pussy was clamping around my cock, catching and releasing it and I was already in ecstasy. She began to moan, and I rubbed her clit with my thumb, desperate for her to come again.

My cock throbbed, and I fucked her harder, deeper, faster. Her moans were coming more rapidly so I suckled again on her incredible tits.

"I'm going to come again."

That was my girl. I cradled her in my arms and kept the friction constant, so we could move together as one. I took her hand in mine, covered her mouth with my lips, and kissed her through her orgasm. I could feel her explode under me and I finally let go into incredible bliss.

Our bodies were entangled in the sweat drenched sheets.

I looked over at this beautiful woman and realized that I couldn't live without her.

I cupped her face and asked her a question. "Babe, will you move with me to Florida?"

CHAPTER TWENTY-THREE

CHAMANGO

"**A**re you serious?"

Excitement twisted with fear in my chest. He was not asking me to marry him, which of course I didn't expect. He had just told me he loved me, and I wasn't trying to rush things any more than they were already rushed. Even so, I needed to know where I stood.

"Dead serious. I love you, Loma."

"I love you, too. But I want to go to San Diego. I don't know if I can move across the country. I mean, I have to support the girls."

"Don't worry about money. I can take care of you and your sisters. Just come with me. I need you. Sky needs you."

I needed them, too. "But what if this doesn't work out? Then what?"

He pulled me into his arms. "It's going to work out, baby. Trust me."

I had never trusted anyone in my life but my abuela. If it didn't work out, I would be stranded in Florida, with no job, and no money. I'd be completely dependent on him. No, I couldn't do that. No matter how much I loved him.

I pulled away from him. "I'm not sure. I need to make my own money. I don't feel comfortable with you supporting us."

His face contorted. "Well, I could still pay you as Sky's nanny."

Though I was positive he meant that offer as a way to give me independence, it didn't sit right with me.

We were sleeping with each other now. I didn't want him to pay me.

I didn't accept money for sex.

I wasn't my mother.

I needed to think about this.

"I'm not sure. I don't know what I want."

He kissed me. "We don't need to decide our future right now. Let's just be happy. We love each other. I want to make you happy. I respect you. I'm not going to abandon you. Let's just take this one day at a time."

I kissed him back but inside my heart wrenched.

I did love him. And I believed him. But I couldn't take this one day at a time. I had fought so hard to leave this town. I couldn't become dependent on a man. I needed to find my own way.

"We have a few more weeks to decide. Let's check in and see where we are at."

His face grimaced. Clearly not satisfied with my answer. I didn't think that Beck was used to hearing the word no.

Well, I may be poor, but I wasn't pathetic. I would stand up for myself and my sisters. I just couldn't put all my trust in a man.

I fell asleep in Beck's arms and he woke me early with kisses and we made love again. This time it was sweeter and more loving. I loved how he could fuck me at night and then make love to me the next day.

For once, I didn't even try to sneak out of his room early. I would no longer keep where I slept a secret from the girls. I felt guilty being so blatant like mama had been, but even so, I still woke up before they did.

I made breakfast and Beck took the girls to school. After I fed Sky, I sat on the floor and started to read to her. She was more and more active by the day and I was pretty sure she would start walking by next month. She was such a fat, healthy baby with a beautiful smile. I adored her. I loved her.

After a few hours of singing songs, crawling, and playing games, I put her down for a nap. I walked into the kitchen to make lunch when I heard a loud knock at the door.

I rushed to open it, not wanting Sky to wake.

My heart stopped when I saw who was standing at the door.

It was my mother. Her hair seemed to have become greyer and her eyes had more lines. And she was holding a cup of my favorite treat—chamangos.

What the fuck was she doing here?

I quickly rushed her inside, so no one would see her.

"What are you doing here? How did you find me?"

She pushed by me. "I'm not stupid, *mija*. I know things. I can find you. I'm your mother."

"How did you even get on base? Did you fuck the guard?"

She leveled me with her eyes. "Your uncle got me on. You got that nanny position the full town has been talking about."

Dammit. My uncle sold me out. I was actually surprised it took her so long to find me. "Doesn't matter. It's a job."

She handed me the chamango cup. When I had been young, she used to take me into town and share chamangos with me. It was the best thing ever—juicy mangos mixed with chamoy, an amazing sauce that was a mixture of pickled fruit and powered chilis. Topped with chili powder, lime, and a tamarindo candy, chamangos had been the happiest part of my childhood.

To hell with my mom—I wasn't going to let this treat go to waste. I sucked on that straw and drank it down.

As I was indulging in my drink, my mom opened her mouth to ruin my bliss.

"Have you slept with him?"

I wanted to slap her. How dare she ask me that? She had no right. No right!

"None of your business."

Then for the first time in years, I saw my mom cry. Her voice broke. "Listen, *mija*, listen. I know you hate me. But I need to tell you something. I was once like you. I wanted to leave this town, too. Until I became pregnant with you. Your father . . ." she paused.

I jerked my head back. My father? She never spoke about my father. Never. Even my abuela didn't know who he was.

"What, what about my father? Who is he?"

"He . . . he was in the Navy. He was here for ten weeks and then left. He abandoned us, *mija*. He told me he would take me away, start a new life with us. He knew I was pregnant with you, but he left anyway."

My hand trembled and heat burned my eyeballs. Oh my god, was she serious? Was my father a Blue Angel?

"You are lying to me."

"I'm not lying. He was a Blue Angel! But he was no *ángel*. He was *el diablo*."

I fought the nausea down my throat. No. No. No. She had to be lying. There was no way this could be true.

"Prove it. You are a liar. You have always been a liar."

Her hand reached into her worn leather purse, and she pulled out an old picture. A Blue Angel pilot with piercing green eyes the same shade of mine was posing for a picture with my mom, who looked just like I did now.

But that wasn't all.

The pilot was holding a little girl around Sky's age.

And that girl was me.

Holy fuck.

My lips burned, and my vision clouded, and it wasn't from the chilies on the chamango. I felt instantly weak.

"Why have you never shown me this before? He could've been

any pilot you took a picture with at the show. Why should I believe you?"

"Look in the mirror! Have you ever wondered why you are so pale when me and your sisters are dark? Why you are the only person in our family without brown eyes? Where do you think your green eyes come from? From him!"

I didn't need to look in the mirror. I always wondered why instead of getting tan my pale skin burned. I knew my eyes were the same haunting pale green as the man in that picture. These green eyes caused my classmates to call me a *gringa*. These green eyes caused my uncle to tease me and say I wasn't a real Mexican. These green eyes were proof that my father wasn't another brown-eyed local.

"What his name?"

She pursed her lips and closed her eyes and said his name as if it was a prayer. "John Emerson."

John Emerson.

Paloma Angélica Emerson.

But I still wasn't sure. "I don't know if I believe you."

"Why do you think I named you Paloma? It means dove. A bird who flies in the sky like a plane. Used at weddings as a symbol of love. I thought if I named you Paloma he would return to me. And Angélica was because your father was a Blue Angel." And with that, she broke into sobs.

And I knew she wasn't lying to me anymore.

I put my hand on her shoulder, comforting her beside myself.

"Why didn't you tell me before?"

"Because I didn't want to hurt you. I tried, *mija*, I did. I know you don't believe me, that you hate me, but I tried. It was so hard. No one would hire me. And I had a baby. I was only a teen. I gave up. But you have to know I tried. And I do love you."

"I don't hate you, Mama." And I didn't. Her confession shook me to my core. Was history repeating itself? Was Beck going to use me and leave me like my father had left my mother? "But it's different. He loves me. I love him. He wants me to go to Florida with him. He wants to take the girls."

She stared at my left hand and I knew what she was looking for.

A ring.

A ring that I didn't have.

"Where's your ring?"

"I don't have one."

She shook her head. "Did he ask you to marry him?"

"No. His wife died last year. But he loves me."

She scowled. "No, he doesn't. He asked his *nanny* to go to Florida. Not his fiancée. You take care of his daughter, wash his clothes, cook his food, keep his home clean, keep his bed warm, why wouldn't he want you? But don't be mistaken, *mija*. You are only his nanny. You will only ever be his nanny. He will never marry you."

That's it. I had enough. "Go, Mama. Go. Don't ever come back. I'm not you. Beck is not my father. He probably didn't love you the way Beck loves me."

ALANA ALBERTSON

"No Paloma, you are wrong. He loved me. He loved me like the air he breathed. Like the stars in the sky. Like the moon loves the sun but they can only meet passing in the night. We could never be together. I didn't fit into his life and you don't fit into you pilot's life, either. Look at you. You are a Mexican nanny. He's rich! Educated. He may be having fun right now, but he will never ever marry you. Leave him now, before he breaks your heart—or you do something stupid."

My muscles quivered as rage consumed me. "What does that mean, Mama. Is that what you did? Did you get pregnant with me to trap my father?"

She looked down at her feet. "Yes, *mija*, I did. I was so desperate. You don't know how much I loved him."

My stomach recoiled. "I can't believe you did that? You trapped him? Of course, he didn't want to marry you. No one wants to be backed into a corner."

"You are no better than me. You don't know what it's like. Two years from now, when Beck still won't marry you, you will do the same thing. Mark my words."

"I would never." But somewhere deep in my soul, I connected with her desperation. I couldn't imagine being out in Florida with Beck, him never wanting to marry me. Would I ever do something like my mom had?

"You are just like me. You will. He had everything. I had *nada*. I thought once he saw your little face, he would love you too. You were perfect, *mija*. But he left us. Never sent money or even a card. For years, I prayed he would come back. And one day he did. You were around two, and he came out for a show. And he saw you. He knows about you. And I could see it in his eyes. He

160

still loved me. But he wasn't man enough to take us away and keep us in his world. We are nothing like them. You should know your place. The world hasn't changed. These men, these Blue Devils, they come here to go slumming and they go back and marry women who look like them, women who are from their world.

I wanted to push her out of the room, I didn't want to hear anything she had to say. I didn't want to listen. Beck was nothing like my father, if she was telling me the truth. Beck didn't care what people thought about him, about me, about us. He had taken me out in public, he had introduced me to his friends. I was even going to meet his mother when she came to town for the airshow.

"Beck is not embarrassed by me. He loves me, too. He's going to introduce me to his mother. Times have changed, Mama. I'm sorry my father left us. That's horrible. But Beck loves me."

"If he loved you, he would marry you, not keep you as the nanny. You are the help. Don't you see? He's using you. He will never ever marry you. You are young, you are beautiful. It's too late for me but don't throw your life away on this man. Move to San Diego with your sisters. Start a new life. But do it on your own. If he loves you, he will come after you."

I thumbed the picture. "Can I keep this?"

She nodded. "Yes, it's yours." She looked toward the door. "I'll go. But *mija*, if you were smart, you wouldn't go to Florida. Take the money and get your sisters far away from here. And one day, when you realize I'm right. Forgive me."

She hugged me hard, and I didn't push her off of me.

Then she walked out the door.

Leaving me alone with all my insecurities.

And for the first time in years, I believed that my Mama actually cared about me. That she loved me and wanted the best for me.

But I also believed something else.

She was right about Beck.

CHAPTER TWENTY-FOUR

NEW YORK STRIP

When I arrived home from work, Paloma had not made my lunch. I didn't mind at all. She didn't have to cook for me. But it struck me as odd.

"Why don't we pick up your sisters and go to lunch?"

She shook her head. "I hope you don't mind, but today I want to walk alone and pick up my sisters."

Great. Something was definitely wrong. "Are you okay?"

"Yup. Never better. I just need some fresh air. I'll be back later."

I leaned over to give her a kiss and she turned her cheek. What the hell? What did I do wrong?

I wasn't the type of man to let her walk away without a fight. I grabbed her by the wrist. "Babe, what's wrong?"

"Nothing."

"Paloma, don't. You are upset, and I care. Tell me what happened."

She reached into her purse and took out an old picture of a Blue Angel pilot holding a baby at an air show. Standing next to a woman who resembled Paloma.

Holy shit. Was that her mother? And was the baby here?

I took a closer look and noticed that the little girl had dark hair and green eyes, just like Paloma, and the Angel's eyes were the same color.

Dammit.

Her lip trembled. "My mom stopped by today. I don't know how she found me, but it doesn't matter. She won't come back. She gave me this. She says he was my father. And even worse, I actually believe her."

Her voice was breaking. I pulled her into me and kissed her forehead as she cried.

"She said he was an Angel. And he didn't want anything to do with my mom. Or with me. Do you know how many times I cried out for a father to save me from this life? How many nights I went to bed hungry? How many times I walked to school with shoes that had no soles?"

"There, baby, there." What an asshole. I would hunt her father down and deal with him myself. No pilot, especially a Blue Angel bestowed with this privilege should ever abuse his power. And abandoning his own child and leaving her to live a life in poverty is inexcusable.

And then it hit me. She was crying over her father for sure, but she also probably feared I would do the same thing.

But I never would.

I needed to soothe her fears.

"Hey, I have an idea. Your sisters don't get out of school for another hour. Let me take you to the officers' club to lunch. You can meet all the other officer's wives."

I thought my offer would cause her to smile, but instead she burst into even more tears.

Man, I really didn't understand women.

"I'm confused, babe. Help me out. You don't want to go with me? That's fine if you don't. We can stay here. I can take you to pick up your sisters and we can get takeout. Or I can cook. I just want you to be happy."

"No, I do. It's just that you are so amazing. You never disappoint me. But you are too good to be true. You have to have a fatal flaw. No one can be as perfect as you. I'm waiting for the other shoe to drop. I'm so damaged. You can do so much better than me. You can find a rich educated girl who knows how to act at the officers' club. Like Laurel. I'll probably use the wrong fork and embarrass you."

"You could never embarrass me. And you are better than all these women. You have fought so hard to survive. Just because I was born into privilege doesn't make me better than you. I always knew that I was going to college. My parents sent me extra money and bought me a car. I still worked my ass off in school and when I graduated to be a pilot. I admire your grit. And I'm not embarrassed by you. I don't want Laurel. I want you."

She finally smiled and I wiped her tears away. "Let's go. I've always wanted to go to the officers' club. I never thought you'd ask."

I gathered Sky's baby bag and we left to walk to the officers' club.

The weather was sunny and crisp and I proudly escorted Paloma inside.

Paloma's eyes widened when she saw the décor, but I cringed in embarrassment.

We were immediately seated at a window table and the staff attended to us. After our waitress read off the specials, Paloma ordered fresh salmon and I had a New York strip steak. I ordered a side dish of bananas for Sky.

"Wow, this place is gorgeous. Thank you for taking me here. It means a lot to me that you aren't trying to hide me."

I reached across the table and took her hand. "Hide you, not a chance. I want to show you off."

She blushed. But even so, I could still see the pain in her eyes. I vowed not to add to her misery. Only to her happiness.

My commanding officer walked over to our table. "Lt. Daly. Who is the lovely lady?"

"Sir, this is my girlfriend, Paloma Pérez.

CHAPTER TWENTY-FIVE

HOTDOGS

I adored Beck for making a me feel wanted and loved. And not some lover to be hidden. We spent the last few weeks in our new routine. Making love all night, waking up together, and hanging out in public as a big happy family when he was off work.

But no matter how much we played house, I was painfully reminded that he wasn't my husband. Sky wasn't my daughter. I was still the nanny. And we had avoided any more deep talks about our future.

But we were running out of time. He would be leaving to return to Pensacola this week.

Today was the first airshow to mark the start of the season. Though I had seen the airshow every year of my life, this time it would mean so much more. My man was the pilot. And this was my final farewell to El Centro.

Beck led me, my sisters and Sky to the executive chalet. My nerves rattled. But I wasn't worried about the safety of his flying.

Today—I would meet his parents.

Beck glanced around the chalet. "My parents aren't here yet, but they will find you. They've seen a picture of you and of course, will recognize Sky. I have to go get ready."

"Okay, babe. I can't wait to see you."

He kissed me in front of all the friends and families in the chalet. See my mom had been wrong. Beck loved me and accepted me. I wished she could see me now.

I would not end up like her.

The crowds filled outside the chalet and the excitement was thick. I had seen the Angels perform many time, but they had always represented this other type of life that I wasn't a part of. And now, I could truly appreciate how amazing they were. How amazing Beck was.

The show started, and I enjoyed the other events first—the U.S. Navy Leap Frogs jumped out of their helicopters, wowing the audience.

There were many other planes doing tricks and maneuvers but I was anxious to finally see Beck fly.

I scanned the chalet but didn't see anyone who looked like his mom. Where was she? She had to be here? She wouldn't miss his first show.

The narrator took to the stage. The sounds of Mötley Crüe's "Kickstart My Heart" filled the air.

But my own heart stopped.

Another piece of the puzzle that proved my mom wasn't lying

about my dad. She always used to play that song to me. I felt sick to my stomach, and it wasn't from the hotdogs I just ate.

What if my father was in this audience? I scanned the crowd but quickly was distracted.

Beck and his fellow pilots walked down the runaway in their matching flight suits. Man, they were so fucking hot. They saluted as they turned and went toward their planes. I couldn't believe I was his girlfriend.

Then they took off—one by one. I pressed Sky's earphones tightly on her head. "That's your daddy."

"Ma ma?"

Oh my god. Did she just call me Mama? I wanted to be thrilled, but instead I was crushed. I wanted to be her mama. But I wasn't.

I was only the nanny.

I hugged her tighter than I ever hugged her and then I noticed that a woman was watching me with Sky. Was she Beck's mom? I'd seen pictures of her but couldn't be certain because she was standing at a distance.

I turned my attention back to the sky. "Ladies and Gentlemen. Please welcome our own Blue Angels."

Mónica clapped loudly in my ear. The planes were now in the sky and my heart raced. They were flying close! Wing to wing. I suddenly realized how dangerous this was. One wrong turn and he could crash.

But he didn't crash. He soared in the sky. Upside down, inverted loops, side by side—Beck did it all. It was so amazing. The music contributed to the adrenaline pulsing in my veins.

Pass after pass, loop after loop, pride filled my soul. I had always known what Beck did everyday while I was watching Sky but until now—I had no idea how much precision and focus it took.

And this amazing man loved me.

He had asked me to move in with him.

And I knew that I couldn't be without him.

I made my decision. I was going to say yes.

I marveled at this house. At my life. Just ten weeks ago I was jobless, hopeless, hungry, and alone.

And now, I was in love with a brilliant, educated, handsome pilot. He loved me too and wanted me to be in his life. He was moving me and my sisters out to be with him.

Dreams do come true.

They made their final pass and I cheered louder than anyone.

Then a woman tapped me on the shoulder.

"You must be Paloma. And there is my beautiful granddaughter."

She pinched her on the cheek and I did my best to smile. Her face was incredibly tight, as if the skin had been pulled and she wore way too much makeup. Her top lip was obviously enhanced, and her blonde hair didn't have a hint of gray. She wore a huge diamond ring on her left hand—a ring that probably cost more than I would make in my lifetime.

I swallowed my nerves. "Hi, Mrs. Daly. So nice to meet you. I have heard so much about you."

She gave me a condescending smile and I felt immediately judged. "I'm sure he did. You know Beck. Always poking his nose where he shouldn't have. Even when he was a young boy, he would try to save all the homeless cats. I used to have to tell him, now Beckett, you can't save them all."

I bit my lip. Was she comparing me to a cat?

I didn't know what to say so I remained silent.

"Paloma dear, may I have a word?"

"Sure Mrs. Daly."

We walked over to the corner of the chalet and I felt everyone was comparing us. From her designer clothes to her expensive jewelry, there was no doubt that she was high class.

Standing next to her, I was sure people assumed I was her maid.

"Now, darling, you are truly lovely. And I thank you for taking such good care of Sky. And my son."

"You are welcome. I love them both. You raised a great man."

"I did, dear. I did. We gave him everything in life. Because we truly believe he can achieve everything. Did you know he wants to be an astronaut?"

"Yes, he mentioned that. I think it's wonderful. I'd support him in any way I could."

Mrs. Daly exhaled. "I'm sure you would, sweetie. I'm sure you would. But these programs are very competitive and very political."

I wasn't sure where she was going with this but I was one hundred percent sure I wasn't going to like it.

I tried to remain calm. "Well, Beck is so accomplished I'm sure they would love him."

"They would. Did you know they interview the family and friends of each candidate? How would it look to them if they know that Beck had slept with his nanny? That kind of scandal could ruin his chances. You wouldn't want to ruin his career now, would you Paloma?"

Nausea overcame me. I did not want to do this. I didn't want to be rude to his mom. "No, I wouldn't want to ruin his career. I would support him in anything. I may be a poor Mexican girl from a border town, but I'm an American. And I'm a great woman. I love your son. And I love your granddaughter. I would. never embarrass him. And frankly, he would be lucky to have me. I treat you son like a king and Sky adores me. I love her like she is my own." Take that, bitch. A wave a satisfaction rippled over me. I had stood my ground. I knew my worth.

I hoped Beck would be proud of me.

"Well, aren't you self-important? Beck may have fun with you now, but he will never marry you. I promise you that." And she stood up and walked away from me, never even kissing Sky goodbye.

I would not let this change my feelings for Beck. Those were his mother's beliefs, not his. Beck was an adult. He didn't need her approval.

Even so, the doubt lingered. I saw the way his buddy Charlie looked at me. The way some of the other officer's wives stared at me around base.

Did I want to be blamed for every bad thing that happened in his career for the rest of my life?

Did I want people to judge me—think I was using him?

Would one day these comments get to Beck and would he leave me for someone more like Catherine?

And though I hadn't wanted to pressure marriage, now I was curious if Beck had any intention of ever marrying me.

Both my mom and his claimed he never would.

I had to hear it from him.

I didn't want to live my life constantly having to prove myself to these pretentious people who cared more about Beck's image than his happiness.

I wanted to be accepted to be loved to be appreciated.

I had to know the truth before I moved with him.

What were his intentions toward me?

Would he ever marry me?

Or would I always just be the nanny.

CHAPTER TWENTY-SIX

CHICKEN MOLE

Man, that show had been amazing. Our formation wasn't as tight as I liked but we had killed it. I couldn't wait to fly for the next nine months.

Once I disembarked from the plane, I walked over to the chalet to see Paloma and Sky, but she was nowhere to be found.

What the fuck? She left?

My mother on the hand was waving me down.

"Beck, darling, that was incredible."

"Thanks, Mom. Where's Dad? Did you meet Paloma? She was here with her sisters and Sky."

"Dad is back at the Navy Lodge. I'm afraid he's come down with a bug. I did meet your nanny. Feisty, isn't she."

Great. I wasn't going to fight with her in my uniform. I lowered my voice. "She's not my nanny—she's my girlfriend. What did you say to her?"

She shook her head but I couldn't read her face because she used way too much Botox. "Really, Beckett. Sleeping with your nanny. What a disgrace. Poor Catherine would be rolling in her grave. I understand the need to have a lover, but the poor girl thinks you will marry her. End this at once before you ruin your career."

I cringed when my mom said lover. "Listen to me, mom. I love her. And Sky loves her, too. She's a part of my life and if you want to be part of my life and Sky's, I suggest you get over yourself."

I walked away from her and went back to greeting the rest of the fans. That was my job. I wanted to run after Paloma, but I had an obligation to fulfill. I glanced back and my had left the chalet. Good riddance.

She would come to her senses. And if not, she could learn to live without me and Sky.

Two hours later, I returned home.

I handed her a dozen red roses. "I'm sorry about my mom. I took care of it."

"It's fine. I understand. My mom is a piece of work too. Let's enjoy our last night together."

My heart skipped. "What do you mean by that? You are coming with me, aren't you?"

She placed her hand on my chest. "We will talk after dinner."

"No, I want to talk now. Are you leaving me?"

Her lips trembled. "Please, Beck. Can't we just enjoy dinner?"

Fine, whatever. I sat down at the table. Paloma had made another incredible meal, chicken mole. We made small talk with the girls who were still talking about how much fun we had at the dance a few nights ago. We'd taken pictures, danced together, and then I took them out for ice cream. Was Paloma really leaving me? She couldn't. I loved her and her sisters. And what about Sky?

After we put the girls to bed, I cornered her in the kitchen.

"Dammit, Paloma. Don't shut me out. What did my mom say to you?"

"It doesn't matter what she said to me. I'm not moving with you to Florida."

Her words knocked the wind out of me.

And for the second time in my life, I knew I had just lost the woman I loved.

CHAPTER TWENTY-SEVEN

CAVIAR

Beck's fist clenched. I couldn't believe what I had just said. But my decision was final.

I was moving to San Diego.

Tomorrow.

"Why Paloma? Why are you doing this to me? I love you dammit. Isn't that enough?"

I shook my head. "No, it's not enough. I deserve more."

"What do you want from me? Babe, I'm crazy about you. Sky loves you. I love your sisters. Of course, it's a good idea"

"But you will be flying around the country. I will never ever see you."

"I come home most weeks for a few days."

"But what about the rest of the time? I won't know anyone. And people will talk there like they talk here." People like his mother.

I had tried to be strong and proud but her words and stung me deep.

"I don't care what people think. Not Charlie, not my mom. I just want to be with you. Don't you get that?"

I believed that he thought that now. But I also thought that his feelings could change.

"Your mom hates me. I don't sip champagne and eat caviar. I don't want to ruin your life."

"You would never ruin my life. You are my life."

He kissed me, and I melted. He was great. I had no complaints at all about him or our relationship. But deep down no matter how hard I had tried to convince myself otherwise, I had always known that we were on a timeline.

And now our time was up.

I had made my decision.

And even if it was the wrong one, I was sticking to it.

Sure, I could go to Florida, and it could work out. We could get married and I could be Sky's mommy.

But I would be alone on the base.

I would be ostracized.

And then—he could leave me.

And I would have nothing.

I couldn't take that risk when my sisters were involved.

My heart constricted in my chest. I couldn't believe I was the one who was ending this. Especially when my feelings for Beck hadn't changed.

When he had walked into the door earlier tonight he had a hopeful look on his face. And roses. A dozen red roses. How was I going to be able to tell him?

I pulled back from him.

"Is this about your dad? I'm not him. I'm not going to leave you. I asked you to move to me with Pensacola. He has nothing to do with us."

And that was when I broke. "How can you say that? He has everything to do with us. Everything. Don't you see that? History is repeating itself."

He clutched me by the arms. "No, you are wrong. I'm not going to leave you. I'm in love with you."

I paused. Was I really going to bring up marriage? Yes, I was. I had to lay it all out.

"But do you want to be with me forever?"

His face turned pale. "I'm in love with you. We have only been together for a month. But I'm getting there, babe. You are incredible."

A lump grew in my throat. "Well, I would marry you. Today. Now."

He shook his head. "Why do we have to rush everything? We live together. You are moving in with me. I just want to make sure it's forever."

"I don't want to be your nanny. I want to be your wife."

His neck tensed. "My wife? We have only known each other for ten weeks, and we have only been dating for a month. I'm not saying I will never marry you. But it's too soon right now. Catherine and I dated for six years before I proposed."

"I'm not Catherine! I'm so sorry that your wife died but I'm not her. And you dated long distance. We live together. I am your wife for all intents and purposes. I cook for you, watch your daughter, clean your house, do your laundry, sleep with you at night."

He held my arms down. "Babe, listen to me. I'm crazy about you. You know that. But I have so much going on right now. With the airshow season kicking up and waiting to get orders. I don't know where I will be next year. I'm sure this is going to work out, but I don't see what's so wrong about taking this slow."

"We are not taking this slow. You will never decide to marry me. I'll always be the nanny. That is not what I want. That is not what I deserve. I love you. And I would make an excellent wife. If you are not ready, I understand. I never expected that you would be. But I can't move the girls across the country on a maybe."

He dropped his hands and paced in the kitchen. "So what? You are breaking up with me? After I opened up to you? Trusted you with my daughter? After I fell in love with you?"

"You trusted me with your daughter before you opened up to me. You hired me as your nanny, remember?"

"Look, I know you are scared, and I get that. This is a risk. But love is always a risk. And you are worth it to me. I'm not going anywhere. I just want to get through this year, figure out where I'll be stationed, and then make some decisions. I've always been practical. And I want to make sure because Sky is involved."

I wanted to scream but I didn't want to wake the girls. "Love isn't rational! Love is passionate and messy and heart wrenching. I already know I would do anything for you. And I want to know that you feel the same way about me. That I'm not just some runner up because your amazingly beautiful, perfect, classy wife who your mom loved died. I want to know that you love me just as much if not more!"

And with that, I knew I had gone too far. But I didn't for a second regret the words that came out of my mouth. I meant every one.

"I can't give you want you want right now. You have no idea what it's like to have your whole world ripped away from you. My feelings for my wife have nothing to do with my feelings for you. I wish you could understand that."

"I do understand that. And no, I have no idea what that's like. But I do know what it's like to have nothing. Because my entire life has been nothing. Until you. And Sky. And I want this so badly that my heart is in knots. I need you. But I need you to need me to."

"Of course I need you. You know that. You are everything. You are beautiful, kind, sexy, loving. I'm just not ready to propose to you today."

"Well, I deserve more. I deserve everything."

And that was it. I had pushed the issue and he had given me an answer. An answer that I didn't want to hear but at least it was honest.

"The girls and I are moving to San Diego tomorrow. I'm buying a car and we will be gone. My mom has agreed to terminate her parental rights."

"So that's it? After everything we have been through you are just shutting me out?"

"Yup. That's it. This will never work. We are too different. Like your mom said, I don't want to ruin our chances."

He shot me a pointed glared. "That's so unfair. I never said that, nor do I think that. I don't bring your mom up."

He was right. That was dirty. But I didn't care. I was mad and lashing out. I had just given up the only man I had loved. "I'm sorry. But it's true. You deserve someone like Catherine. Not me."

He walked over to me and held me, and I didn't push him away. "But I want you."

I want you too. "We can't always have what we want."

"What about Sky? She loves you."

And that broke me. "I love her too. But I don't want to be her nanny anymore. I want to be her mom."

CHAPTER TWENTY-EIGHT

ENCHILADAS ROJOS

Paloma did not sleep in my bed that last night.

And when I woke early the next morning, she had already left.

She didn't even leave a note.

I walked through the empty house, pitying myself, pitying Sky.

I grabbed her from her room. She had grown so much these last ten weeks.

She looked up at me. "Da da?"

I kissed her. She had been calling me da da for weeks. Her voice melted me. But I wasn't prepared for the words that came out her mouth next. "Ma ma?"

Ah fuck. Maybe she said Loma.

But then she said it again. "Ma ma?"

I doubted that Paloma taught Sky to call her Mama. Sky probably learned it through books. Even so, I was just crushed.

Sky had lost another mother figure. And I wasn't going to be around enough to make it up to her.

Who was going to watch her? I would have to hire another nanny.

But I didn't want another nanny. I wanted Paloma.

I opened the refrigerator to get some milk and noticed a casserole dish covered in foil.

I lifted the foil off and found a full batch of enchiladas rojas.

In Paloma's final moments in my house, she had wanted to take care of me.

Fuck, I missed her already.

The doorbell rang. I jumped up, hoping it was Paloma and that she had come back.

But it was my mother. The last person I wanted to see.

I reluctantly let her in.

"Beck, darling. Why so glum?"

"What the fuck did you say to Paloma? She left today. You are so fucking pretentious. Just because she isn't rich and educated? Who the fuck do you think you are? I'm a grown ass man. I will love who I choose to love."

She opened her mouth and just stared at me. I had never gone off on my mother like that. But she deserved it.

"You will get over her one day. She left. What does that tell you about her character?"

"Everything. That she wasn't going to give up her goals for a man. She loves me. You see her as a gold digger, but she didn't want my money. I offered to pay her in Florida and she turned me down. Just go. I want to be alone."

She exhaled. "I'll go. Call me when you come to your senses."

She walked out of the door and never even said goodbye to Sky. I hadn't realized how cold she was until now. I didn't want Sky to be raised by a cold woman, like my mother. I wanted her to be raised by someone like Paloma.

I wanted her to be raised by Paloma.

Fuck.

I fed Sky and placed her in her Pack n Play. And then I went to my room. I opened my dresser drawer and took out a sealed envelope.

Beck

My wife had handed my this letter as she was dying. She had told me not to open it until I had fallen in love again. I had wanted to rip up the letter at the time but she made me promise to keep it.

Now was the time. I opened it and the sight of her beautiful handwriting gutted me.

My Dearest Beck,

I have so much to say to you and not enough time to say it. Loving you has been the best part of my life. You were the prince that I dreamed of when I was a little girl. You are handsome, kind, generous, brilliant, and so sexy in that flight suit. You have given me everything I have ever wanted in my life—love, a purpose, a home, and our beautiful little girl. By the time you read this, you will have met someone new. And it's okay. It's more than okay. I'm thrilled for you. Our baby needs a mommy. Someone who loves her as much as I do. Someone to talk to her about her first crush, hold her when she is scared, wipe her tears away when she cries, style her hair into the latest craze, paint her nails the hottest shade, and teach her how to become a young lady. You will never leave the military and our daughter needs a parent, not a caretaker, when her daddy is fighting a war a world away. I know you have chosen a wonderful woman because you would never let anyone unworthy around our child.

And I want you to be happy. You deserve to be loved by someone who loves you as much as I do. Or someone who loves you more than I did. As much as I love you, I never allowed myself to totally lose myself in you. I was scared and proud and never able to fully express how much you mean to me. But you need to know that my world started the day I met you.

Your love for your new wife will never take away our love. You are not betraying me by loving another woman. You have my blessing. And I'm not gone. I'm beside you and our little girl everyday. All you need to do to visit me is fly. I'm in heaven, loving you both, waiting for you to come and kiss me in the sky.

I love you, always and forever. Until we meet again in the clouds.

Love,

Your wife, 'til death do us part, Catherine.

The tears came and I was unable to control my sobs. It was almost as if she had chosen Paloma for me and Sky. She had told me to hire a local nanny—forcing me to let someone into our life.

I would love Catherine until the day I died.

But I also loved Paloma.

And I was going to get her back.

CHAPTER TWENTY-NINE

CUCUMBER SANDWICHES

I left this morning like a coward, driving straight to San Diego. Tomorrow I would go apartment shopping, but today we checked into an extended stay hotel.

I handed Mónica a brand-new cell phone.

"Oh my god! Are you serious? Is this mine?"

"Yes, I have to go somewhere now. But I'll be back in an hour. If there is an emergency, call me. I'll just be down the road."

"Okay. Where are you going?"

I didn't want to tell her in case it didn't happen.

"I'll tell you later."

"Okay. Bye. Don't worry. Ana María and I will be fine."

I gave them both kisses and left the room. As I drove away from the hotel, my nerves rattled. I should've told Mónica where I was going, who I was going to see, and why this was so important to me. But I needed to see this stranger alone.

The stranger who was my father.

I drove down the Coronado streets. San Diego was glorious, even better than in the pictures. I was so excited to live here, where I could drive to the ocean and dip my feet in the sand. No blistering summers to keep me indoors.

I finally found an old Spanish house with a blue and gold sign out front.

Home of a Naval Aviator.

John Emerson.

A chill took over me. In my twenty years, I had dreamt of meeting my father. What would he look like, would we share any interests, was he quirky like me, did he love cooking?

But most important of all, would he accept me.

I checked the address from the background report. And then I checked it again. This was it. I was about to meet my father.

I parked the car and could see the raised hair on my arms. Was he living alone? Was he married? Did he have kids?

It was now or never. I had to meet him. I had to go in.

I opened the car door and slowly walked outside. The salty ocean air hit my face. Twenty years of dreaming and wondering had come down to this.

The Spanish style house had an arched doorway and talavera tiles lining the entrance. Adorned with a red clay roof and a turquoise frame around the windows. Did he ever look at his home and remember the poor Mexican girl he had left behind?

My hand pressed the buzzer, and I pushed the nausea down my throat.

I heard footsteps. But instead of a man greeting me at the door, a woman with brown hair in a crisp bob opened it.

"May I help you?"

Ay. I couldn't do this. What if she didn't know? I had no right to break up his family by revealing his secrets.

"Oh hi. I . . . I'm sorry. I must have the wrong house."

I dashed down the steps and fumbled for the car keys. God, I had been so stupid. I had no right to meet him and demand answers.

I finally opened the door and began to cry. I had chickened out. I wasn't brave at all. And now I would never know my father.

I turned the key in the ignition when I was startled by a rap at the door.

And there, standing outside my window, was my father

I knew it the second I saw him; his green eyes were the same shade of mine and we had the same chin.

He motioned for me to roll down the window, and I complied.

"You must be Paloma. I had hoped you would find me."

He recognized me?

"Wow, let me look at you. You are beautiful, just like your mother. Please come inside."

I emerged from the car and he pulled me into a long embrace and just held me. Held me so close and I breathed him in. My father. How many nights had I cried dreaming of this moment. Even a grown woman sometimes needs her father to hug her. Especially, when she never had that closeness growing up.

My father led me into the house. "Jill, I'd like you to meet Paloma. My daughter."

Jill's lip quivered, and I didn't know if she was horrified by my presence or thrilled. Our pause was awkward, but after a few minutes she pulled me in for my second hug of the day.

"Nice to meet you dear, we have been waiting for you. I'm your step-mother."

To hear this strange woman tell me she was my step-mother was almost too much to bear. My mom had warned me that his family would reject me, want nothing to do with me, just like Beck would. But so far, I was sensing this was exactly the opposite.

My father sat on a chair across from a sofa. "Please sit down. We have a lot of catching up to do."

That seemed like the understatement of the year. He turned to his wife. "Would you get us some tea?"

"Of course." She placed a hand on my shoulder.

The house smelled like roses. Though it wasn't lavish by any means, I knew how expensive homes were in Coronado. I knew this home must be worth over two million dollars, a number that was mind boggling.

"You knew about me? Why didn't you find me?"

The creases on his eyes deepened and a pained look fell across his face. "I tried. God knows I tried. I came back to El Centro once I found out your mom was pregnant. Your mom demanded that I marry her. And I loved her, but I wasn't ready to get married." He looked toward the door and his expression became vacant. "My family kept telling me that marrying your mom would ruin my career. I didn't listen to them. But then 9/11 happened and I was given orders to deploy. I was so overwhelmed with my career—I just needed time to sort everything out. I sent your mom money, but she wouldn't let me see you."

"I understand." And I did. It was complicated. Probably how Beck felt about me before I dumped him.

"But I came back. You were almost two and I remember seeing you at the air show, my own eyes looking back at me. I had spent the next year deployed, and all I could think of over in Iraq was you and your mother. I vowed that if I made it out of the war alive, that I would marry your mom. But by then, it was too late. She wanted nothing to do with me. Wouldn't let me see you. Wouldn't see me. I proposed to her, offered to share custody, but she wouldn't even let me see you. I should've fought harder, Paloma. I should've fought harder for you and for her. I sent money and cards for years, but she would send them back. After a few years, I gave up. I met Jill and we have been happily married, but we unfortunately weren't blessed with children. I had always hoped that one day you would come back to me. That you would forgive me. And now you are here. You are like an answer to my prayers."

I was legit speechless. Should I believe this man? Why on earth would my mom not take him back, and worse yet not let him see me? And why would she send back money when we were so poor. It was unfathomable to me. Was he lying?

"I don't understand. You could've filed for custody. You could have supported me. We were so poor. I spent my entire childhood hungry. My only daily meal was free lunch. I had nothing, and you have everything. Why would she cut you out?"

Jill returned with the tea and a china plate filled with cucumber sandwiches. She had a kind face and blonde hair. She looked to be in her early forties. Had this man fought harder to see me, I could've lived with them. Maybe I would've had a close relationship with Jill. Maybe she would've braided my hair, cooked for me, taught me how to be a woman.

Maybe she would've loved me.

"I don't know. You will have to ask her. It never made any sense to me either. I knew she never forgave me for not marrying her when I found out she was pregnant. Maybe she was afraid I would take you away from her. And you know, that was probably a valid fear. Had I known everything you had just told me, I would've filed for custody."

I exhaled and I felt as if this world was closing in on me. The information overload was too much. Had my mother truly loved me when I was a little girl? Done everything in her power to keep me close? And this man just admitted that her fear would've been founded. He would've taken me away. And I would've lived a privileged life.

What happened to my mom? Why didn't she want this man back? And when did she stop loving me?

"Did you really love her?"

"I loved her with every fiber in my body. She was beautiful of course, looked just like you. I met her when I went to eat in town. She sat across from me at the table and introduced herself."

That definitely sounded like her. My mother had never been shy like me. "Go on."

"Well, I was immediately taken in by her. She was so full of life and simple, and I don't mean that in a condescending way. I'm from Connecticut and I was used to girls with money who always wanted to be pampered. My high school girlfriend had left me when I joined the Navy because she had wanted to be with a wealthy guy. So your mom was refreshing. She could have fun with a blanket and a picnic. She loved riding in my truck, stealing kisses in the moonlight. I fell deeply in love with her."

I wanted to scream at him. Then why didn't you marry her? And then I wanted to scream at my mom, why didn't she take him back?

But unfortunately, I didn't need to ask those questions. Because deep down, I knew the answers.

"I don't expect you to forgive me, but if you will let me, I'd like to have a relationship with you. We can take it slow. Tell me about yourself. What do you do for work?"

Ha. Was this man clueless? Maybe this was why my mom didn't want him back. He would never understand the realities of my life, the realities of the poverty that I lived in. Did he really think a poor girl from El Centro could just get a job?

"I just moved here last week with my little sisters, Mónica and Ana María. Mónica is fourteen and Ana María is six. I was vale-dictorian of my high school class, but I didn't go to college because someone had to take care of my sisters. My mom is a mess. She's an alcoholic. Luckily, this year a Blue Angel hired me to be his nanny, his wife died. He paid me ten thousand dollars and I used the money to move out here. I plan to rent a small place for us in Chula Vista and I'm looking for work now."

And there it was. My story. I left out the part where I fell madly in love with Beck, where he had fallen in love with me also, where he had begged me to move with him to Florida, where I had told him no and had broken his heart. Where I had left little baby Sky, an angel who loved me, an angel who relied on me.

And then it hit me like a ton of bricks. My mother had been right. I was just like her.

If I believed this man, then she had rejected him, not because she didn't love him, but out of fear. Fear that she wasn't good enough, fear that he would never really love her, fear that she would never be accepted.

And that fear had ruined her life.

And mine.

¡Ay, Dios mío! What had I done?

Instead, she settled. Believing she only deserved a man like Mónica's father, a drunk or even worse, Ana María's father, an abuser.

And now, her life was a mess. She probably drank to forget the love of my father.

And she had rejected him because she loved me. And now, she didn't even have me. For her own daughter hated her.

I sipped the tea and the jasmine calmed me down. For the first time in my life, I felt like I understood my mom.

And maybe, I could even forgive her.

"You live here now? Wow. That's a blessing. Why don't you bring your sisters over to Sunday dinner and we can get to know each other."

"I'd like that."

He gave me a tour of his beautiful home, and I pushed back a twinge of jealousy. This should be my home. I could've grown up here.

I had to be certain he was my father. "Sir, do you mind if we take a DNA test? I brought a test. Just to know for sure."

"Not at all. But Paloma, one look at you and I know you are my daughter. Here, let me show you something."

He went into the house and then returned a few minutes later with a picture. The edges were frayed, and the picture looked yellow. But there was no mistaking the woman in the picture. It was my mother, her long dark hair flowing in the wind. But the oddest thing about the entire picture was that she looked just like me.

We swabbed our cheeks and put the swabs into a plastic bag. I would mail it tomorrow. And then I would know for sure.

We sat in the garden and discussed his long military career. He had been an Angel and then had flow fighter jets. They had lived all around the world and finally settled in Coronado. He had been stationed here for the last five years.

My father had lived two hours away from my house for the last five years and I didn't even know.

"Paloma, may I ask you a question?"

I nodded, craving an intimate moment with my father. The kind of talk that I had always dreamt that fathers and daughters would have.

"Did you date the pilot you were a nanny for?"

Another lump grew in my throat. "Yes. I did."

He exhaled and it almost sounded like a gasp. "Then why aren't you with him now?"

And then, I broke. "I don't know. I love him. He is a kind, great man His wife died in childbirth. And he loves me too. He asked me to move with him to Pensacola, but I told him no. I don't even understand why I told him no. I love him. I'm just so scared. The pilots' wives I met were nice to me, but I always felt like they truly didn't like me. And his mom pretty much told me I would ruin his life. I just felt that at some point, he would leave me, and I would never be good enough. He was good to me and my sisters. And I love his daughter like my own. I'm an awful person, just like my mother."

"Don't ever say that. No, you aren't. You were scared. I get it. When you are a Blue Angel, you are treated like a God. It's hard not to get caught up in all that. But to be a pilot, to truly achieve that level of success and be chosen an angel, you have to be honorable, you have to be the best. I'm sure he loves you, just like I loved your mom. Don't let your fear of being accepted by the pilot community and his family ruin your life. I know I'm not one to be giving advice, but I have lived my life with this regret. I don't want you to go through this also. Give him a chance. Let yourself love him."

"I'll try."

I said goodbye and left. I knew exactly what I had to do. I had to call Beck and beg him to come back to me.

CHAPTER THIRTY

DUNGENESS CRAB CIOPPINO

TWO MONTHS LATER

A s I stood out in front to the restaurant in Old Town, kneading the tortillas for all the tourists, I felt a set of eyes on me.

I looked around the crowd but the heat from the press blew hot in my face and I couldn't focus on any faces.

I turned my attention back to the tortillas.

Life for the past month had been incredible. My father had embraced me and my sisters. After the DNA test came back positive, he had invited us to move in with him. I had resisted at first, but he and Jill insisted. We lived in his guest home and the girls were lucky enough to attend the high rated public school in La Jolla. Jill loved the girls and has so happy to help raise them, since she had always wanted children. I worked part time at this restaurant and attended the local junior college part time. I had wanted to work full time but my dad insisted that he pay for my tuition and pay our bills. He said it was the least he could do after being gone for so many years. It was so hard to accept help, but I finally relented. I couldn't be more blessed.

As for Beck, we had been talking on the phone. I had apologized to him for my behavior. I was dying to see him, but I knew he had been doing shows around the Midwest and unable to see me, though he would be in San Francisco this weekend. Charlie's wife Brittney was watching Sky when Beck doing the shows. But I still felt immense guilt for not being there for Sky.

But I was hopeful for our future.

I looked up again. I knew I was being watched. The line was wrapped around the building and I almost jumped when I heard a voice say, "I'll have two carnitas tacos."

I knew that voice. I had dreamt of that voice ever night since I had left.

I looked up, and my handsome pilot was standing there in front of me, holding flowers with a big grin on his face.

"Beck, oh my god! What are you doing here?"

I quickly asked my supervisor for a break and ran out of the booth into Beck's strong embrace. Though it had been months, since I had seen him, it felt like we had never been apart. His lips crashed on mine and kissed me passionately, as the now growing crowd clapped.

"Nice dress."

I blushed. I was wearing a traditional Mexican dress with a huge colorful skirt and ruffled low cut top. And my hair was bound in braids with ribbons.

"Glad you like it. You didn't even get the tacos you ordered."

"That's okay. I'll eat you instead."

I blushed and punched him in the arm. "What are you doing here —you are supposed to be in San Francisco?"

"I couldn't wait to see you. Would the girls be okay without you this weekend? I want to take you somewhere."

My heart fluttered. "They will be fine with my dad. Where are you taking me?"

"San Francisco."

His hometown. Then it really was true. Everything he had said on the phone. He wasn't embarrassed by me. He truly did love me. And he saw a future with me.

"I'd love to go. Should I drive and meet you there?" I said, knowing that he had to take his plane.

"No. You're flying with me."

My hands shook. "Are you serious? In your Blue Angel plane?"

He smirked. "Yup."

I wanted to jump for joy. This was just like a fairytale. "You aren't going to do some crazy tricks are you? I don't want to black out in the plane."

"I'll be good in the plane. But I'll show you some tricks when we get to the hotel."

He pulled me to him and we kissed again. My break was over, and I refused to lose my job. Luckily my boss understood and let me off early for the day and gave me the weekend off. Beck followed my car back to my place. We picked the girls up from school. And took them to dad's.

Beck and my father instantly hit it off. They were like the same person.

We finally said goodbye to Jill and the girls and we went just down the street to the air station. My father accompanied us and checked out Beck's plane.

"Wow, they have really upgraded these."

"I'll take you on a flight next time."

My father said goodbye and Beck helped me into his shiny blue jet.

My nerves wouldn't calm down. I had never flown. What if I puked all over Beck. But he took off as smooth as silk. I watched Coronado get smaller in the distance as we flew over the coast.

"You okay, babe?"

"Yup! This is amazing."

I couldn't believe how beautiful California looked from the Sky. To think I had lived in this state my whole life and never seen its beauty.

After an hour and a half, we landed at a base near San Francisco. Beck had a car rental waiting for him and we drove into the city.

It was so gorgeous. Old historic buildings, curvy streets, cable cars, Chinatown. San Francisco was so different than San Diego. I couldn't wait to spend more time here.

Beck drove across the Golden Gate Bridge. It was even more breathtaking in person. I couldn't believe I was finally here, a place I had never in my lifetime thought I'd see.

The harsh waves crashed below, and the fog rolled in over the mountains in the distant. I marveled at the beauty of my home state.

"Babe, we fly right over the top. I can't wait for you to see it."

I paused. The airshow in San Francisco was next weekend. I couldn't possibly stay here for another week.

"Wow, I'd love to! But I don't think I will be able to go. I have school and work, and I mean my dad and Jill are fine with the girls but I have to get back."

"Well, they will all be here. I'm flying them out."

"Wait what? Why?"

Beck didn't say anything but he had a sheepish grin on his face. We drove across the bridge and entered the rainbow colored tunnel.

"This is Marin. I grew up here."

"It's so beautiful. I love it here."

"Well, maybe we could move here one day. Marin could use a great Mexican restaurant."

"Stop, teasing."

He laughed. and grabbed my thigh. I leaned over and kissed him. My hair blew in the wind. This was the life. I was so carefree, so happy.

He exited the freeway and told me he was taking me to his hometown. We parked in downtown Tiburon and I was charmed by the quaint little shops. The downtown area overlooked the ocean.

We stopped in a coffee house and I indulged in a rich, velvet mocha. Since I had moved to San Diego I had developed a taste for expensive espresso. It was a treat that I didn't have every day, but San Diego's culture of coffee houses and craft beers had influenced me.

As I was waiting for my drink, I noticed this drop dead gorgeous girl standing next to me. She wore a long flowy dress and had perfect sun kissed hair. She posed her drink next to flowers and a book. Then she sat at a table and took out a selfie stick out and snapped a shot of herself. Wow, she must've been one of those Instagram girls I heard about it. I was so behind the times. I still didn't even have a smart phone. I wondered what it must be like to make a living being pretty.

Beck put his hand on my back and took to Sam's Anchor Cafe, a seafood restaurant that was packed. I ordered Dungeness Crab Cioppino and Beck had a flat iron steak.

I had never been happier than I had been at that moment. We were a normal couple. We were together. I no longer felt insecure. But I still wondered what the future would hold. I didn't need any more guarantees.

The waiter brought dessert to the table with a cover on top. Seemed fancy for this restaurant but maybe they wanted to keep it cold. When he lifted the lid, I gasped.

There was a small black velvet box underneath.

¡Ay, Dios Mío!

I couldn't even control myself. I burst into tears before Beck even dropped to his knee.

He took my hand and I was shaking. "Paloma look at me. You

came into my life when I needed you the most. I'm proud of you. You make me a better man. You say I saved you, but you are wrong. You saved me and Sky. I don't want to live another day without you. Will you marry me?"

CHAPTER THIRTY-ONE

STREET TACOS

"Yes, yes, yes!" Paloma screamed.

I scooped her into my arms. For the past two months, I knew more than ever that I loved her, that I couldn't imagine my life without her, that I wanted to marry her.

And she said yes.

"We're having an engagement party tonight. Brittney organized it. She flew out with Sky."

Paloma's eyes welled up in tears. "I love you. I can't believe you did all this for me."

"I love you, too. I don't want to live without you. Our life won't be easy. I'll be gone all the time, but I'll always come home to you."

I slipped the ring on her finger and we finished our lunch. Then I took her shopping for a new dress and heels. She even got a manicure and a pedicure, which she had never done.

We showed up at six to Guaymas, a Mexican restaurant in

Tiburon. I had gone all out. There were mariachis, a margarita bar, and a taco bar. My fellow pilots made their way in but I was most happy when Brittney walked in, holding Sky.

Paloma ran to Sky and grabbed her from Brittney's arms.

"Hi baby! Oh I missed you so much,"

Brittney pulled Paloma into an embrace. "Congratulations, Paloma. You look so beautiful. And Catherine would really like you."

Those words caused Paloma to cry again. I took her around and introduced her to all the other pilots and their wives. Then the door to the restaurant opened.

And my mother and father were standing there.

I walked over to her and greeted my father.

"Congrats, son."

"Thanks, Dad."

I glared at my mom.

"Mom, please. Don't ruin our day."

"I will do nothing of the sort." She walked over to Paloma. "Darling, I'm sorry how I treated you. I was just looking out for Beckett. But he loves you. Welcome to the family."

And we all hugged.

And finally, after losing Catherine, my world was complete again.

CHAPTER THIRTY-TWO

STRAWBERRIES

I drew myself a warm bath, knowing that Beck was waiting for me outside the door.

Tonight was the night. The night I'd dreamed of since I had moved in with Beck.

I poured in a capful of bubbles and slipped into the warm water. This tub was luxurious—a white stand alone on a marble floor with views of the Golden Gate Bridge. A view of the ocean. To think just a month ago, I had never seen the ocean. I had never flown on a plane. I had never left El Centro. And now I was in San Francisco. I was in love. And I was engaged.

As the hot water filled the tub and the bubbles began to form, heat rose between my legs. I closed my eyes and allowed myself to get lost in the moment. I sipped on champagne that Beck had poured and snacked on a few strawberries that room service had brought into the room to celebrate our engagement.

I slowly emerged from the bath and rubbed coconut lotion all over my body. Then I pulled on a white silk slip and matching panties.

For once I wasn't going to think about my mother, my sisters, or Sky. Tonight was going to be the first time in my life that I was going to live for me.

I took a deep breath and opened the door. Beck's jaw dropped when he saw me in my slip.

"Come here, babe."

I walked over to him. Confident, feeling sexy and not shy.

I placed my hands around his neck and straddled his lap. "I love you."

A sly grin graced his face. His lips crashed on mine and my pussy throbbed. "I love you, too. I love you so much, baby."

"Lay down."

Yes, sir.

He took one finger and slowly pressed it inside me. The pressure felt so good, so right, but I want more of him. He kissed my neck as another finger entered me. His technique was incredible, and I felt the pleasure build again. We stared into each other's eyes and all I knew was that I never wanted anything more in my life.

"Ready, babe?"

"Yes. Please."

He removed his fingers and dropped his boxer briefs and I stared at his cock. He slowly pressed it inside me and I gasped, as I felt myself stretching to take him. Pleasure and pain intricately bound together. Inch by inch, until he was fully inside me. Then he cupped my head. "Look at me. I love you. You saved me."

I didn't want to cry but I couldn't help it. He kissed away my tears as we made love. We moved together as one. We were finally one now. Body and spirit and soul. Our rhythms synced and the pleasure filled my soul. He kissed my lips, kissed my neck, my breasts.

After a loving eternity, he flipped me over so I was straddling his lap. I rubbed my clit over him as he suckled on my nipples.

"Come, baby."

I wrapped my arms around his neck and rode him until another orgasm pooled in my belly and for the second time tonight I came. He quickly came after me as I collapsed in his arms.

After our bodies remained connected for a few moments longer, we finally separated.

He wrapped his arms around me. "I can't wait to marry you."

CHAPTER THIRTY-THREE

BLUEBERRY MUFFIN

Beck and I had a beautiful wedding on the beach of Coronado. My father walked me down the aisle and even my mother attended. She took one look at my father and burst into tears. He hugged her and they talked about the past. I prayed that she found some piece.

My sisters were thriving in school. Ana María took dance classes and Mónica decided to go out for the swim team. She was still boy crazy but at least, she now had other interests. She also wanted to attend college.

Beck and I had moved to Coronado, a few blocks away from my father. The girls spent so much time with them but they lived with us. My father and Jill were also happy to watch Sky any time I needed them too.

And Sky and I had so much fun together. We took mommy and me yoga, and mommy and me music. Every day I thanked my blessing for her and Beck.

I had quit my job but still attended school, where I planned to study sociology. And I still wanted to open a restaurant one day. But for now, I was content.

I placed a blanket down at Tidelands park in Coronado. Sky sat in the middle of it and snacked on her blueberry muffin. A stunning woman with icy blonde hair, designer sunglasses, a huge diamond and even a bigger belly walked over to me. She must've been at least eight months pregnant.

"Excuse me, you are so wonderful with that little girl. I was wondering, are you happy with your current job? I hear you speaking Spanish and I would love to have a bilingual nanny. How much are they paying you? I'm prepared to offer you a healthy bonus and health insurance. I'm due next month and we haven't found a nanny."

I gulped. Wow, did rich people just think they could buy people off? Even if I was still a nanny, I clearly was bonded to Sky. How horrible. But I gazed down at Sky's happy face, bouncy blonde locks, and bright blue eyes. When I reached for her hand, her creamy skin contrasted with mine.

"Oh, congratulations. I appreciate your offer, but I'm not Sky's nanny. I'm her mom. But nice to meet you. I'm Paloma. My husband and I just moved here. We love Coronado. I live up the street. Do you live nearby?"

The woman's jaw dropped. And I got it. No matter what, I still didn't look like I belonged in this sea of wealthy people. I might never fit in with the wealthy residents of this town.

But I no longer cared what other people thought of me. When Sky looked up at me, she didn't notice that my skin was darker and hers was lighter. All she saw was that I was her mother. Beck and Sky loved me. They saw me as part of their family.

And I finally realized, that was all that mattered.

Thank you for reading my book.

If you liked it, would you please consider leaving a review? **_Blue Sky_**

Please stay tuned for **_Blue Moon_**_, the next book in the Blue Devils series._

For the latest updates, release, and giveaways, subscribe to **_Alana's newsletter_**.

For all her available books, check out Alana's **_website_** or **_Facebook page_**.

Follow me on **_Bookbub_**.

Read on for Conceit, the first book in my best selling Se7en Deadly SEALs Series.

CONCEIT

SE7EN DEADLY SEALS #1

Conceit
The Se7en Deadly SEALs Series
Episode One
Copyright © 2014 by Alana Albertson.
Cover Designer: Regina Wamba of Mae I Design
(https://www.facebook.com/MaeIDesignandPhotography)
Cover Models: Callan Newton and Dani Cooper
Interior design and formatting by JT Formatting
(http://www.facebook.com/JTFormatting)

Bolero Books LLC
11956 Bernardo Plaza Dr. #510
San Diego, CA 92128
Bolero Books

Publisher's Note: This is a work of fiction. Names, characters, places, and incidents are a product of the author's imagination. Locales and public names are sometimes used for atmospheric purposes. Any resemblance to actual people, living or dead, or to businesses, companies, events, institutions, or locales is completely coincidental.

It was **pride** that changed angels into devils; it is humility that makes men as angels

SAINT AUGUSTINE

Se7en Deadly SEALs bound to secrecy about a night that ended in tragedy

6ix months my brother Joaquín has spent in jail for murder

5ive hours a day I've trained to go undercover to learn the truth

4our plastic surgeries to transform into a pinup to gain access to their world

Thre3 shots of tequila I knock back before I strip and dance for the SEALs

2wo years since I'd left my soul mate, Grant, the only man who can help me now

1ne dead stripper found strangled and drugged

Zer0 room for error

I'm Joaquín's only hope for freedom. No sin is too depraved, no challenge is too great. Even if it means destroying my soul.

CHAPTER ONE

MIA

THE PRISON GUARD LED ME down the hall to the waiting room. A pregnant girl cowered in the corner, an older couple embraced each other, and a pale, skinny woman bit her nails as a young boy fidgeted in her lap. The rancid smell of vomit loosely masked with bleach made me gag. This scene was so pathetic. We were all here to see our loved ones incarcerated in this hellhole.

"Your boyfriend will be out in ten minutes," the guard sneered, his eyes undressing me.

"He's not my boyfriend. He's my brother, and he's innocent."

The guard laughed and wiped the beads of sweat from his forehead. "Sure, he is, sweetheart, never met a guilty one."

Jerk. That guard wasn't fit to polish Joaquín's boots.

After an agonizing wait, the prisoners stumbled out into their partitioned section of the room. My brother came last. All my girlfriends were in love with Joaquín—who could blame them?

Even in this pit of despair, he still looked like the ultimate alpha male. His muscles bulged in his orange prison jumpsuit, the elbow-length sleeves barely covering his tattoos.

At least I didn't have to worry about anyone screwing with him in jail; he was trained to kill a man with his bare hands. Joaquín had everything going for him. Until he was charged with a crime he didn't commit. I knew my brother, and he simply couldn't be guilty of what he was accused of doing.

Joaquín was an easy target—a poor Mexican-American orphan with no trust fund, no senator endorsements, and no college education. But my brother had integrity, loyalty, and honor. He would never disgrace his Teammates, betray his country, or destroy his brotherhood. And he could never hurt a woman.

He tapped on the glass, and we both reached for the phone. "Thanks for flying down, Mia. Are you okay?"

I threw my free hand in the air. "Yeah, I'm okay. I'm not the one in jail facing the death penalty for murder. I took the first flight I could get. What the hell happened?"

The man on the other side of the glass wasn't the brother I'd grown to respect and adore. He was still strong, still resolute, and seemingly impenetrable. But his eyes ... I looked right into his eyes. Though his long dark lashes covered his pain, I knew him too well. To anyone else, he would seem formidable, but to his baby sister he looked broken, torn.

"I didn't kill her. I can't talk about what happened in here." His eyebrows motioned toward the cameras in the corner of the room. "But you have to believe me."

I swallowed. I'd watched the incessant news coverage. It didn't look good. Two weeks ago, one of Joaquín's commanding officers,

Paul Thompson, had thrown a huge party for his SEAL Team at his parents' oceanfront home in Encinitas. Witnesses interviewed by the police said they heard loud music and saw women coming in and out of the place. Guess the neighbors weren't exactly going to call the cops on a group of SEALs.

In the early hours of the morning after the party, Joaquín had discovered a lifeless stripper named Tiffany in his bed. He called 911, and the paramedics determined that she'd been dead for hours. Joaquín told detectives that he'd slept with her the night before, but that she had been fine when he fell asleep. The police didn't charge him immediately and waited for the autopsy results. Two days ago, the coroner ruled that she'd died from asphyxiation and had the date rape drug Rohypnol in her system. Since Joaquín had admitted to having sex with her, he had been arrested and charged with her murder.

He already said he didn't kill her. He would never lie to me, and we kept no secrets from each other. Well ... we never used to. I held my own deep secret close, never wanting to add any burden to Joaquín's intense life.

"Can't anyone clear you? Are the other guys in the Team trying to help or did they desert you? What about Grant ..." My voice trailed off.

My ex-boyfriend Grant Carrion, Joaquín's swim buddy in BUD/S, had been there that night. And I knew the rest of the guys on their Team pretty well. After our parents had died, Joaquín had become my legal guardian, and I'd moved to San Diego to finish my senior year in high school. I met Grant right before I graduated, and we started dating at the beginning of my freshman year at San Diego State. I'd transferred to San Francisco State as a junior two years ago because it had the best drama department. Well, that was the official excuse for me fleeing—I could've finished school in San Diego. The reality was much more painful. Too painful for me to think about, let alone deal with.

Joaquín pursed his lips; his eyes leveled me. "Stay away from Grant. I'm not going to ruin his career, too. I slept with Tiffany, but I didn't drug her. None of the guys are talking to me right now, probably under orders from the command. Our Team doesn't need this publicity, especially with all the rumors going around about Pat saving Annie from that brothel. My brothers don't have a choice but to obey. My lawyer thinks I should take a plea. If it's the best for the Team, then I will."

I seethed. The public should still be happy that Joaquín's Team just saved a group of USO cheerleaders who had been taken as hostages in Afghanistan. I didn't even know what to say about the Pat and Annie mess, except that I wasn't buying the Team's cover story. "Take a plea? Have you lost your mind? You're gonna confess to murder because that's best for your Team? Who cares about your damn Team—can't you be selfish for once in your life?" I knew the bonds of these SEALs ran deep; they'd kill for each other; they'd die for each other. I couldn't fathom the pain Joaquín had to be going through, but pleading guilty to a murder he didn't commit was insane.

He blinked hard, too hard, as if he was trying to stop tears from escaping. "You don't understand. You never could. I'm not going to ruin the rest of the guys' lives and tarnish our Team's reputation further. It's complicated, and I really can't talk about it."

I didn't want to hear about his Team loyalty. "Who's your lawyer? Is he any good?"

"Daniel Reed. He's a former Team guy."

Sure he was—the world's most exclusive fraternity. Even when these guys left the service, they only hired their own. "What did he say about bail? I'll find a way to raise money."

"We won't know until the arraignment, but he thinks the judge will probably make an example of me. No bail."

"But you're a SEAL."

"Exactly, no playing favorites."

From his posture, the edge in his voice, I knew I was treading on his patience. I needed to garner any information I could before he cut me off. "What's the last thing you remember? The girl, did she pass out?"

His nostrils flared, and he bared his teeth. "Knock it off, Mia."

Whoa. He never raised his voice to me. There was no use arguing with him. Joaquín was a stubborn Taurus—I'd never win. I bit my lip and tried another approach. "You can't tell me anything about that night? Who was the dead girl? Were you dating her?"

"No. I'd never met her before." Joaquín shrugged. He wasn't really a relationship guy. A complete player, he claimed no one could ever be faithful to a SEAL, which was bullshit. I'd never even looked at another man when I was with Grant. I still hadn't, even though we'd been broken up for what felt like forever.

"Who invited her?"

His tone became more agitated. "One of the Team guys invited a bunch of strippers."

Yeah, I'll bet. Strippers and SEALs went together like rum and cola. At least Joaquín wasn't a cheater. I couldn't count the number of times wasted SEALs had called Grant to be picked up from Panthers, the local sleazy strip club. Grant would drag me along, and then his buddies would beg him to act as an alibi to give to their wives. We used to fight about him covering for the philanderers all the time. I had to make small talk with their wives at the family barbecues, knowing that their husbands had their dicks sucked by strippers the night before. Grant always told me to stay out of it—it was their marriages and not our place to get involved. I argued that we were involved because covering for them made Grant an accessory to their infidelities. At least Grant never went to the strip clubs; he swore it wasn't his thing.

I tried to stop myself, but I had to know. "Which guy asked the strippers to the party? Mitch?"

He let out a growl. "One more word, and I'll drop this phone and walk back into my cell."

My gaze darted around the room. I was grateful that this crime had been committed off the naval base so at least he wasn't stuck in the brig. Under a civilian justice system, I could find him the best lawyers. I'd do whatever it took. "I'll get you out of here. I'll find out the truth."

He laughed, and although it was nice to see him smile, I knew he didn't have a shred of faith that I could help him. "How are you going to do that, Mia? You're a theater student. We're talking about a bunch of Team guys."

I preferred the term "highly trained actor," but I wasn't about to correct him. Plus, who was he trying to protect anyway? Did he suspect one of his Teammates? Did he know who killed the girl? "I know. I'm just trying to help." But my mind started racing. Why *not* me? Joaquín was my brother—the same blood ran through our veins, the same dedication, the same stubbornness. Just because I lacked testosterone didn't mean I was any less capable than he was.

He studied me. "I know that look. Don't get involved, Mia. That's a fucking order. I didn't drug or kill Tiffany, which means someone else did. I don't have a clue who, and I can't protect you from in here."

I cringed when I noticed that his hands were shaking. This was real, not some fucked-up nightmare. "I can protect myself." He'd always protected me, been my savior. It would kill him if he knew what had happened to me years ago. But it wasn't his fault. He and Grant had both been deployed, and there was nothing either of them could've done to save me that night. Telling them the truth would accomplish nothing.

"No, I need you to trust me on this." His voice firmed. "I'll be fine. Don't worry about me." He was proud, pigheaded, and I knew he didn't want me to see him defenseless. Just like Grant. These macho SEALs never allowed themselves to be truly vulnerable, not to their families, and most certainly not to their women. Though I completely understood—I was too proud to admit my own weaknesses.

He focused on me. "Mia, I can't take care of you anymore. This is important. I need you to hear me. You have to be strong for me. Remember that place in Marin we used to hike to?"

How could I forget? On the top of Mt. Tamalpais, on a ridge overlooking the fog, was a group of rocks. Joaquín and I used to go up there and spend hours playing make-believe.

"Of course I do. Why?"

"If you need to feel my presence, go there."

What on earth was Joaquín talking about? He hated what he called my "New Age bullshit" about vortexes and spirit guides. But my spirituality guided everything I did. I didn't care if he didn't understand it. "I won't need to. I'm going to take a leave of absence from school, move down here, and visit you every week until you're free."

"Don't you dare. You only have one semester left. Don't ruin your life, too. Listen to me. I don't want you to visit me again. Promise me you won't come back to San Diego."

I bit my nails, and my stomach clenched. He was the only person I had in my life since I'd ended things with Grant. Without Joaquín, I couldn't breathe. I didn't exist. He would never ask me to abandon him. It was then that I knew in my heart something was gravely wrong. Not just the murder of Tiffany and the charges against Joaquín, but something else. Something hidden deep in the secret realm of the SEAL brotherhood. "I promise."

I nodded and placed my hand on the thick plexiglass. He did the same. Would this be the closest I ever came to touching him again? "I love you, Joaquín."

"I love you too, *Angelita Mia.*"

My little angel. He hadn't called me that since we were kids. That name had always meant so much to me. I wanted to be that angel for my brother. No, I *needed* to be that angel. And I would. I would live up to my birth name and become Joaquín's angel.

We only had a few minutes left, so I tried my best to cheer him up. My hands trembled, my body froze. He'd worked so hard to be a SEAL. It was all he ever wanted. The possibility of his career being destroyed was almost worse than him being accused of a crime he didn't commit.

The bell rang, and the guard came and escorted Joaquín out of the room. I stared at him walking away, praying that this nightmare would end soon. This couldn't be goodbye.

I walked out of the San Diego County Jail. Determined. Dedicated. Definite.

I would clear my brother's name. For my entire life, he had protected me, lifted me up when I had fallen. It was my turn to rescue him.

I took off in Joaquín's truck, a brand new Ford Raptor. The scent of the fresh leather tickled my nostrils. For a second, I actually questioned his innocence. How could he afford this new truck? He'd told me he'd saved up during deployment, but I knew he spent most of his money on my tuition and housing. Even though I worked part-time as a makeup artist, living in San Francisco was not cheap. Paul was a second-generation Navy SEAL officer and came from old money—was Joaquín involved in something shady that had resulted in him being framed for murder?

I pushed the thought of his guilt out of my head. My gut wrenched for even questioning his honor.

Speeding on Harbor Drive, I rolled down the window and allowed the crisp San Diego breeze to blow all doubt away. Though it was January, the sun was still bright in the sky. As Joaquín's words replayed in my head and the look on his face haunted my thoughts, I choked back tears.

The Raptor seemed to have a mind of its own, and I found myself driving toward Grant's place. I had to see him. I had no choice. He was my only hope. I needed to ask for his help. I prayed that he would be able to fix everything like he once had. He'd been with Joaquín at the party that night. He must've seen something.

My insides twisted. The intersection of excitement, desperation, and guilt left me unable to focus. Grant was the one man who rivaled my brother in his steadfast character. He'd been my first love, my only lover, and I'd shoved him away. Like every great thing in my life.

I pulled up to his tiny apartment in Point Loma, praying he wasn't off somewhere training. The sight of fresh mud on the door of his lifted truck alleviated that fear.

My fingers traced the doorbell. His dog Hero let out a friendly bark. There was no turning back. I pressed the button.

"Hello?" Grant's deep, sexy voice sounded groggy through the door.

He must've been asleep even though it was three in the afternoon. Probably another balls-to-dawn training rotation. Back when we were together, I'd make sure to have his place clean, his favorite meals cooked, Hero walked and fed when he came home from those all-nighters. It was some of the only times he allowed me to take care of him. "Hey, it's me."

His tone turned bitter, dark. "What do you want, Mia?"

I couldn't help but smile that he still recognized my voice immediately, even though we'd been broken up for two years and hadn't seen each other in six months. I knew what I had done to him—abandoned him in his hour of need, secretly blaming him for being gone when I needed him the most. I had been unwilling to allow him to see me at my lowest point, and unable to open up to him and confess my secret. My fatal flaw had ruined our love. My conceit.

Joaquín would never turn his back on someone he loved. He would embrace his anxiety. Shake hands with fear.

Somehow I would have to learn to do the same.

"I need to talk about Joaquín."

Grant opened the door, and I gasped at the sight of him standing in front of me wearing only pajama bottoms. I'd forgotten how incredible his body was; his broad shoulders and V-shaped torso displayed no body fat, just a perfect eight-pack of abs. His skin glowed in the afternoon sun, highlighting his sculpted arms, which were covered with ink. My eyes focused on his huge hands, remembering how they had explored every inch of my body. He ran his fingers through his golden hair, and I imagined those fingers deep inside me, sending spikes of pleasure to my core. The scruff of his beard hid the deep scar on his neck. His green eyes seemed to shoot beams of kryptonite at me, exposing my soul.

Right, I came here for my brother.

"Let me in, Grant." I pushed my way inside the door, scanning the place for signs of another woman. All clear. Hero, his black lab/pug mix, gave me a lick on my face and lay by my feet.

The last time I saw Grant was at an awkward run-in at my brother's apartment last summer before they deployed. Grant had ignored me the entire time. No matter how hard I'd tried, he refused to engage with me.

Today, he had no choice.

CHAPTER TWO

GRANT

THE VIXEN STANDING IN FRONT of me barely resembled my beautiful ex-girlfriend Mia. Her waist length brown hair that had once carried the scent of coconut milk and vanilla beans was now tinted fuchsia and chopped off into a long, angled bob with spiky bangs. Her freckled skin was painted up like a streetwalker's. Her soft curves were hard, skinny, angular. Her nails, which had always been kept short and pale, were filed into sharp points and polished black, like daggers. I fucking hated her full look. Like some bull-shit revenge breakup make under meant to ensure that I wasn't attracted to her anymore.

It didn't work—I still wanted her.

My eyes lingered on her small breasts and fell down to her wide hips. "There's nothing I can do. No one remembers anything—and if they do, they aren't talking. I'm sorry. For what it's worth, I don't think he's guilty."

"Of course he's not guilty. But you can help him, right. You know the men on your Team. You were at the party. We can find out who killed that girl. I'll do whatever it takes."

"Whatever it takes? What the hell are you talking about?"

She inhaled deeply through her nose and then exhaled through her mouth. "I don't know. I haven't figured it out."

I laughed. "Well, let me know when you do. Until then, you can get the fuck out of my place." I urged her toward my door.

Her eyes darted around my place, but she held her body firm, refusing to budge. "I know we can figure out something if we put our heads together. We can do this."

I sneered at her. "We? There is no 'we.' You made sure of that."

A flash of guilt must have caused her to avert my gaze, as she looked down at her feet and bit her nails.

"Maybe I could go undercover? I'm a chameleon. An actress, a makeup artist. I've reinvented myself so many times even you wouldn't be able to recognize me."

This bitch was crazy. "You can't be serious. You're five-feet-four inches tall, one hundred thirty pounds. I used to have to open spaghetti jars for you. You think you can defend yourself against a SEAL? No way can you outsmart my Team. Sorry, Mia. It will never work. You're delusional. I could recognize you no matter how you changed." I had memorized every inch of her body, the sound of her voice when she whispered my name, the way her lips parted when she was embarrassed, the glint in her hazel eyes when she wanted her way, and the flush on her cheeks when she came.

I loved you.

Picturing her smile had gotten me through those long muddy

nights freezing my balls off in the frigid water during BUD/S. Her faith, her love, her belief in me had kept me from quitting, from ringing that bell.

Too bad it was all complete bullshit.

She touched my face, tracing the beard that hid the scar on my neck. "I just need one of them to talk."

I pushed her hand away. My stomach churned, I couldn't stand the sight of her anymore. Couldn't she see the hurt in my eyes? I'd once looked at her with warmth, love, devotion. Now only her betrayal lingered in the air. "SEALs don't talk."

She let out a laugh. "You did. You used to tell me everything."

Smartass. My fist clenched. "Yeah, I did. Only because you were my girl. What are you going to do—fuck them all?"

A wicked smile graced her lips. "Why the hell not? I'm single, remember? You made it clear you never wanted anything to do with me again."

My chest tightened. She was taunting me. The thought of her, my girl, being screwed senseless by my friends made my palms sweat. She was mine—only mine. She'd lost her virginity to me, and I'd always found comfort knowing that no other man had ever touched her. Images flashed through my head of another man kissing her, fucking her, making her come, her screaming out his name.

I swallowed hard and steadied my breath. "Stop, Mia. We both know damn well you were the one who fucked things up. Even if you were that much of a bitch and wanted to fuck me over more than you already have, none of them would touch another Team guy's woman. Especially since you're also Joaquín's sister. I only got away with sleeping with you because we started dating before

Joaquín and I became SEALs. And no matter what you think, in their eyes, you will always be mine."

She cringed, and I noted the look of shame on her face. Had she cheated on me back then? I would never believe that. Like a wild animal, I was confident that I could've sensed another man's scent on my woman. Even so, Mia was hiding something from me. There was more to her leaving me than being too young for a serious relationship. Unfortunately, I didn't have a fucking clue what her secret was. She never even gave me the chance to fix it.

She leveled her gaze at me. "Yeah? Yet you are sure quick to abandon Joaquín at the first sign of trouble. So much for leaving no man behind. You know if the situation were reversed, Joaquín would do anything possible to set you free."

Dammit, I shouldn't have let her in the door. This was already too intense, too emotional. "It's not that simple, and you know it. I'm under orders not to talk to him. I don't have a choice."

"Fine. I understand that you are forbidden to talk to him. But I can. You need to help me help him. This isn't about us; this is about Joaquín. Can you tell me about the girl who died? Who invited her? Was Joaquín dating her?"

I clenched my teeth. Some people thought that since I was a SEAL, I'd have a wicked temper, but I had complete control of my emotions at all times. That composure allowed me the mental strength to point a loaded gun at my enemy and still be able to make a conscious decision not to pull the trigger. I'd never raised my voice to Mia, ever. Even so, she knew when I was pissed off.

"What the fuck? Do you think you can just walk in here like you didn't rip my heart out and I'm just going to comfort you and fix this mess? I already fucking told you there's nothing I can do. And I don't owe you anything."

Her chin dipped to her chest, her shoulders slumping. "I know you don't believe me, and I don't expect you to, but I had to leave. I didn't have a choice."

"There's always a choice." I looked back at the rumpled covers on my bed. I remembered watching Mia sleep, the way she always curled up in a ball, with Hero at her feet. I never told her, but she used to talk in her sleep, sometimes even said my name. "And we aren't in this together. My world started and stopped with you. All my friends told me that we wouldn't work, that we didn't have a chance because we were so young and because of my job, but I told them you were different. That you would have my back no matter what."

Her voice cracked. "For what it's worth, I've never even looked at another guy. I want you to know that."

My eyes bore into her. "That's supposed to make it better? That I'm the only man you've ever been with, but you still don't want to be with me? Well, I wish I could say it was that easy for me. Since you left, I've fucked a bunch of girls, trying to get you out of my head." But she was still fucking there every night when I closed my eyes. I prayed her face would soon fade from my mind.

Her mouth tightened. She wasn't stupid—she had to know from her brother that I'd been with other women since her. But she only had herself to blame. "Please, Grant, if what we had meant anything to you, please help me exonerate Joaquín."

My eyes met hers, and I cupped her face, fighting the urge to kiss her. "You meant everything to me. You know that."

She pulled away from me, her bottom lip quivering. "I'm back now. I still love you."

"You left me. Period. And you didn't come back for me; you came back for Joaquín." As much as I loved Mia, I could never give her another chance. I refused to let myself rely on any woman after she had abandoned me. I didn't need that type of stress. My job was consuming—my personal life had to provide me stability and comfort. Or at the very least, simple release.

"But—I need you."

I'd needed her once also. Now, I needed her to leave. "I can't help you. I'll do anything I can to clear Joaquín; you know that. But my hands are tied. You need to leave." I pushed her out of the entryway and slammed the door behind her, never looking back. I wished I could say it was easy, shutting her out of my life again, but her scent still lingered in the air, and my heart remained with it.

I hoped I never had to see her again, which was now a realistic option since her brother was in jail.

Still, my heart ached for her, and for my swim buddy. There was no way Joaquín could've intentionally killed that stripper. Maybe he'd just gotten too rough in bed. Regardless, the reputation of our Team was now tarnished. The public was supposed to see us as heroes who rescued hostages from ISIS, freed boat captains from pirates, and assassinated leaders of terrorist regimes. Not as a bunch of sex-crazed, hard-partying hooligans with no morals. The average American citizens would be blown away if they learned the truth about our lifestyle—just last month we had rescued some kidnapped USO cheerleaders from insurgents and my boy Pat had saved his wife Annie from a sex-ring in Aruba. We worked hard, but we partied harder. And no way would I ever apologize for what any of us had to do to relieve our stress. The intensity of our lives was unfathomable to most.

Even so, Mia had been it for me. I'd once found enough comfort in her touch to forget my daily burdens. But no more. I would never allow another woman to distract me from being a warrior. Plenty of girls wanted to be fucked by a Navy SEAL, some real-life hero to step off the pages of their favorite romance novel. I was now more than happy to use them the way they used me. Mia was the only woman I'd ever loved, and when she left, I'd closed my heart to anyone else.

CHAPTER THREE

MIA

I SPENT TWO DAYS SCOURING every inch of Joaquín's apartment, but came up empty-handed. I found nothing—no shady receipts, no weird email messages. Everything was clean. Too clean, as if someone had already scrubbed any evidence from the place.

I wanted to crash Tiffany's funeral to search for clues, but I definitely didn't want to affront her family, who would no doubt kick out the sister of the man they thought had murdered their beloved daughter. I skipped the service, uncertain what to do next.

Any day now, the remaining men on Joaquín's Team could be deployed, and after that, who knew when I'd be able to see them again. I'd lost my inside connections, no Grant, no Joaquín. I had only one way to see them all.

Today I was going to head to the Pickled Frog. The bar was a dive where all the SEALs went any time one of their men had passed. The looming death toll never seemed to wane—a training accident, a downed helicopter, an embassy upheaval. I'd been to enough SEAL funerals during the two years I dated Grant to know the drill. One by one, each man would pound down his trident, the SEAL insignia, on the deceased man's coffin. Then they'd get wasted. Even though Joaquín was still technically alive, I was pretty sure they'd be mourning the loss of their Teammate.

The Pickled Frog was more than a watering hole; it was a safe haven for heroes. Men who needed to drown their sorrows in hard liquor, men who wanted to forget the faces of the terrorists they killed, men whose wives had cheated when they'd been deployed, men whose kids didn't even recognize their own fathers. I shuddered, imagining all the times two years ago Grant might have sat in the seedy bar, getting hammered, trying to get over me.

I needed strength before I saw Grant again. Time to meditate. I sat on a chair in Joaquín's apartment and straightened my spine, my feet placed firmly on the ground. Resting my hands, I turned my palms upward and prayed. I alternated my breath, from tense inhales to relaxed exhales. Focusing my attention on my spiritual eye, I uttered a quick chant and closed my practice. I needed to remain calm and centered, today more than ever.

I locked up Joaquín's place, jumped in his truck, drove along the coast, eventually parking in an alley behind the bar. A deep sigh escaped my lips. I was sure I was the last person these men wanted to see.

When I pushed back the front door, the acidic stench of whiskey and sweat overtook me. It was two in the afternoon on a random Saturday, and the place was mostly empty. Despite being in the heart of Ocean Beach, no college coeds or surfers hung out here. This was a SEAL bar; SEALs and frog hogs were its only customers, though the occasional SEAL wife or girlfriend would make an appearance. But on this day, even the frog hogs must've taken the day off from their groupie duties. I was the only woman in this dump.

My feminine scent gave me away. No sooner had my heels touched the Technicolor, puke-stained, carpet than the heads of seven men turned toward me: Grant, Paul, Mitch, Joe, Vic, Pat, and Kyle. The seven other men on Joaquín's eight-man SEAL squad. Had they all been at the party that night?

I avoided Grant's suspicious glance and stared at the walls, studying the pictures of fallen SEALs. So many gorgeous men. Bearded, tatted, ripped.

Gone. Dead.

Never to kiss their wives again, never to cradle their babies in their strong arms. I might as well put Joaquín's picture on the wall. Man, this place was depressing, but it was a thousand times better than jail. Now I was the one who needed a drink.

I sat on the bar stool closest to the only friendly face, Kyle, who was tending bar. The gummy pleather seat clung to my thighs as he gave me a welcoming smile.

Kyle Lawson was a SEAL and former NFL linebacker; he was also the new owner of the Pickled Frog. He was gorgeous—smooth mahogany-colored skin, trimmed dark beard, warm chocolate eyes. At six foot five, his body seemed sculpted by Michelangelo himself. Kyle was like a celebrity in the Teams. After he'd given up a multimillion-dollar football contract to become a SEAL, the media had hailed him a hero, even before he rescued a group of cheerleaders who were kidnapped on a USO tour. But he'd refused all interviews to the press and was as humble as any of the Team guys. "Hey, beautiful. Sorry to hear about your brother. What can I get you?"

His buddies, Pat and Vic, both gave me forced nods. Their loyalty must've been torn between their hatred of the woman who broke Grant's heart and their protectiveness of Joaquín's sister.

"Malibu and Coke."

"Coming right up."

I glanced down the bar at the other SEALs. It was like a buffet of rock-hard men. My eyes watered; I was high on the testosterone levels in this place.

Kyle placed the drink in front of me. "How's your brother?"

"I saw him after he was arrested, and he looked horrible. Now he's refusing my visits." I took a sip, the warm rum coating my throat. "Were you at that party?"

"Look, honey, I wish I could help, but Joe, Pat, Vic and I left before the strippers arrived. I'm sure you're trying to help Joaquín, but no one is going to talk to you about that night." He glanced at Pat and Vic. "We keep each other's secrets to our grave."

Kyle wasn't kidding. Pat was married to Annie Hamilton, a famous missing American who had vanished on spring break in the Caribbean. Initially, the public was fed a story that she'd just run away, become a missionary, had a kid, then decided to return to the States. I never bought that tall tale for a second. I'd interrogated Joaquín about what he knew, but he just played dumb, until a recent news story broke. Apparently, Annie and another missing American girl, Nicole, had both been kidnapped and forced into sex slavery. A Marine who recognized Nicole recently discovered her in Venezuela. She had amnesia and didn't know who she was or what had happened to her. And a former SEAL named Dave supposedly saved Annie, though I think Pat was involved in her rescue.

As much as I had a window into these SEALs' worlds, as both a girlfriend and a sister, I knew that I wasn't privy to their world of secrets.

I adored Pat though; he was such an amazing guy. He adopted Annie's son, and Annie was now expecting his child. My own womb ached—had I stayed with Grant, I was sure we'd be married, and we'd probably have started a family by now. But instead of celebrating a new life with my soul mate, I was trying to salvage my brother's future.

I bit my lower lip and threw back my drink. I didn't have a plan. I didn't have a strategy. I didn't have a clue what I was doing.

Here goes nothing. I pushed myself off the seat and squeezed between Paul and Mitch, to at least try to see if I could get them to admit some details about the night of the party.

Paul resembled a young Tom Cruise—brown hair, blue eyes, dimples. He had even more arrogance than the rest of the men. As one of only a handful of second-generation SEALs, he'd been bred for this life. "Mia, I'm sorry about Joaquín, but the brass has forbidden us to talk about that night."

"I know. Grant told me the other night."

Grant, who was sitting on the other side of Mitch, didn't even look at me. "Why are you here exactly?" he demanded, his voice cold. "You should leave. You're not welcome."

"Yeah, well, you don't own the bar now, do you? Kyle doesn't seem to have a problem with me being here. It's a free country." Grant's short-sleeved blue T-shirt teased me with glimpses of his tattoos. I gulped when I noticed he'd covered up my name with some sort of vine. At least I hadn't tattooed his name on my ass, though I'd strongly considered it. My lack of ink didn't matter; Grant's name was permanently embedded in my heart.

He turned toward me, his green eyes digging deep into my soul. "What do you want from us? We aren't going to talk about that night, none of us are. We've all given statements to the police and to our commands. When this goes to trial, we will be forced to testify, and it will ruin our careers." He stood up and came over to me, placing his hand on my thigh. An electric shock pulsed up my leg. I was addicted to his touch, longed for him, dreamt of him at night. "Why don't you just go back to your 'I hate the United States military' city and leave me the fuck alone?"

How could he be such an asshole to me? He knew how much I loved Joaquín—our love for my brother was probably one of the only things we still shared. I turned to Mitch, my eyes pleading for some mercy.

Mitch's long dark hair skimmed his shoulders; his full sleeves of tattoos decorated his huge arms. He put his strong hand on my back and gave me an icy stare. "Sorry, Mia. I was passed out and woke up with some bitch sitting on my face. I don't remember anything."

"Dammit, Mitch. Why do you have to be so disgusting?" I hopped up from my chair. Grant was right; this was pointless.

But the stakes were too high to just give up. I couldn't imagine my brother spending the rest of his life caged like an animal.

As I turned back toward Paul, the doors flew open. Paul's wife, Dara, and Mitch's wife, April, came bouncing in, laughing as if they were about to meet their hubbies for date night at a five-star restaurant instead of a drink in this hellhole.

Dara gave me an insincere hug. "Oh Mia, honey. So sorry to hear about Joaquín. But who knew he was into fucking strippers?"

"Fuck you, Dara. Where were you that night? The party was at your in-laws' house, right? Maybe it was your husband fucking strippers." I hated her and her perfectly blow-dried hair, her designer purse, her lime skinny jeans, probably in a size twenty-six. Typical SEAL officer's wife; thought she was better than anyone else. She was a few years older than I was, and never forgot to mention her Ivy League education and her vacation home in Lake Tahoe. I didn't need her pity.

Dara shoved the hair out of her eyes and shot a bitter glare toward Paul. Without a word, he clutched her wrist and led her away from me. Paul went to great lengths to hide his other women from her. Dara loved him, unconditionally, and I knew that no matter what bullshit he pulled she would never be able to leave him.

April put her arm around me. "I am sorry, Mia. Joaquín is a good guy. I hope he's exonerated. Call me if you ever need to talk."

I thanked her. April and I had been good friends—once. A long-suffering SEAL wife, she was painfully aware of Mitch's philandering. I never understood their relationship. Grant's theory had always been that they got off on making each other jealous, but to me, it just seemed deeply dysfunctional.

I glanced at Grant, but when he turned his back on me, I decided I couldn't take any more. My heels touched the gravel outside, and the bar door slammed behind me. I felt the clang inside my heart as well. He was done with me. I was alone. Again. No Grant. No Joaquín. No parents. Alone.

This was not the Grant I knew. He was cold, aloof, distant. Something was off. Wasn't he outraged about Joaquín's false imprisonment? Could he be hiding something? Grant said he didn't think

Joaquín killed Tiffany. Had Grant witnessed the murder? What in the hell was going on?

Stop, Mia. Just stop. I was clearly stressed out and not thinking rationally. I'd dated Grant for two years; he was a good guy, a hero. He wouldn't hesitate to give his own life to protect the ones he loved. Like he'd said, he was under strict orders not to talk about the case. I didn't want him to sacrifice his career. His Team needed him, especially without Joaquín. Hell, our country needed him. Grant was the best of the best.

Unfortunately, I needed him, too.

But that ship had sailed. *He'll never be mine again.*

I wasn't going to give up on Joaquín that easily. With or without Grant's help, I would clear Joaquín's name. My brother was innocent. He'd sacrificed everything for me since our parents died, and it was time for me to repay his loyalty.

There had to be a way to free my brother. And nothing would stop me until I found it.

Grant had been right. SEALs wouldn't talk.

I had only one clue left.

Time to make strippers sing.

CHAPTER FOUR

MIA

PANTHERS, SAN DIEGO'S PREMIER STRIP JOINT, was located in an industrial area, tucked between used-car dealerships and noodle shops. I never understood the allure of strippers; paying women to pretend that they were interested in you seemed pathetic, not flattering.

I sat in the parking lot, staring at the entrance. I didn't want to go into the building. What was my plan? Ask the women if they'd been at the party where Tiffany was murdered? These ladies were her friends. I'd get the door slammed in my face.

I hugged my shoulders, tucking my chin into my chest. I didn't have a clue what I was doing.

My window rattled. I looked up and saw a busty redhead in a tight sweat suit standing by the window of Joaquín's truck.

I opened the door.

"Honey, you okay? Is your boyfriend inside?"

I swallowed. Here I was judging these women, yet this stripper was showing me compassion. "No. I don't have a boyfriend. My brother used to come here."

Her eyes narrowed, her gaze intent. "Hey, wait. You're Mia, aren't you? Joaquín's sister? I knew I recognized this truck. Oh, honey, I'm so sorry. Your brother is the nicest guy. Not like his friends, especially that jackass Mitch. None of us think Joaquín killed Tiffy."

I jumped down from the seat, my breath bottled in my chest. "You know my brother? Were you at the party? I know he didn't do it. Can you help me exonerate him?"

She gave me a warm smile. "I was at that party. But nothing was out of the ordinary. It was just some Team guys and some girls from here. The police interviewed us all. I've racked my brain trying to think of something, anything that stood out. Maybe it was an accident? I'm so sorry, honey. I wish I could help."

My mind raced. There had to be something she could tell me. Some clues to give me hope. "Which guy invited you?"

"Grant. Tall, amazing body, tattoos, blond hair, green eyes."

I gasped and almost tripped on the cracked asphalt. "Grant Carrion? You must be mistaken. He hates strip clubs. I know—he's my ex-boyfriend."

She let out a laugh. "So, you're the girl who fucked him up? Sorry to be the one to tell you honey, but Grant's a regular. Comes in here every Tuesday night when he's in town. He has a thing for bleached blondes with huge tits and fake lips. We call him Ken because he's always scouting for his newest Barbie. Shows them a good time when he's around, deploys, then moves on to the latest model when he returns." She gave me a sad smile. "Look, I have to go to work. My name is Emma, but my stage name is Pepper. If you have any more questions, don't hesitate to stop in and find me. I'd be happy to help any way I can. Best of luck with your brother."

"Thanks, Emma." I hugged her, and she waved goodbye to me.

I got back into the truck and drove out of the parking lot.

Heat rose in my body. Could she be right? Had Grant become addicted to the strip clubs since I'd left him? Spending his free time here, drinking himself into oblivion, finding comfort with women who had no expectations, women who could never disappoint him the way I had?

I winced, pushing away the image of Grant getting a lap dance from some troubled woman with ragged extensions and fake tits.

But Emma had given me what I needed, what I craved. Hope.

I now had a clue. *Grant* had invited the girls. This man, who I thought I knew everything about, was nothing more than a stranger to me. Maybe he was hiding something.

Seven Deadly SEALs—Seven Achilles' heels. I would smoke out their secrets and figure out what happened that night.

CHAPTER FIVE

MIA

I'D BEEN BACK IN SAN FRANCISCO for two weeks. I attempted to honor Joaquín's wish and stay in school, but I couldn't focus. Even attending guided meditations and kirtan chanting hadn't helped. My mind raced in class. I hadn't slept well since I'd returned.

I glanced around my room in the tiny North Beach apartment I shared with two other San Francisco State students. Scripts lay across my desk, with stacks of books huddled against the wall. Just a little over a month ago my life had been so simple, so easy. One focus, one goal. To be the best actress possible. How stupid and trivial my dreams seemed now.

I swiped through my iPhone to the San Diego News app, scanning for headlines about Joaquín. I didn't have to even scroll down the page. There it was at the top. *Bail denied for U.S. Navy SEAL accused of murdering a stripper.*

Fuck.

My ears pounded and my vision blurred. I couldn't even read the article. No hope. This was it—the realization finally sank in that he might get convicted of this crime.

I called Joaquín's lawyer, but the secretary told me that my brother had given instructions not to talk to me anymore. The secretary had only one thing to say: Joaquín had transferred the title of his truck to me. I knew Joaquín too well—this was his way of ensuring I went on with my life. But what he didn't realize was that I would never be able to enjoy my life unless I fought for his.

I needed to clear my head, meditate, try to find some peace. Find a way to connect to Joaquín.

Despite being desperate for sleep, I climbed into his truck—my truck now—and headed over the Golden Gate Bridge toward Mt. Tamalpais. It was a clear day; San Francisco's famous fog seemed to have cleared the way for this mission. The winding hills through Mill Valley reminded me of the weekend adventures Joaquín and I had gone on with our parents.

Mt. Tam was more than a mountain to me—it was a sacred place, a vortex of energy. Grant and Joaquín never missed an opportunity to tease me about my spiritual beliefs. I was raised Catholic, but after my parents died, I'd become deeply spiritual. I practiced yoga, became a vegan, attended kirtan chants, and meditated. My dedication only grew stronger after I'd left Grant. For me, my spirituality was a way to center myself, develop a personal relationship with God, and feel closer to my parents.

As the Raptor approached our favorite trailhead, my breathing slowed, and a memory took hold of me.

"Let's do a time capsule!"

Joaquin, a skinny boy around age twelve with a devilish grin, led me down the trail. Our parents slowly lagged in the distance. Always the Boy Scout, Joaquin took a Swiss army knife from his pocket and notched a hole at the base of a tree.

"Give me your bracelets."

I shoved the candy-colored beaded bracelets off my wrist and handed them to him without a second thought. A big deal, considering at age eleven, those tacky things were my prized possessions.

Joaquin's eyes twinkled. He loved going on adventures, and I was always his right-hand girl. Most brothers and sisters fight, but we were truly best friends.

He took a small leather pouch out of his back pocket. "This was made by the Miwok Indians." He slipped his Swiss army knife inside, wrapped in my bracelets, reached deep between the roots of the tree, and dropped the pouch inside.

"One day, when we're older, we'll come back here and find our treasures."

I thought it was stupid, but I would never tell him that. I just hugged him, and we ran off toward the voices of our parents.

Centering myself back in present day, I touched the damp soil. I closed my eyes, and I could hear my parents' voices calling us. "Mia, Joaquin. Where are you two?"

The voices became quieter in my head, and I found the tree. Eleven years later, the old oak had seen better days, but it still stood, leaves gathered at the base.

I knelt beside the trunk, my hand wrestling with the soil, which was surprisingly loose like it had been disturbed not long ago.

Digging faster, furious. *It has to be in here.* I'd all about given up when my fingers touched something smooth. I reached down and grabbed ... the pouch!

I tore it open, now weathered with dirt and rain. My bracelets flew out, but instead of Joaquín's knife, I found a small wooden box.

He's been back here?

The box was new. When had he come up here? He hadn't visited me in at least a year.

I flipped the box open, and inside was a small key and a dog tag. I pulled the dog tag to me and squinted at the etched numbers. WF #1459.

WF—Wells Fargo? I examined the plain key. It looked like the safe deposit box key from our bank. Joaquín and I had opened this box for my mom's jewelry once I turned eighteen, but I'd forgotten all about it. I had my own key somewhere back at my place, but I would've never thought to look in the box.

My jaw dropped. I knew he hadn't killed Tiffany. He must've known something was going down. Joaquín was so smart he had planned to send me on this chase. He believed in me and knew I could save him.

My watch read four thirteen. The bank was open until six. I stuffed the dirty pouch into my pocket, raced back to the truck, and sped down the hill.

After stewing for twenty-five minutes in traffic, I reached the bank. I handed the teller the key, she asked for my ID and gave me the signature card.

Joaquín's name was signed above mine; the date entered was a week after the murder.

Holy shit! He'd come up here just the other week and not told me?

I scribbled my name on the card, and she led me to the safe deposit boxes. When she placed the bank key in the lock with mine, it clicked open, and she handed me the box. My heart fluttered.

I took the box to the room, anticipated what I would find. A note? Instructions?

I slowly opened the lid. There was a certified check made out to me for seventy-five thousand dollars. Also dated a week after the murder.

Where did he get this money? Was this money dirty? Related to Tiffany's death?

A note floated out of the box. *Mia, here's the rest of Mom and Dad's life insurance. Please spend it wisely. I love you.*

Please spend it wisely. He knew. He knew he'd be arrested. But why? How could he possibly have known? It was a testimony to our close relationship that he knew he could provide the one hint that would send me here. It was also testimony to how much he loved me that he wanted to provide for me, look after me. Just as he had always done.

The only thing I could conclude was that he was in over his head in something...I didn't know what. His last gesture, which didn't surprise me, was to make sure I was taken care of. It brought tears to my eyes. My heart ached.

I emptied the safe deposit box, desperate for another clue. But it was completely barren.

But I had other plans. I would take this money and find out the truth. I'd clear his name.

I slammed the box shut and walked out to the teller. "I'd like to deposit this check."

CHAPTER SIX

MIA

THE FAINT SMELL OF CURRY, chickpeas, and fried pastry from the Afghan restaurant below wafted through my tiny apartment. A potato sambosa sounded amazing, especially washed down by a cherry blossom iced tea, but I was running late again. I'd taken leave from my college, moved out of my place, and quit my part-time job applying makeup at the MAC counter at Nordstrom, styling the drag queens in the city.

Now, four months after Joaquín had been arrested, I was living in San Rafael, across the San Francisco Bay. I hated isolating myself, but I couldn't afford to make any mistakes. If Grant came looking for me, any connection to my former life had to be erased. That meant no catching the latest indie band at Bimbo's 365 Club with my girlfriends, no hikes to Mount Tam with my old friends from high school, and no spring auditions for Marin Shakespeare Company's summer season with my drama cohorts. Whenever I thought of my passion for theater, my chest ached. For so long that had been my dream. Sometimes your dreams would simply remain that: a dream. It was hard not to feel sad, bereft.

Still, I actually loved being back in my hometown of Marin—the cool, creative vibe, being among the musicians and artists who flocked here. But I wasn't here to make friends, and this time I wasn't running away from my problems. This was my BUD/S. Joaquín had undergone six months of rigorous training to become a SEAL. I was training just as rigorously to make sure he could keep being one.

I threw some gel into my hair, pulled on a vintage Mötley Crüe T-shirt and some faded jeans. It was a relief to be back home, away from the flock of picture-perfect *Baywatch* bitches who inhabited San Diego. I never fit in there. Not that I was doing an excellent job of blending in here, especially with my new looks, though I was doing a better job after trading Joaquín's monstrous Ford Raptor for a Honda Accord Hybrid. The Raptor was too conspicuous among the eco-friendly Teslas, Toyota Prii, Nissan Leafs and Chevy Volts of Marin.

Saying goodbye to Joaquín's truck gutted me. Every time I drove it, I'd thought how it should be him behind the wheel, free from shackles, and my resolve to clear his name grew. But I had to erase any connection I had to my old life, to Joaquín, in order to go undercover and save him.

I locked up my place, filled up a bottle of water, and hopped into my car. Today I had a long day of training in San Francisco: a Russian lesson in the Richmond District, kung fu in Chinatown, pole dancing at a studio on the unfortunately named Bush Street. Tomorrow was equally packed with weapons training, CrossFit, an acting workshop, and computer classes. I was so exhausted and sore every night I would usually stumble back to my place, soak in a warm bath filled with Epsom salts, and crash.

The lessons and training were actually fun, but I had done something drastic. Something I swore I would never do, something that was completely against my belief system.

I'd gone through an extreme makeover.

As a rule, I was fundamentally against plastic surgery. I loved my body, my unique looks, my distinct features. I was half Latina—I had flat breasts, wide hips, almond-shaped eyes, a weak chin, and a cute bump on my nose. At first, I didn't even consider surgery as part of my plan,

After Joaquín was denied bail, I'd gone to San Diego one more time and, as promised, my brother had refused my visit. But I refused to give up on him—I drove like a madwoman across the Coronado Bay Bridge. I was no longer a military dependent, so I didn't have an ID to gain access to base. I parked at the Del and headed toward the beach that borders the SEAL compound.

I hoped one of Joaquín's friends would see me, take pity, and offer me some help or guidance. As luck would have it, Grant and his buddies were helping to train the BUD/S recruits. Grant's face flashed a notice of recognition toward me, but he ignored me. I might as well have been a stranger.

Then a wicked idea crossed my head. What if I *was* a stranger? To not just him, but to his entire Team. Could I find out what really happened that night? Go undercover with the strippers at the club and discover the SEALs' secret sins? Learn about them with their masks off, from the vantage point of a fantasy temptress instead of the good girl they wanted to protect.

It was the only way. I drove back to San Francisco that night and booked an appointment with a surgeon.

Having to go under the knife last month was excruciating, especially without anyone to take care of me. The nurse I'd hired to help me recover kept lamenting that such a pretty young girl would ruin her face and body. I agreed with her completely, but she didn't have a clue what was at stake.

I was trying to go undercover with Navy SEALs, men who were impossible to fool, and I couldn't take any chances, especially with Grant. He knew every inch of my body. So I'd had breast implants, a nose job, a chin implant, fillers in my lips and cheeks, lipo on my neck, lasers to remove my freckles, and Botox on my eyebrows. I looked like a plastic freak, but the doctor swore my features would get less tight and I might someday resemble a human again.

Still waiting.

My entire body throbbed, the chin implant burned through my skin, my nose was still swollen. Blinking was a daily struggle. These silicone balloons on my chest strained my back.

I forced myself to stare in the mirror, not recognizing my own reflection. The rest of my body had transformed also. As soon as the doctor cleared me, I'd started weight training. Squats to give me a nice butt, weights to make my skinny body toned and lean. Was this the type of woman Grant really desired? A stereotypical plastic blonde bombshell with perfect features devoid of any uniqueness?

I reminded myself I hadn't changed my appearance to win Grant back. I'd altered my looks to lure Grant to me so I could go under-cover and clear Joaquín's name. After all I'd done, this had better work. Failure was not an option. I wasn't sure I could survive the heartache if I didn't complete this mission.

I was used to being alone, but I missed my brother. And I missed Grant. What was he doing now? I had always kept tabs on him through Joaquín—but for the first time since I'd met Grant, I didn't have any clue where he was. Was he deployed? With another girl? Training somewhere? Bastard didn't even have a Facebook account I could stalk. His Scorpio ass had become even more elusive since we broke up.

When we were together, I never doubted his fidelity or love; he was honest and open with me. But I also felt that I could never penetrate his core. Even after dating him for two years, he always held a part of himself back. Like he was afraid to let me see his true self. Joaquín and I shared so much with each other that Grant's exclusion had sometimes made me wonder if he really wanted me in his life. But I was far from innocent—I kept my secrets too.

I crossed the Golden Gate Bridge, and my heart raced when I viewed the city skyline. This was my hometown, the last place where my life had made sense. The Transamerica Pyramid, where my father had worked nights cleaning, glowed in the distance. My dad had been so proud, so principled. In a way, I was glad he never lived to see his only son accused of murder.

I turned off Geary Boulevard and pulled the car in front of Blue Danube Coffee, grateful to the parking fairy for finding me a spot. I dashed out of the car but paused before opening the front door of the coffee shop. The *San Francisco Chronicle* stand held a paper with the headline—*U.S. Navy SEAL Joaquín Cruz Murder Trial set for August.*

I pushed four quarters into the metal slot and grabbed a paper from the top. My muscles quivered, and I ground my teeth. I hated not being there for him, showing him support and unconditional love every step of this mess. I had to make this work. I was his only hope.

My instructor, Roman, was waiting for me at a back table. I ordered myself an almond milk Mexican Mocha and slid into the chair across from him. This gorgeous man was the polar opposite of Grant. Roman's jet-black hair skimmed his eyebrows, highlighting his almost black eyes. His lips were full, his skin was pale, his body was lean. His accent was so alluring; every time he pronounced the word *pleasure* "plea-shure" my knees went weak. In another life, another time, I could fall madly in love with the man sitting across from me sipping a single black espresso. But I was focused on Joaquín, and unfortunately for me, Grant had a permanent hold on my heart.

He slowly eye fucked me. "You're late."

"I'm sorry, it won't happen again, Roman. Traffic."

"Call me Roma." His eyes focused on my swollen breasts. "Why it is that you want to learn Russian? You never told to me."

Of course I didn't. I found you on Craigslist.

"It's a sensual language. Always wanted to learn. I'm an actress. I would love to perform Chekhov in his native tongue."

He smirked, clearly not buying my story. I now started to doubt my acting skills. "You will tell to me when you are ready. *Davai. Kak vas zovut?*"

Let's go. What's your name?

I took a sip of my mocha, the warm liquid coating my throat, helping me slip into my character. "*Menya zovut Ksenya.*"

Ksenya, derived from the Greek word *xenia,* which meant stranger. My eyes perked when I found it on a list of Russian names. I was a stranger now, a stranger to Joaquín, to Grant, to myself. Grant had been right. Mia couldn't help Joaquín. Mia couldn't break the SEAL code. Mia couldn't get anyone to talk.

But none of those SEALs stood a chance of resisting Ksenya.

CHAPTER SEVEN

KSENYA

AS I REINVENTED MY LIFE, Joaquín rotted in a jail cell for five months. Per his request, I made no further contact. Just one final call to his lawyer, telling him that I'd been accepted into a theater program in England and that I'd check in when I could.

I missed Joaquín so much, every day, but I couldn't focus on that pain. Today was game day.

I pulled my car into the parking lot at Panthers. Was I really going to do this? The thought of taking my clothes off for a bunch of leering men made my throat burn.

Roma had helped me secure a new driver's license, social security number, and birth certificate. He'd even found me a place to live —a tiny room in an elderly Russian lady's apartment in El Cajon. The place reeked of pierogies and tea, but it didn't matter. I was pretty sure Roma had Mafia ties, but we'd both adopted an unspoken rule about not asking about each other's activities.

One final glance in the dashboard mirror and I was ready to go.

My hair was now bleached and blended with platinum blond extensions, my hazel eyes were masked with brown contacts, accented with heavy dark eye shadow and false eyelashes, and my lips were painted pale pink and frosted. And thanks to the combination of my depression and my physical training, my skinny frame now looked like it could grace the cover of a Victoria's Secret catalog.

And I hated to admit it, but I loved the way I looked. Conceit. Vanity. Pride. My lack of humility saddened me. Though I would've never gone under the knife in any other circumstance, this dilemma forced me to fix every one of my physical insecurities. As a woman, it was almost empowering, no longer having to worry about my thin lips or crooked nose. I did realize through the recovery that my previously low self-image didn't matter, that my soul and dedication was what was important. I just wish I could've understood this new truth without having to change myself.

I'd transformed myself from cute girl next door to, according to Emma the stripper, Grant's ultimate fantasy. It was still hard for me to believe her; I would have to see it with my own eyes. But if Grant dreamt about blonde bombshells, I would become the woman of his nightmares. I was unstoppable. I was in control.

I pushed by some guys in the parking lot, made my way to the entrance, and spoke to the bouncer. "I have meeting together with Jim," I said in my affected Russian accent. Roma kept telling me no one would be able to distinguish me from any other Russian speaker. I'd studied not only the language but also the grammar mistakes the recent immigrants often made when they spoke in English.

The bouncer eye-fucked me. "Ka-sen-e-ya? Jim is expecting you. In his office."

I nodded and made my way toward the back of the club, watching the girls on stage out of the corner of my eye. Smoke filled the place from the adjoining private hookah lounge. The sweet, musky smell made my eyes water. Better get used to it.

Jim greeted me at the door. Bald, fat, hairy, pretty much what I expected the owner of a strip club to look like. "Welcome, Ksenya. Wow. You're a little minx, aren't you?"

Gross. I'd made a strict pact with myself—I'd go rogue, but under no circumstances would I sleep with a man who disgusted me. "Good to meet together with you." I hated using improper English, but it was a necessity now.

"Come into my office and relax. Tell me about yourself. Where are you from?"

His office consisted of a squalid cum-stained couch, a desk with papers piled all over it, and walls of framed pictures of him mugging with celebrities who had come to this joint.

I perched on the edge of the sofa. "I'm from Kharkov, in Ukraine. I was ballroom dancer. I come here with my baba, my grand-mother, who was engineer. But she is dead and so I must work. I do not disappoint you. I hear you are the best, and me, I always want to be the best."

He motioned me to stand up and twirl around, and I obliged, wiggling my hips.

"Let's see what you've got. We have striking girls come in here every day, but I need to know you're the real deal. You can give me a dance in the VIP lounge."

He led me to the room, which was painted electric purple. The pole in the middle glowed from the bright lights.

"Undress."

I slowly took off my sweat suit, fighting the urge to flee. Now stripped down to my matching pink bra and panties, my cheeks burned, and I hid my blush behind my hair. I'd always been modest; the only man to ever see me naked was Grant. The music started, almost as if it sensed my presence. The hypnotic rhythm of the R&B song seemingly overtook my body. Centered, calming, crafted. Seducing this dirty old man with my moves would be easy—tricking Grant would be the true test.

My eyes focused on Jim, but I didn't see him. I wasn't dancing for Jim. I wasn't even dancing to save my brother. I was dancing for Grant—I saw Grant's face, his lips, his eyes trace my movements. Slow and seductive rather than fast and frenzied. How many times had he sat in this room, watching a broken girl dance for him? What had these women given him that I hadn't been able to? Did he open up to them? Truly let them in instead of how he always tried to be tough and resilient for me?

As I made love to the pole, my heart pounded, my stomach fluttered. This was where I was meant to be. After seeing Grant again and having him shut me out, literally and figuratively, I realized I wasn't done with him. As much as I didn't want to admit it, I missed him, despite the fact that he had been an asshole to me. I'd hurt him, but behind his vicious words to me, I wondered if he still loved me no matter how much he tried to fight it.

A loud clap sprang me from my haze. "Bravo. Ksenya, you are enchanting. Can you start tonight? We have a huge party booked. VIPs, extravagant spenders. They love seeing a new gem. Are you game?"

I wasn't sure if this transformation would work, that I could even get close enough to any of the Team guys, but I had to try. My plan was to strip here until I saw Joaquín's Teammates. I'd focus on the first one who paid me any attention, entertain them at a similar party, and try to figure out what happened to Tiffany.

"*Da*. Thank you, Jim. I won't let you down."

I put my clothes back on, and Jim gave me a bunch of forms to fill out. Surprisingly, he actually ended up being quite nice and went out of his way to make me feel comfortable.

VIPs. It was Thursday night. I'd done my research—driven by the houses of my brother's Teammates, seen their cars in the driveway, the "Welcome Home Daddy" banners in the windows. They must've just returned from a training exercise or a deployment. Which meant they were due to make their appearance here any day.

When Grant walked through these doors, I'd be on that stage. And I would be able to dance for my man. In the shadows.

CHAPTER EIGHT

KSENYA

UNFORTUNATELY, JIM'S BIG SPENDERS THAT first night didn't include Grant. Or the night after that. Or the next. Days turned into weeks. It seemed as if I'd been stuck in this hellhole forever, and there was still no sign of my former lover, or any of his Teammates. I'd gone from star of the SFSU drama department with a promising future, living my dreams, moonlighting with the best thespians at American Conservatory Theater, to a lowly stripper with limited hope, stuck in a nightmare, dancing—if you could call it that—for lonely men.

I hated it—the baby talk, the lap dances, the inappropriate touches, the lewd remarks, the constant propositions. I kept telling myself—*You can do this, Mia. You're preparing for the role of a lifetime.*

The other strippers were nice at least. I was surprised that they weren't as messed up as I'd assumed they'd be. Emma was long gone though. From what I could glean, this place had a high turnover rate.

It was Taco Tuesday—carne asada, salsa bar, Coronas, churros. I'd decided to have a little bit of fun with the crowd and dressed up in a sexy border patrol costume, enjoying the irony since I was an undercover Latina. I was dancing to a Latin pop song when the doors flew open. The loud laughter of deep male voices perked my ears.

Then I saw him—my man was standing right in front of the stage.

Jolts of electricity coursed through my veins. The sweat on my back moistened my costume; the heat from the dazzling lights burned my skin. Could I really pull this off? Would Grant take one look at me and call my bluff? My mouth became dry and my heart palpitated.

We were in the same room, breathing the same smoky air. Dreaming of his face every night for months made him seem like my own mirage. But this time he was very real.

"Blurred Lines" started playing. Well, at least the song was appropriate. I glided to the pole, my partner in this urgent dance, a dance that could help me enter into this new world I so desperately sought to infiltrate.

My hips swayed, I licked my lips. Climbing to the top of the pole, I spread my legs, determined to get Grant to notice me. I had to remind myself to stay the course, not blow my dance or run over to him.

I made eye contact and he winked. I knew that wink, that look of desire. The first time he'd winked at me, sitting across from me at a coffee shop, I'd completely melted. Back then the giddiness of first love consumed me. Now, I had to hold back tears, since I was pretty positive that he had no idea I was Mia. Just some sexy stripper he hoped to see naked.

I pranced up and down the catwalk, narrowing my gaze on him. Dancing for him, willing him to connect with me. His eyes turned hungry as he followed my every movement. Soon I could barely see him through the bright lights and smoke. My hair whipped in the air, my body seduced the pole. The song ended, the smoke waned, the lights dimmed. And Grant was relaxed in a chair, motioning me to come toward him.

The plan. Stick to the plan, Mia. Watch which girls go over to his group. Don't approach him immediately, take your time. You have dreamt of this moment, planned, prepared—now it's showtime.

I gave him a coy smile, blew a kiss, and walked off the stage. I headed to the bar to get a better vantage point and some liquid courage. A quick shot of vodka calmed my nerves. Grant's skin looked darker, perhaps he'd just returned from the Middle East. His massive biceps bulged out of his black T-shirt, looking bigger than when I'd last seen them. His hair was longer, his beard fuller. And he was looking right at me.

I waved and he moistened his lips. If I avoided him, he might suspect something. I was just another dancer, and if a customer was staring at me, it was my job to flirt back.

Shoulders back, tits up. I reapplied my red lipstick, locking my gaze on his. I'd turned myself into his dream girl, his personal fantasy pinup. But I was real—well, mostly. And he was still the only man who had ever sent ripples of pleasure pulsating throughout my body.

A casual flaunt of my blond locks, a batting of my false eyelashes, and I made my way over to him. "Hi, handsome. My name, it is Ksenya. How are you doing tonight?" My accent was crisp, I rolled my *r*'s, my tongue touching the top of my mouth.

"Much better now that I saw you, sexy. I'm Grant. Where you

from?" He pulled me onto his lap. I ran my fingers through his hair. He smelled the same as I remembered—pine, lemon, and vodka, as if he had just chopped down a Christmas tree and drunk a spiked lemonade to refresh. Did I smell the same to him? Could he recognize my scent despite me switching to new brands of lotion and shampoo?

"Kharkov, Ukraine." I figured my recent-immigrant ruse would explain my terse conversation. Reduce the chances for him to find me out.

His eyes zeroed in on my chest. I arched my back to give him a better view. My mind flashed to him sucking on my nipples, cradling my small breasts. He'd always seemed so pleased with me, with my body—did he really want a girl with fake tits and silicone lips?

"I've been around the world twice, but never to Ukraine. Maybe you could show me around some time." His words were slurred.

I've been around the world twice? Really—he was actually quoting the Navy SEAL "Ballad of the Frogman"? His bloodshot eyes told me he'd been wasted before he ever set foot in here.

I focused my energy on controlling my facial movements, ensuring that my eyes didn't shift or my nose didn't twitch as I spewed out my lines. "I'd love to show to you whatever it is you like to see, handsome." Had he gone to strip clubs behind my back when we were together? My heart wrenched, thinking of those nights I'd spent practicing lines from a script for class in his apartment, waiting for him to come home from boys' night, supposedly at bars and steakhouses. He'd always sworn to me he was the designated driver, that the older Team guys had forced him to join them, since he was merely a SEAL pup.

By now, every Team guy was talking to a girl. My gaze scanned to the other present members of Joaquín's Team—Paul and Mitch. Had one of them murdered Tiffany and framed my brother?

I turned back to Grant. Rules for keeping a SEAL's interest: #1 always make him the center of attention, #2 never let him see you checking out his Teammates, no matter how insanely gorgeous. "Can I dance for you?" Talking too long would arouse suspicion. He thought I was a stripper. I needed to earn my tips.

"Sure, sexy. Follow me."

Follow me? Even now, even in here, he was taking charge. I usually led my customers—emasculated husbands, inebriated frat boys, insecure businessmen, even conceited rock stars—back to the VIP room. But no, Grant was in control. He was a regular. He knew the drill.

He grabbed my hand, and instead of recoiling at his touch and being disgusted about his ease in this place, I couldn't fight my arousal toward him. What the hell was wrong with me for still wanting him? Especially in here, when I looked like a porn star. When would this pain end? The combination of disgust, sadness, and guilt crashed through my mind. Had my abandonment driven him to seek comfort with these women? Or had he been seeing them all along?

But I didn't have a moment to reflect. I needed to give the performance of a lifetime.

I LED KSENYA—HOWEVER THE fuck you pronounced it—to the back room. After months on a mission, I couldn't wait to see her peel off her clothes. Alone with me, without a group of guys also getting off on her.

She was so fucking hot. Physically, she was exactly my childhood fantasy pinup, as if she had been designed for me. Long platinum-blond hair. Full, round breasts which busted out of her black negligée. Plump, pouty lips. Definitely not the girl-next-door type, like my ex Mia, the only woman I'd ever loved.

But I could tell something was off with this chick. I was a regular here, and she didn't seem the type to take her clothes off for money. She was too stunning, almost too sexy. Why was she stripping?

Strippers were the best; I didn't care what anyone else thought. They were fucking hot, listened to your problems, loved sex, didn't nag you, didn't expect anything in return. Sure, they danced practically naked for money, but men paid for women no matter how you looked at it. Whether it was nice dinners, designer clothes, expensive jewelry—nothing was for free. At least with strippers, you got what you paid for. I hadn't been this callous, cynical man when dating Mia. This was who I was now.

Fuck it, I didn't care. I wanted to see her naked. That was the problem with these titty bars—rules, cameras, bouncers.

I sat on the blue velvet sofa. "Dance for me, baby."

Her mouth turned up into a smile, and her long hair brushed against my face. That sweet, citrusy scent of her skin—smelled like Mia, even though she had always masked it with coconut products. I pictured Mia naked, rubbing lotion all over her thighs, an image I could recall to my head anytime, anywhere, day or night—a useful skill when I was stuck in a dirt hole in Afghanistan. I wondered if Ksenya tasted like Mia, too?

Fuck. I couldn't think of Mia now. I had a sexy woman in front of me and refused to think about my ex. All those nights when I was alone in the hospital, missing her, hoping she would come back to me. She had made it clear she didn't want me. I had moved on.

A slow melodic beat started playing, not the upbeat dance crap the strippers usually chose. I recognized the song, a power ballad by a hair metal band. Interesting choice. Why had she picked that song? Doubtful she was even born when it came out. Whatever—Eastern European chicks were live wires.

I relaxed, took a swig of my beer. Ksenya's chocolate-brown eyes locked onto mine. Though the color was different, something about the shape of her eyes reminded me of Mia. Dammit, what was wrong with me?

Without prompting, Ksenya turned around, her fingernails, filed short and painted red, dug into my jeans, her tits rubbed my chest. A coy glance, a warm touch. She was totally into me. Not in the normal stripper bilking her client way, or off in her own mind dancing and thinking about her problems. This chick seemed one hundred percent present and focused on me. I loved it.

I needed her to come home with me. "Baby, how long've you worked here?"

She turned away from me. My only way to connect with her was through my voice—I wasn't allowed to touch her, which was so hard since her juicy ass was only inches from my tongue.

She shot me a glance over her shoulders. "Few months. It is job."

Her broken English was charming. The only foreign girls I had met were overseas. Some of the Team guys liked going to brothels, but I refused to pay for sex, especially after what happened to my buddy Pat. He'd hired a hooker in an Aruban brothel, and she turned out to be a sex-trafficked American. I couldn't help thinking that all those women overseas in those places were forced into the sex industry, victimized, abused. I refused to be a part of their nightmares.

Besides, I could get plenty of women right here. I was used to San Diego coeds, no challenge at all once they found out I was a SEAL. Ksenya hadn't even asked me what I did for a living. "Yeah? You're too gorgeous for this place. I've seen some other Eastern European women here, but most of them seemed harder. You seem fresh. What's your deal?"

She bit her bottom lip; her eyes glanced down at her clear stripper heels. I paused for a second to catch my breath, Mia always used to bite her lip when she was nervous. "I have no story. I need it, the money, and my English is not so good. I have no family. Dancing it is what I am good at."

"Do you have many regular clients?" Strippers lied, would tell you whatever you wanted to hear. But I was pretty talented at detecting bullshit.

"Few. But I don't do extras." She squeezed my thighs. "Not even for you, handsome. I just dance."

Fuck, I hadn't gotten laid in months. I didn't want to get blue balls or waste my time trying to meet a girl in a bar. I didn't do the fuck-buddy thing either. Way too much drama, and if I was fucking a girl, she better not be foolish enough to cheat on me. At least Mia never screwed around with other men. And my dumb ass had been faithful to her too. "Hey, when's your shift over? I'd like to see you out of here. I know this great little sushi place downtown."

"I have plans tonight." Her eyelashes lifted. "I'm not hooker. Only dancer."

"Hookers hold no interest for me. All I want is to grab a bite to eat." I wanted her to know I didn't see her as just a stripper. She had an angelic face, and I needed to get to know her, carnally.

She nuzzled my neck, cupped my face in her hands. "Tomorrow? I get off at eight."

"It's a date." I took out a hundred dollars and handed it to her. She started dancing again, but I stopped her. She could give me a private dance tomorrow night. And fuck if that couldn't come a moment too soon.

CHAPTER TEN

KSENYA

SUSHI? HAD GRANT SERIOUSLY ASKED a stripper out to dinner? He couldn't possibly know I'm Mia. Emma must've been right when she said he wooed the girls at Panthers, taking one out whenever he was in town. I knew he was single—no steady girlfriend since me—but when had this stripper fetish started? What if he'd cheated on me when we were together? Bile rose in my throat. Was I simply naïve expecting him to have been faithful to me?

Dinner with Grant was not the plan. I wanted to observe him with the strippers. See who else talked to the guys, try to figure out which girls were at Paul's place the night of the murder.

But I couldn't say no to Grant. I was in character. I was Ksenya, and she wanted someone to save her.

I seethed inwardly. I didn't need a man to save me. The only good thing that had resulted out of this nightmare was that for the first time in my life I had proved I could take care of myself. Without my parents, Joaquín, or Grant to pick me up when I fell. Yes,

Joaquín had left me the money in the safe deposit box, but every red cent had gone toward this plan. Once my brother was free, I refused to ever rely on anyone but myself again.

What was I going to wear? I'd just finished my shift twenty minutes ago. I rummaged through my duffel bag in the dressing room—stripper costumes, Victoria's Secret PINK sweats, and a skintight black dress I'd worn last week for VIP night. Mia would've worn sweats, but Ksenya would choose the dress. And heels, earrings, and makeup. Playing Ukrainian Barbie was hard. I just hoped she was hot enough to get her Ken doll to talk.

What I would give to go home to my room in El Cajon, shower, scrub off this makeup, crawl into my pajamas, and binge-watch *Dancing under the Stars*. The arches in my feet were cramped from those ridiculous stripper shoes, my empty stomach was craving a heaping plate of pesto pasta, not sushi, and my eyes were heavy from lack of sleep. Not to mention these humongous tits were killing my back. But I wasn't going to blow my big chance.

I waited by the back entrance for Grant. My goal for the night was to get him to open up to me, even just a little. Then maybe he'd invite me to the next stripper party he and his buddies had. But I had no intention of sleeping with him—not now, not ever again. I was confident in my acting ability, but I couldn't control the way my body would respond to his touch. If we made love, he would know I was Mia. I closed my eyes, imagined the warmth of his chest pressing on my skin, the stubble from his beard tickling the nape of my neck, the tender way he used to hold me.

I stared down Convoy Street, scanning for Grant's truck. Our club was next to used-car dealerships and Korean barbecues, and the scent of burning animal flesh and kimchee made my skin crawl. A few customers catcalled me, and I resisted the urge to flip them off.

The roar of a motorcycle shook the air. Grant had bought a bike? I was so pissed at him. He'd always wanted one when we were together, but I refused to let him get one. It was one thing for him to risk his life overseas defending our freedom; it was another to end up as road kill for a drunk driver and die the way my parents had.

I wanted to go off on him, but I highly doubted Ksenya would nag him. I took a deep breath and centered myself, slipping back into Ksenya's world.

His windblown hair framed his face. I loved his masculine jaw line, his beard, his intensity. The deep scar on his neck beckoned me to reach out and caress it. I had clearly underestimated the hold this man still had over me.

"Hey, gorgeous. Hop on." He handed me a helmet.

"You drive motorcycle? Is dangerous, no?" Screw it, I figured Grant would like a little bit of sass from Ksenya.

"Nothing's dangerous when you're with me. Let's go."

Cocky son of a bitch. In the past six months, I'd never once considered how hard it would be to shut my mouth and not call Grant out on his bullshit. I pulled the tight helmet over my head, wrapped my arms around his waist, and held on.

The wind chilled my legs as we entered the freeway, my skintight dress riding up around my thighs. I'd never been on a motorcycle, fundamentally refused to ever ride one after my parents died. But gliding through traffic, I had to admit, for the first time since Joaquín had been arrested, that my pulse steadied, my heartbeat calmed. For our brief ride I vanquished memories of my parents,

Joaquín's troubles, my heartache—this overwhelming sense of urgency. I was truly enjoying living in the moment.

We pulled up to some hole-in-the-wall sushi joint. We weren't in the ritzy part of downtown. No, we were on Broadway, a few blocks from the county jail where Joaquín was being housed.

I'm here, Joaquín. I haven't abandoned you.

It was hard being so close to him and not being able to reach out to him, but I had faith I was on the right path.

I removed my helmet and crinkled my nose. The stench of urine and tar churned my stomach. Grant would never have taken me to a restaurant like this. This was a place where a guy took a girl to hide her, not to show her off. Was he shrouding me because I was a stripper? Or did he have a girlfriend somewhere who he was cheating on?

Last night, I almost felt guilty for using him to find the truth after having dumped him in the past. But he chose to date a stripper, who on the surface was clearly not the type of woman to get serious with. So if he wanted a fling, at least he would be spending time with a woman who actually cared about him.

Grant studied my face. "This place is great, I promise. I know it doesn't look like much, but the food is incredible."

Great, he could still read me even as Ksenya. "I'm sure it is wonderful. I'm excited for good meal."

His eyebrows lifted. "It's refreshing to meet someone who looks beyond outward appearances."

I bit my lip. "Compared to where it is I am from, this place is like palace." Grant had a point. This could be the best sushi in the city, but I would've never agreed to go here when we were dating.

I'd never considered myself to be pretentious, but I admit I'd been a tad judgmental. I wondered if Grant had held himself back with me, afraid to push me to try new experiences. Why hadn't I just been more open when I was with him?

The waitress sat us at a cramped table, stuck between the sushi bar and the restroom. Grant ordered a bunch of rolls, Asahi beer for himself, and saké for me.

He held my hand across the table. "So, how long have you been in San Diego?"

"Few months. I lived together in San Francisco with my baba. She died, and it was too much money for me there to live. I have friend here who was dancer and made good money, so I come down. The clubs in San Francisco are good, but houses are not so cheap." My story was solid—I'd gone over it a thousand times—but gazing across at a man who regularly interrogated terrorists caused my palms to sweat.

The waitress brought us the first batch of rolls. Grant swirled a neon green mound of wasabi in the soy sauce with such concentration I shuddered from his intensity. "So you live with your friend?" he asked.

"No. She got boyfriend and quit the club. I live with older woman. She gives to me room in home, and I help with cleaning and cooking." I tasted a piece of sushi—the Motion in the Ocean roll. The spicy jalapeño sauce lit my lips on fire while the sweet citrus put out the flame. I swallowed the tuna, the slithery fish sliding down my throat. *Dear God, please don't let me gag.* I had been a vegan for years. But I knew there was no chance I could remain one in front of Grant.

"You could clean and cook for me."

"Very funny."

He popped a crunchy soft-shell crab roll into his mouth. "I'm serious, I travel all the time for my job. I could use some help."

Was he kidding me? He had to be joking—he did not invite a stripper he had just met to move in with him. I dated this jackass for two years and we hadn't even lived together.

"No, thank you. I do not know you."

His eyebrow lifted, and his mouth widened into a sly smile. "Well, get to know me."

My head pounded and it wasn't from the cheap saké. Who was this man who sat across from me? Was it possible to change that much or did every man reinvent himself when dating someone new? I fought the desire to kick Grant in the balls, hightail it out of there, and get back to my life.

"What is it you do for living?"

"I sell pharmaceuticals." His nose didn't even twitch; he'd become an expert at hiding his lies. Though this fib didn't bother me. SEALs never told civilians what they did for a living. Joaquín told everyone he met that he drove an ice cream truck. That guy you met in a bar boasting about being a SEAL? He was a liar.

"Let's get out of here. I want to take you somewhere." He signaled to the waitress and paid the bill in cash.

We slid onto the back of his bike, and I placed my arms around him. I wanted to vanish into this moment, go back to the way we were when we had first fallen in love. Before he deployed that first time. Before I'd done something stupid. Before I didn't have the guts to confide in him.

Grant headed down to the pier, in front of the USS *Midway*, a retired Naval carrier turned maritime museum. The millions of lights from the ship illuminated the ocean, as the view of Coronado's Hotel Del beckoned in the distance. Grant might be lying to his date about his job, but he was also sharing his love of the Navy. Maybe he didn't see Ksenya as just a conquest.

We stood under the world-famous *Unconditional Surrender* statue, which portrayed a sailor kissing a nurse at the end of World War II.

Grant took me into his arms, and I was sure he was going to kiss me under the moonlight. "You're so incredibly hot. Let's go to a hotel."

"*Nyet.*"

"Come on, babe. We'll have a great time. If you feel uncomfortable, I'll take you home. I just want to spend some time with you."

My first instinct was to slap him. But my panties became damp as I imagined what this new Grant would do to me. Which way should I go—sweet, shy, good girl forced into stripping? Or nasty, freaky, bad girl who owned her sexuality?

I had vowed when this deception started—hell, when this date started—to never sleep with him again, fearful that he would discover my identity. Now I decided I wasn't going to make any rules. I'd fooled him so far—maybe I could fool him in bed as well. I'd spent every night for the past two and a half years imagining making love to him. As Mia, I'd been the girl next door, a young inexperienced virgin, petrified to ask him to act out my deepest fantasies. But I had always harbored a secret desire to play the temptress.

If Grant wanted to party, I'd be ecstatic to rock his world. This time, I wouldn't hold back. I couldn't. Ksenya would have to be a wildcat in bed for me to pull off this deception.

Sleeping with Grant might be the only way to truly have him let down his guard and open up to me. But this time, sex would be on my terms, on my timeline—and for once in my life, I'd be in control.

CHAPTER ELEVEN

GRANT

I WASN'T BUYING KSENYA'S GOOD-girl act, but I was game to play along. Her eyes had dilated at my request, but she still agreed to go to the hotel with me. She was, in fact, a stripper, not that I cared. It was about time I dated a girl who loved sex.

I'd worshipped Mia—we'd been each other's firsts, and I would've never made it through BUD/S without her support. But whenever I wanted to ask her to try something new in bed, I'd chickened out, afraid of how she would react. I didn't want to lose or disrespect her, so I'd repressed my desires. She was a "good girl," and I'd figured that making love to her should only be about tenderness.

Since we'd been apart, I'd had mostly one-night stands with chicks in bars and flings with messed-up strippers. I wanted to be with a girl who could fulfill my every fantasy. I wanted to *fuck* this girl, not marry her.

I sent a quick text to my buddy to reserve the Bachelor Pad Suite at the Coronado Bay Hotel. Equipped with its very own stripper pole and a huge mirror over the bed, I couldn't think of a better place to watch Ksenya ride me. The trip over on my motorcycle was sexy as all hell. Her tight little body wrapped around mine, her huge tits pressed into my back.

The regular girls who worked at Panthers didn't seem to have any light inside them. Their eyes were cold, their hearts dead. Fuck, I felt dead when I dated them. But not with Ksenya. This chick was different. There'd been other damn sexy strippers from there, but this girl seemed almost innocent. Her immigrant-orphan hardship story was way more compelling than the typical stripper drama. She awoke something inside me.

Even so, I wasn't going to chase her. I had enough willing women ready to drop their panties and suck a SEAL's cock.

I'd only pursued one woman in my life. And frankly, I didn't have the time to put into getting to know someone when I was deployed nine months out of the year. How could I ever build a relationship with a sweet girl who'd always be there for me if I didn't have any time to spend with her? I'd done that with Mia and failed.

I pulled up to the hotel entrance with Ksenya and tossed the valet my keys. I pressed her against the building. My lips met hers, and her fiery mouth tasted as sweet as freedom.

She let out a slow, sweet moan. My cock hardened in my jeans—only a fine layer of denim between it and her wet panties. Navy SEALs rarely wore underwear.

I checked in at the front desk, the key already waiting for me. One of my Team guys knew the concierge; whenever one of the suites was vacant, he was happy to let one of us use it.

Ksenya's mouth dropped when I opened the door to the suite. The pad was pure decadence: a black leather sofa faced the gold stripper pole, a mirror overhead. A full bar beckoned to me.

"Oh, Grant. This place it is very beautiful. It must be very expensive. Do you come to here many times?"

I studied her face; she looked almost dazed.

"Don't worry about it, baby. I have a friend who hooks me up. Would you like a drink?"

She smiled in agreement, so I poured her a glass of wine, myself a shot of whiskey. She studied the pole. "You want me to dance for you now?"

Hell yeah, I did. But I didn't want her to feel cheap. "Let's just relax for a bit."

"Can I look around?"

"Sure. Make yourself at home." She walked around the suite, examining the pole, the gaudy painting of a naked woman to the right of the bar.

I downed my shot, and poured another, then another. My head buzzed from my earlier beer.

She sat on one of the barstools, slowly sipping her wine.

Then I saw it. Her lips. Big and pouty, but the left edge of her mouth curled when she smiled. Just like Mia's used to.

Fuck. I was still so hung up on that girl that even sitting here with a beautiful woman, all I could think about was my ex.

I studied Ksenya's face. It was perfect. Completely symmetrical, as if an artist had sculpted it. No imperfections, like the small bump Mia had on her nose. Still, I'd loved Mia's face; she was unique. She had been all mine. I was still not sure why I was never enough for her. But that was history. This was my present.

Ksenya bounced her knees, fidgeting in her swivel chair. I turned the satellite stereo on in the room. "Undressed" by Kim Cesarion was playing. Perfect.

"Dance for me." I relaxed on my sofa, the bottle of whiskey in my hand, waiting for my private show.

Her skin flushed, and her fingers brushed down her side. My every nerve tingled.

A wicked smile slowly built on her lips, and she pranced up to the pole. She teased me with glimpses of her tan thighs, the round curve of her back. She was baiting me, fondling her chest.

"Take off your dress."

She obliged and it slid onto the carpet. Man, she was incredible. Easily the finest woman I'd ever laid my eyes on. Including actresses, porn stars, and every stripper I'd ever fucked. She was too good to be true.

"Now your bra." I set the bottle down.

With one hand, she unhooked her red lace bra. I motioned her to the sofa, and she rubbed her breasts in my face. My tongue lashed at them, but she slapped me away and backed to the other end of the cushions. The friction from my jeans reminded me how much I wanted her, and my breath hitched. Fine, I'd play—for now. I couldn't wait to have my way with her.

"Show me your pussy."

Her fingers traced down her stomach, and she pushed off her panties. Her skin looked soft and warm, a thin landing strip begging me to devour it.

I lowered my voice, touched my tongue to my upper lip. "Come here."

Naked except for her heels, she crawled over to me. She pushed herself on top of me and straddled my lap. I closed my eyes for a second, just to feel her sensational body pressing down on mine. I lived for this moment, the moment of anticipation before I hit my target. I leaned in for a kiss.

"I told you, I don't do extras," she hissed before my mouth found hers.

"Don't tease me, baby."

"I gave you the dance you paid for yesterday. If you want to see me again, you can come by club. Tomorrow."

She kissed my neck, my face, her warm tongue tracing my ear, and I imagined her tongue dancing around my cock. Her lips pulled away from me, and she quickly gathered her clothes, dressed, and slammed the door behind her.

Fuck.

My balls burned. I could've easily stopped her, but I knew I was being an asshole. After having my heart ripped to shreds by Mia, I just couldn't allow myself to see women as good for anything other than sex. Women treated me like this too—none of the San Diego coeds wanted to get to know Grant, they just wanted to be fucked by a Navy SEAL, something to brag about to their sorority sisters. I figured after getting fucked over by Mia, these types of emotionless hookups with no future were the only way for me.

Maybe I was wrong and Ksenya was just a typical stripper playing me—after money, fame, or power—getting me all worked up so I would give into whatever she demanded. But I had to have her. I was ready to play her game.

CHAPTER TWELVE

KSENYA

I RACED OUT OF THAT hotel suite and headed to the elevator—pressing those stupid buttons and begging those doors to take me away from this nightmare. I reached into my purse to grab my cell phone and call for a cab.

Had I just squandered my best chance to find out the truth and save Joaquín? After everything I'd gone through to get here, how could I be so careless?

I flicked off those ridiculous heels and threw them in my purse. I was wrong—I didn't have what it took to accomplish this. I couldn't handle being treated like a whore. Not by the love of my life. I fantasized about unbridled passion with Grant, nothing off-limits. But I had to feel like he saw me as more than a random stripper to get off with. I'd just wanted to tease him, bait him, but I panicked when I couldn't control my emotions. I needed to regroup.

The blue light on the elevator button taunted me. *Open!*

Thump, thump, thump.

I didn't need to look back. The rhythm of Grant's gait gave him away.

I shuffled back a step. He'd always been protective of me as Mia, but I was impressed that he'd come back to retrieve a stripper.

He placed his hand on my shoulder, and I shuddered. "Ksenya, I'm sorry. You're so fucking sexy, and I can be a prick when I'm drunk. I can call you a taxi or you can stay here with me. I won't touch you."

The elevator door opened. My resolve forced my feet to stay put and not hightail it inside. I had to see this through, stay with him tonight. His false bravado masked his loneliness. I knew the real Grant. Deep down, I wanted to comfort him, hold him, make love to him, be the woman he needed, and apologize for abandoning him.

But my only goal now was to get him to trust me. "I forgive you."

His arms extended to me, and he pulled me into his chest. For a second, I tried to resist, retreat into my shell, but I found comfort in his embrace. His bulging arms seemed almost twice the size they had when I saw him at his apartment in January—how was that even possible? Sure, he was twenty-three now, not the same lean nineteen-year-old boy I'd fallen in love with. But his biceps were massive, like one of those slicked-up bodybuilding guys you saw on television. Was Grant using steroids? I'd seen him only six months ago, and he hadn't been this ripped.

I couldn't dismiss this thought, especially now. I had to find out what had happened to Tiffany, and I refused to allow myself to let my feelings for Grant get in the way of my mission.

What was the link, where were the clues? Drugs, sex, money? Maybe that saké and wine were too potent, because not a thing about Grant, or this night, made any sense to me. This man standing in front of me, who could easily be Thor's stunt double, was nothing like the man he'd once been, the man I'd given my heart to.

"Let's go inside. I'll sleep on the couch."

I nodded, and we walked back into the hotel room. He poured me a glass of water, and we snuggled up on the sofa. This was more like it. He stroked my hair, and I nuzzled his chest. I had so many questions, but I couldn't decide which ones to start with.

My throat burned. "Why did you take me to here? Do you have girlfriend at your home?" My heart thumped. I didn't want to know the answer to this question, not that I had any reason to believe he would tell me the truth.

He swallowed and his voice softened. "Nah, babe. I just thought you'd like this place. I just wanted to take you somewhere nice, figured you weren't used to a place like this. I had a girl once, a few years ago. She left me when I was in an accident."

This time he wasn't lying. I blinked back tears; my brown contacts itched. After my parents died, I couldn't imagine loving someone so deeply and losing them. Being the sister of a SEAL was bad enough; I couldn't fathom being the widow of one.

"I am sorry, Grant. I don't understand how she could leave you when you were not well."

But I did know. I had left Grant, but it wasn't because I didn't love him. I loved him more than anything—even more than my own brother, though I'd never admitted that to anyone. But seeing Grant laid up in a hospital bed, a deep scar under his neck, his chiseled face bandaged, I couldn't...I wouldn't go through that agony again. I'd watched my parents cling to this earth hooked to respirators, and I'd had to help make the agonizing decision to turn off their life support. When Joaquín called and told me Grant had been trapped in a vehicle that had been destroyed by a roadside bomb, I knew I couldn't go through the pain of losing someone I loved so deeply again. I was too young, too fragile after losing my parents, too scared to trust again. So I'd walked away from him, from us, and had regretted it ever since.

And that wasn't the only reason. Something had happened to me while Grant was deployed. I'd done something stupid and paid the consequences. My shame for my lack of judgment bore at me, and I didn't want to explain myself to Grant. So I took the easy way out and ran, like a coward.

He lifted my chin with his hand. "Look, I'm sorry. You're different than the other strippers I've met, and I thought you were into me. One of my buddies is having a rager tomorrow at this townhouse he's housesitting in Pacific Beach. Would you like to come with me?"

Hooyah! There it was. The golden ticket. The invite I'd been waiting for. This was actually working. Old Grant never invited me to the beach parties—I'd been relegated to family days with four-year-olds running around with melting Popsicle sticks. I remembered the rules—no wives, no girlfriends. Men only. But I wasn't dense—I knew their bashes had no shortage of willing women thrilled to be in the presence of sexy SEALs. These women were peripheral ghosts to every SEAL wife and girlfriend.

I knew I was in.

"I would love to go to beach." I wrapped my arms around his neck, nuzzled his ear. He attempted to kiss me, but I turned away. The sharp stubble from his beard grazed my cheek. I wanted him to pin me down and ravage me, but it was completely out of the question.

"I'll pick you up at the club at seven. Feel free to invite any of your hotty friends."

You got it, buddy!

I clenched my hands to contain my joy, fearful that Grant would somehow realize my true intentions. "Oh, I will. They will love to come. I not want you to think I go home with all man I meet at strip club. You are first, I promise this to you."

He leaned into me and made firm eye contact. "I believe you."

I already knew Grant would never forgive me for deserting him when he was injured. But once he found out I'd completely deceived him, I would be dead to him forever. There would be no coming back from this second betrayal—ever.

As a SEAL, he had to trust his partner implicitly, know she would be faithful during his never-ending deployments, confident she would be by his side and support him when he was silently suffering from witnessing the horrors of war. We could never be together again. If anything, being with him tonight confirmed that belief.

It's okay, Mia. This is about Joaquín. Freeing Joaquín. Your sacrifice for him.

I'd made my choice. I chose exonerating Joaquín over getting Grant to trust me. And as long as I could free Joaquín, I vowed never to regret my path.

CHAPTER THIRTEEN

GRANT

L AST NIGHT COMPLETELY SUCKED. I couldn't even score with a stripper. But I wasn't about to blame myself. Call me a conceited prick, but I didn't usually have a problem with the ladies. Ever. Maybe I should've told her what I did for a living. Like the magical phrase "open sesame" opened the cave's mouth for Ali Baba, the words "I'm a mother-fucking Navy SEAL" usually opened a woman's mouth to my cock.

But who knew? This chick wasn't American—the SEAL line probably wouldn't work with her anyway. Her ignorance about SEALs suited me fine. I didn't want to deal with another Frog Hog, begging to start a relationship or bragging to her girlfriends she fucked a SEAL, only to cheat on me once she got what she wanted. I wanted one woman I could fuck whenever I desired, no talk about our futures or our pasts. Ksenya was perfect.

I'd sacrificed so much for Mia, hadn't tried out for any East Coast Teams so I could stay close to her, spend weekends with her instead of bonding with my guys. What she didn't know was that

I'd planned on proposing to her, had even asked Joaquín for his blessing. Then she'd left me while I was in a hospital bed, her engagement ring clutched in my hand.

But being injured was the best thing that ever happened to me. Otherwise, I'd have married that bitch, and she would've divorced me the second we had any problems, which was inevitable being married to a Team guy.

Last weekend we had the big welcome-home family day, though this homecoming had been bittersweet. No Joaquín, no Mia. For a while they had both been like family. All the Team guys loved Mia then. Despite my anger toward her, I wondered how she was doing without Joaquín. She was completely alone now—no parents, no brother. I was almost surprised she hadn't tried to contact me again. I couldn't blame her for giving up after the way I'd shut her down after Joaquín's arrest.

Our last homecoming rager ended with a dead stripper and my best buddy getting accused of her murder. My Team needed this party for morale, since we were struggling to get back to normalcy. And rebuild our trust.

I believed Joaquín was innocent. I hoped that I would see something tonight, a trigger, and could figure out what the fuck went wrong that night. Even on deployment, none of the guys remembered anything. Kyle, Vic, Joe, and Pat had left earlier that evening; the rest of us had all been in rooms with strippers. No one remembered anyone else being at the party, but I had to admit we were all pretty fucked up. I'd actually vowed to stop frequenting strip clubs after that girl's death, but I went back to the club to see if I could find any clues. Ksenya hadn't been at the party that night, but maybe she'd heard some girls talk.

My truck pulled up at the strip club. Ksenya stood out front, wearing a thigh-skimming black-and-pink skirt, with a tight black tank top. I could see her nipples beading, begging me to suck on them. Tonight. I had to have her tonight.

She leaned into my window and kissed me on the cheek. "Hi, Grant. These are my friends Brenna, Eden, and Kristi."

Another bottle-blonde, a redhead with tacky lipstick, and a brunette with sparkly nails. My friends would love these women. But unfortunately none of them had been at the party that night. "Nice to meet you, ladies." I nodded, and they piled into my truck. The scent of cheap perfume and self-tanner filled the air.

I headed to Pacific Beach. The girls chatted in the back, but I could only focus on Ksenya's hand rubbing up my thigh. The closeness of an exquisite woman who had not once peppered me with questions was comforting. She hadn't interrogated me about my job, mentioned my family, or asked me what I wanted from her. It was probably the language barrier.

"You look beautiful tonight."

"Thank you. You look to me very handsome."

I laughed. Her accent was cute. I'd never understood the obsession some men had with foreign women. I was a diehard patriot— I bled red, white, and blue. It had never crossed my mind to date someone who hadn't been born in the United States. But maybe I had been too closed-minded. I allowed myself to entertain the thought of dating a woman who would be there for me even if I lost a leg, who would nurse me back to health. Someone who would never betray me. Like Mia had.

Fuck. It had been so long since I'd given so much thought to Mia. Yes, I had missed her dreadfully, but that pain had soon turned into anger. Why was I thinking so much about her now? I had been with dozens of women since we split, and none had ever caused me to scrutinize our relationship so much. Was it Ksenya? Was it because I felt connected to her? Her mannerisms? *Why now?*

Stop. Don't even think about it.

I'd enjoy the attention she was giving me while I was in town. Then I'd deploy again and I was sure she'd move on to her next client.

But this woman's voice, the sound of her laughter, the way she looked at me, there was comfort in her presence. I couldn't explain this unshakeable feeling that no matter how hard I tried, she was more than a one-night stand.

CHAPTER FOURTEEN

KSENYA

G RANT BARELY SAID A WORD on the car ride. I couldn't tell if he was beginning to figure me out, if he had something on his mind, or if he was losing interest in me after only one date. Despite my protests, I didn't know how long I could play the full virginal stripper act. If Grant grew sick of my games, he could toss me aside, and I'd lose my only shot at exonerating Joaquín. I really needed to pull myself together and solidify my plan.

Grant parked his truck a few blocks from the beach. A crush of tourists swarmed the streets. A young couple headed toward the water, basking in the glow of the sunset. I paused and watched them, a stolen glimpse into what had to be first love. The man gazed at the woman, their movements in sync, walking quickly, as if to erase the distance between them.

Grant had looked at me like that once—as if he thought I could do no wrong, that we would be together forever. Now he looked at Ksenya with a combination of hunger and suspicion. His skin was flushed, yet his eyes were narrowed. Was he suspicious of me? I was pretty confident that I had him fooled. Even so, I knew Grant would never look at me with such tenderness again.

Focus, woman.

I was so pathetic, thinking about my relationship with my ex-boyfriend instead of clearing my brother's name. No more. From here on out, Grant was nothing more than a job to me.

He draped his strong arm around my waist. I pursed my lips.

We approached the door of the townhouse, and my fists tightened. I had to be on my game tonight. This was my big chance to find a clue. The last time Joaquín had been free was at a party like this. I said a silent prayer, closed my eyes, and hoped our parents were watching over me, guiding me toward the right path.

The door opened. Damn, guess I wasn't the only one who'd brought friends. It was like bring-your-own-stripper night, with a proper threesome ratio of two women for every SEAL. At least twenty women in various stages of undress were cuddling the men, limbs draped over each other, bodies entwined. I counted thirteen men besides Grant, but I only cared about Mitch and Paul for now—SEALs on Joaquín's squad. I needed to either eliminate them as suspects or focus my investigation on their actions the night of the murder.

My friends from Panthers dispersed and were quickly introducing themselves to the other guys. I'd chosen the girls at random, the ones who had been nicest to me, but these ladies clearly knew how to work the room. And as any girl in her twenties who partied hard in San Diego knew, these men—no matter what they claimed they did for a living—were clearly Navy SEALs.

Once you'd been to Coronado a few times, SEALs were easy to identify. Longer hair, fuller beards, massive muscles sculpted from carrying Zodiac boats, tan skin, weathered hands, cocky attitudes that oozed through the air. Basically a gang of hard bodies who could easily star in the latest summer blockbuster.

Grant seemed distracted, his gaze focused on something or someone. "Ksenya, can I get you a drink?"

I glanced in the direction of his gaze and saw a young woman with short blond hair standing near the refrigerator. "Yes, please. I want vodka and the cranberry juice."

Grant headed to the kitchen. My eyes followed his movements.

Mitch eyed me from across the room. He could be the one who killed Tiffany. I recalled his vile comments to me at the Pickled Frog. April, his long suffering wife, was probably sitting at home, doing his laundry and putting their kids to bed, while he was out getting lap dances from strippers.

Mitch walked over and sat down next to me. "So you're Grant's latest piece of ass? Nice to meet you. I'm Mitch."

I studied his face—something was off about him. His massive dilated pupils crowded out the pigment of his brown eyes, and his nose was shaded red. "Nice to meet with you also. You sell the drugs, too?" I contained a laugh, delighted at my pharmaceutical pun.

His eyebrows lifted, but his calm face didn't react. These men were used to covering for each other. "Nah, I'm a tattoo artist. My brother has a shop." He leaned into me; his alcohol-spiked breath blew hot on my neck. "Man, you're a knockout. Have I seen you somewhere before?"

I scanned the room, but Grant had vanished. And so had the girl

I'd seen earlier. Did he know her? "I work at Panthers. I saw you other night when you came in together with Grant."

He laughed and placed his hand on my upper thigh, squeezing my skin so tight I was sure he had left a mark. "No, baby. Not then. You're a porn star, aren't you?"

I pressed my hands against my stomach. Where was Grant? Why was he taking so long? In all the time I dated him as Mia, not one of his Teammates ever so much as winked at me. They knew the rules—a Team guy's woman was off-limits—no exceptions. But I wasn't Grant's woman anymore. I was a stripper. Not an equal partner, a mere possession. Did he intend to pass me around to his friends?

"No, I am not in those type of the movies. Sorry, you are wrong."

His grip tightened on my jean skirt. "I'm never mistaken, bitch. I've fucking seen you somewhere before. Maybe I've even fucked you." His finger moved up my thigh and hooked the lace trim on my panties. "Quit the virgin act. Go dance for me or something." His words shot off like rapid fire, and he forced my hand against his cock.

I considered screaming, but the blaring music would've drowned out my voice. What was wrong with this man? With all these arrogant sons of bitches? I was in some alternate bizarro reality, where these men I'd always looked up to as honorable, steadfast heroes of character were exposing themselves to be misogynistic pricks.

But I knew this asshole from all of April's tearful late-night phone calls. Mitch loved a challenge; I was just shocked at how disrespectful he was toward me. I squeezed him hard, his cock already rock solid in his jeans. "Ah, you are right. We did fuck. But you did not last. Better luck to you next time."

His mouth raped mine, and I was too blindsided to resist. My lips numbed; a bitter, metallic taste filled my mouth.

Holy shit! Mitch was high as a hot air balloon. Was it cocaine? I'd heard about some SEALs in Aruba who were arrested for smuggling kilos of coke. Was this connected to Tiffany and Joaquín?

I shoved his hands off me, recoiling from his touch. The last time I'd felt this disgusted had been that night years ago, when I'd been young and careless—the night that I had ruined my relationship with Grant forever.

He laughed and knocked back his beer. "I like you. You're a feisty bitch. Most of the strippers here don't put up a fight. You're a wildcat. Tell you what, when Grant gets sick of you in a few weeks, which he will, you can come suck me off. Let me get your number." He took out his phone.

I steadied my nerves, desperate not to screw this chance up. "Let me put it in your phone."

He didn't hesitate to hand it to me. He scanned the room for Grant, and I knew I had to be quick. I stroked my long hair while his eyes were averted and I popped the tracking chip, which Roma had given me, from my hair clip. As I typed my contact info into Mitch's phone, I pressed the chip into the back under the leather case, praying it would work.

I handed him back the phone, and he winked at me. What a creeper. I wanted to shove my fist up his coke-filled nose, but before I could do anything Grant appeared, holding my drink, a jealous scowl on his face. I fought the desire to dump vodka and cranberry juice over Mitch's head. For all I knew, that chip could lead to texts, phone numbers, some type of clue about what had happened that night. Maybe he'd come on to Tiffany after

Joaquín had slept with her, and she had rejected him. He could've become pissed off and choked her.

"Everything okay here?" Grant studied my lips, then glared at the lipstick stain on Mitch's face.

"Never better. Hey, man"—Mitch sniffled—"I'm pretty fucked up. You guys gonna fuck upstairs? Can I watch?"

I expected Grant to just laugh it off. But he shoved Mitch against the wall using a chokehold.

"You have ten seconds to unfuck yourself, Mitch. If you ever talk to her like that again, I'll slit your throat. Got it?"

The rancor alerted some of the other guys, but none of them approached.

"Relax, man. She's a fucking stripper."

Grant removed his hand from Mitch's neck. "Get the fuck out of here."

Mitch let out a laugh and walked away.

"Sorry about that, babe. He's a jerk. You okay?"

I blinked back fake tears. "Yes. Thank you. Is there a bathroom?"

He pointed upstairs. "First door on the left."

"I come right back."

Away from Grant, I let out a deep, gratifying sigh. This was actually working. No one knew who I was.

I pushed back the door to the bathroom and saw the girl Grant was looking at earlier. She seemed younger than me, maybe not even twenty. A crisp blond bob framed her round cheeks as she reapplied pink lipstick.

"Oh sorry, I can come back." I turned away.

"Hey, hon. It's okay. So you're Grant's new girl? I'm Autumn. I used to work at Panthers. Grant's a good guy."

My eyes widened. "I'm Ksenya. You know Grant?"

"Yeah." She paused, glanced toward the window. "We hung out once at another party. But things got crazy. There was this murder. I'm sure you read about it in the papers."

My breath stopped. *She was there.* "I'm new to area."

"A SEAL killed one of the girls there. I was so scared. Grant and I were in the next room when this guy Joaquín found the girl dead. So tragic. Grant hasn't told you about it?"

"No. We do not know each other so well."

"I get it. Well, good luck with him."

"Thank you." My mind raced. I needed to grill this girl, find out every detail about that night. But I had to get her away from this party—away from Grant. "What do you do now for work?"

Her mouth twisted. "I work at this new club downtown, Diamond. It's very high-end, very classy. We don't even go topless. Guys respect you way more. I'm sure the owner would love to have you. You're a knockout."

I couldn't tell if she was just super friendly or she was hitting on me. Either way, I didn't care. I couldn't let her go. "So are you. Can I get it your number and I can go to see it the place?" I reached inside my purse.

She snatched my phone, didn't say a word, and tapped in her number. "Call me anytime. Nice to meet you, Ksenya."

She shut the door. Holy shit. This was huge. I bet some of the other strippers who were at the party that night worked at Diamond. Maybe even Emma? I was getting closer to the truth, to Tiffany's real killer.

I scrubbed Mitch's touch off of me and met Grant back downstairs.

"Babe, come to the rooftop deck with me. I want to show you something."

I kissed Grant on the cheek, grateful to him for inviting me to this party. His sharp stubble burned my lips. A warm flush ran through my body, imagining that stubble grazing my thighs.

I followed him upstairs—a light giggle, a deep moan, and a passionate scream pierced my ears. Was he taking me up to one of these hidden rooms? My palms were sweaty, my hands trembled.

We passed the bedrooms, and he led me out to a small deck.

My heart stopped. I knew what he wanted to show me.

"Sit, babe. Make a wish."

A wish. Grant had brought me up here to watch the sunset. To see the Green Flash.

The Green Flash wasn't a myth, or even an optical illusion. If you ever sat on a San Diego beach at sunset and noticed a group of people staring silently in the same direction, they were looking for the Green Flash. That moment when the sun set and emitted that last glimpse of light, a flash the color of the Emerald City in Oz.

Grant pulled me to him, and I sat in his lap. His arms wrapped around me. "Babe, study the sky. Legend has it if you see a flash of green light, your wish will come true."

Was he feeling a real connection with me or did he share this with all of his dates? It took every ounce of training I had not to question him. I wanted to know how many other women he'd taken to see the flash. He'd taken me to a restaurant on this same beach on our first date, but I'd been unable to spot the flash. My eyes had been clouded by my love for him, the sadness for my parents' death still fresh in my heart. We'd planned to go back and see it together for our second anniversary, but we broke up a week before. Tonight I vowed I would finally see it.

I made my unspoken wish. My throat felt thick, my pulse quickened. I wished for Joaquín to be free, as a good sister should. But another brief wish passed through my head for Grant to forgive me and for us to fall in love again.

His arms tightened around me and I studied the fogless sky, determined to experience this phenomena with my true love. The hues from the sunset hung over the horizon; the sun dipped toward the water. Every nerve ending tingled and stirred inside me. My eyes focused; the final ray of light beamed right at me. My heart beat strongly in my chest. This glorious green spark filled my soul.

Grant whispered into my ear. "That was it, babe. This writer Jules Verne described it as 'the true green of hope.'"

Oh my God. He was quoting Jules Verne now? "You are so romantic to me."

His shoulders fell. "You just seem to have so much on your mind. I've gone through some rough shit too. When I'm really down, I look at the sunset and the flash pulls me through."

A chill pulsed through my body. Grant had told me that during BUD/S looking for the flash had kept his determination not to quit strong. I remembered nursing him back to health afterward, so proud of him and my brother for finishing. Surviving five and a half days of extreme training on less than four hours of sleep was still unfathomable to me, though I had gone through my own version of Hell Week to get here.

After taking care of him then, I'm sure he was baffled why I left him when he had been injured. But I could never tell him the truth.

My resistance to Grant was weakening, despite my disgust for this new version of him. I loved the real Grant, knew now I always would. He was the only man I ever wanted to be with—if I couldn't find my way back to him, I'd rather be alone.

I relaxed into his embrace. Having his warm mouth claim mine would be even better than finally seeing the flash. We'd kissed at the hotel, but I'd pulled away, worried, a deep longing kiss would be too intimate, too risky. But now...

He held my hand. "You want to get out of here?"

"Yes. I want to go together with you."

I texted the girls I had brought, and they all told me they could find rides home. Grant and I would be alone tonight.

CHAPTER FIFTEEN

KSENYA

THE ENTIRE DRIVE BACK TO his apartment, I bit my nails and fidgeted in my seat. There was no going back now. The natural progression of our relationship beckoned for us to become intimate. I wanted him to act out all the fantasies I'd ever had about him. Only the thought of him discovering my identity held me back.

Images rushed through my head of our tame sex life. Warm, gentle, loving, definitely not hot. He'd been my first, my only. I'd never allowed myself to relax, exhale, let pleasure guide me.

Tonight would be different. I was no longer a shy eighteen-year-old virgin—I was now a twenty-two-year-old woman who feared nothing but failing her brother.

He parked, and I hopped out of his truck, chasing after him in the moonlight. He went ahead, opened the door to his apartment, let Hero out in the small yard, and then invited me in. I remembered the first time he took me back to his place. He'd been so nervous, shy even. We'd sat on the sofa, just talking all night until he finally worked up the courage to kiss me.

He wasn't shy anymore. His strong hand grabbed the back of my head, pulling me toward his mouth. I offered my neck, refusing my lips. I had something else planned for them.

My hand reached to unbutton his jeans, making its way down his chest. I knelt before him, and a deep breath escaped me. I'd never done what I was about to do. Grant had never asked, though I could recall many times that he placed his hand on the back of my neck, gently urging me to go south. Not that I hadn't loved him, not that I didn't think he was beautiful, not that I wasn't curious. I couldn't even explain my resistance. It had been just as much about fear as it had been about shyness. Despite his desire, I was afraid I'd disappoint him. I was frightened that the fantasy of me taking him in my mouth would be better than the real thing.

I popped his jeans open, his huge cock freed, stood at full attention. He still never wore underwear, it seemed. That at least hadn't changed. My hand grasped his beautiful cock, harder, thicker, and longer than I remembered, but then again, I'd never seen it from this viewpoint.

"Suck me."

I obeyed, responding to his orders. But despite his words, his dominance, I was in control. I wrapped my palm around his base, and swirled my tongue along his length. He groaned, his eyes hooded.

"Harder, babe."

My mouth clamped down on his cock, sucking as strongly as I could. He tasted spicy and a tad sweet—like chili and chocolate. I wanted to drink him up, please him, make him need me again.

A groan left his lips, his back arched. "Deeper, Ksenya. Fuck."

He didn't know I was Mia. I was Ksenya to him. It almost made me cry, knowing he wasn't in any way thinking of me. He was simply using yet another woman to give him pleasure. My heart ached.

Despite that, I also felt a measure of pride. He liked what I was doing. My confidence rose. The power I had over him caused a flutter in my stomach. My panties were soaked, wanting more, wanting to feel this same strong cock inside me, filling up any space between us.

He was pulsing inside my mouth. I gripped his thighs, pulling him deeper into my throat.

His hand pressed on the back of my head. "Ksenya, stop, I..."

I had no intention of stopping. He was mine. My man. Forever. I wanted to be the only woman to make him feel this way.

He exploded into my mouth, and I lapped his salty cum up, wanting to taste every last drop of him. A lazy grin spread across his face.

"You're incredible." He pulled me up from the floor, placed his arms around the curve of my back. "Your turn."

No. No way. I needed to remain in control. I'd won the first round, no reason to give in now. I fought the desire to feel his tongue devour me like I was his last meal. "Tonight it was for you."

He didn't fight me, gave me a kiss on the forehead. "Stay with me?"

I nodded, wrapped myself in his arms. This was the only way I could spend time with him, so I would treasure it and lock it away.

CHAPTER SIXTEEN

GRANT

I GAZED AT THE GIRL in my arms, purring beside me. She'd just given me an amazing blowjob, though I could tell she wasn't that experienced. She seemed nervous at first, almost shy. And she asked for nothing in return.

I wiped the sleep out of my eyes, restless but afraid to move and wake her. What was her deal? She wasn't a typical stripper. She wasn't asking for anything—money, a commitment, not even love. I didn't have a fucking clue what she wanted from me. There had to be a catch.

Her body flipped over, and I escaped from the bed. I glanced around my bedroom, typical bachelor pad; any trace of a woman had been erased. My eyes focused on a picture of Joaquín. We'd survived Hell Week together, vowed to hold each other up, never let each other quit. Then he'd slept with a stripper and she'd wound up dead. How could I be dumb enough to tempt fate and allow a stripper in my bed too?

A pain grew in the back of my throat. I hated myself for not being there for him in his hour of need.

Just a few years ago, my life had been filled with such purpose. My inner circle was tight, and I'd been secure in my path.

Now I knew that nobody was who he or she appeared to be. Not my fellow SEALs or this stripper slumbering in my bed. I trusted no one. Not even myself.

I opened the sliding glass door, prepared to prevent Hero from barking at Ksenya and jumping all over the bed—the way he always greeted a stranger.

Hero bounced in the door, his nose sniffing Ksenya's scent. But he didn't jump. A friendly bark, and he lay at the end of the bed, Ksenya curled in a ball on the mattress above him. He'd never done that with any girl I'd brought home.

Except for Mia.

I studied the chick in front of me. She and Mia were the same height, but any resemblance ended there. Mia was soft and round, with tiny breasts and a perky butt; Ksenya was lean and sculpted, with tig ol' bitties and a plump ass. Mia had hazel eyes with flecks of gold, and Ksenya had chocolate brown eyes.

But I'd noticed the outline of her contacts in the moonlight earlier. Ksenya bit her lips when she was nervous. When she smiled, her mouth curled at the edge. On the left side. Like Mia.

A crazy thought flashed through my head—what if Mia hadn't been fucking kidding about transforming herself to exonerate Joaquín? The words Mia spoke last time I saw her rang in my head. *"I'll do whatever it takes. Maybe I could go undercover? I'm a chameleon. An actress, a makeup artist. I've reinvented myself so many times even you wouldn't be able to recognize me."*

Could she possibly be that insane to get plastic surgery to fool me? Mia had been in school for acting. I'd never seen her onstage since I'd always been too busy training. It was impossible for her to be that great of an actress, wasn't it?

She had vanished—I'd even called her roommates, and they said they didn't have a clue where she went. But I knew she would never abandon her brother, ever. Even though she had turned her back on me.

No way. No fucking way.

But it was hard to ignore Hero's reaction to her. He almost seemed to...*know* her. Surely it couldn't be? Was this a game?

From the outset, Ksenya had targeted me. But why? Did she suspect me of killing Tiffany? Did she want to use me to find out who did? She wasn't in it to fuck me. Otherwise the deed would have been done already.

You're crazy, Grant. Not everything is a conspiracy. After BUD/S, it took me months to walk down the street and not look at everyone as a potential threat. I was clearly paranoid.

There was only one way to know for sure.

I have to fuck her.

TO BE CONTINUED

SE7EN DEADLY SEALS BOX SET

I DON'T TRUST THE NAKED woman asleep in my bed, the one with the bombshell body and eerily symmetrical face. The edge of her mouth curls when she smiles, she smells like citrus, she bites her lips when she lies.

This imposter is lying to me—she claims she's a Ukrainian stripper named Ksenya, but I'd bet my Trident that she's my ex-girlfriend Mia, her face and body masked with plastic surgery. Her brother is in jail for murdering a stripper, and she must have kept her promise that she'd stop at nothing to exonerate him.

But I'm not going to call her bluff. Hell, no. I'm going to play her game, test her strength, see how far she's willing to go to keep up this ruse.

My beloved girl who shuddered at the thought of lowering her inhibitions is playing my game now. She wants to get wild? I will fulfill her every fantasy.

But I control the game now, not her. It will end when I say it ends.

I'm a Navy SEAL, and I will be the last one standing.

Buy Now!
Se7en Deadly SEALs: Season One Box Set
On Sale until January 28 for $0.99!
Normally $9.99

And she will never be part of my world. ***Triton***

Meet Dax! He left fame, fortune, and willing groupies behind to serve his country as a Navy SEAL. ***Skin***

Blue Devils

Military Pilots Contemporary Series

Meet Beckett! I'll never let down my guard for this Devil in a Blue Angel's disguise. ***Blue Sky***

Rescue Me

Romantic Comedy Series

Meet Preston! When it comes to doggy style, he's behind you 100%. ***Doggy Style***

Military Contemporary Stand Alones

Meet Shane! I'm America's cockiest badass. ***Badass*** (co-written with ***Linda Barlow***)

Meet Bret! He was a real man—muscles sculpted from carrying weapons, not from practicing pilates. ***Love Waltzes In***

ACKNOWLEDGMENTS

I WOULD LIKE TO THANK my wonderful husband, Roger, for supporting my dreams, making Hello Fresh for me, and entertaining our boys while I write.

I would like to thanks my parents for showing me an example of true love.

I would like to thank my boys for being the best part of my day.

I would like to thank my editor, Kim Kincaid for not giving up on me with this book.

To Nicole for putting up with my whining.

For Everafter for being so wonderful to work with.

To Wander for this amazing picture.

To Aria for the cover.

And to my fans! I love you!

ABOUT THE AUTHOR

 ALANA ALBERTSON IS the former President of RWA's Contemporary Romance, Young Adult, and Chick Lit chapters. She holds a M.Ed. from Harvard and a BA in English from Stanford. A recovering professional ballroom dancer, she lives in San Diego, California, with her husband, two young sons, and five dogs. When she's not saving dogs from high kill shelters through her rescue Pugs N Roses, she can be found watching episodes of UnREAL, Homeland, or Dallas Cowboys Cheerleaders: Making the Team.

For more information:
www.authoralanaalbertson.com
alana@alanaalberton.com

CPSIA information can be obtained
at www.ICGtesting.com
Printed in the USA
BVOW08s1105270318
511728BV00001B/1/P